Awesome Reviews for

Evidence

"Thanks for writing an amazing book! I enjoyed every part of it. Changed my perspective on everything especially my marriage! Bless you!" – Lisa B.

"This book is AMAZING! Very compelling, very emotional... the characters have realistic problems that every day couples and marriages face all of the time. Excellent writing!!!!" – Jessica G.

"This book is a great masterpiece. This book covers so many issues that we as people and more importantly as Christians need to deal with; everything from forgiveness of family, friends, and spouses/lovers. This book was divinely inspired to reach a generation of people who need to know there is a God and He loves you, and He wants to have a relationship with you. He also wants to heal you of every hurt, whether it be emotional, physical or mental. This book covers that and deals with those issues. I could not stop reading this book. I finished it in two days and was asking for more. I'm excited about the next installments of this series of books. Terri T. Thrash is a brilliant author and definitely reflects the heart of God for this generation through her writing. I look forward to seeing more from this young rising star." – Minister James C.

"AWESOME!! FAITH IS MANDATORY IN THIS WORLD TODAY!! I'm sure that this book is going to lead someone to salvation and reassure/increase somebody else's faith, as well as teach a lot of people on the importance of forgiveness!! I've laughed, cried, and praised while reading this book!!! It really touched my heart!! Job well done!! You definitely let God use you!!!" – LaQuana O.

Evidence

Also by Terri T. Thrash

Ulterior Motives

EVIDENCE

Terri T. Thrash

Creative Hearts
Publishing

Creative Hearts Publishing, LLC

Evidence (Revised Edition)

For more information about special discounts for bulk purchases, please contact Creative Hearts Publishing, LLC at www.creativeheartspublishing.com

Cover Designed by: Jazmin Jernigan with Aesthetic Innovations

Cover Models are simply models portraying the characters in the book.

ISBN (Softcover) 978-0-9888002-4-3

ISBN (e-book) 978-0-9888002-7-4

Printed in the United States of America

First Printed Edition (Revised) January/2013

Dedication

This book is dedicated to all of my loved ones and to our beloved who are no longer with us: Bryant Bernard Thrash, John Graggs, Mary Lizzie Graggs and Ethel Lee Thrash. "We are confident, yes, well pleased rather to be absent from the body and to be present with the Lord. Therefore we make it our aim, whether to be present or absent, to be well pleasing to Him." II Corinthians 5:8-9

Acknowledgements

First and foremost, I have to give praises to my Heavenly Father. Thank you for being who you are and for that, I love you. You are the God who has given me the ability to create and without you, I am nothing. Thank you for giving me the mind and ability to create such a story line. You are the one who made this all possible and I could not have done this without you. Without you, there is truly no me. If it had not been for your grace and mercy, I wouldn't have made it thus far. You have given me the gift of writing, and for that I thank you. I will use this gift to glorify you and to build up your Kingdom. I give you all the glory, honor, and praise. You are truly worthy of my worship.

To my father and mother, James and Marilyn Thrash, thank you for setting the spiritual foundation and instilling the fear of God in my life. You introduced me to the greatest gift of all, salvation through Jesus Christ and I thank you for that. It was you who also instilled in me the value of education. I am grateful for all you have done and I love you both. Thank you for all of your love, prayers and support.

To my beautiful daughter, Tierra Thrash, thank you for being my greatest inspiration and motivation. You are truly amazing and you are my greatest accomplishment. Thank you so much for your input with some of the names of the characters. You are one of my biggest supporters. I love you so much, baby girl.

To my sister, Shereka Thrash-Stephens, thank you so much for all of your love, prayers, support and words of encouragement. You have been such an amazing help and a big part of this process. Thank you for being an encouraging sister and legal counsel. You support me in all that I do and I love you. Thank you so much for being there and for believing in my vision.

To my brother, Derrell Thrash, thank you for all your love, prayers and support. Thank you for always being a big brother to me and being there whenever I need you. Thanks for believing in me and all of my hopes and dreams and for supporting me in all I do. I love you.

To all of my beautiful family and friends, you all have been super supportive and I thank you for all your love, prayers, support and words of encouragement. I appreciate all of you and all that you have done. You all are truly awesome and words can't express how thankful I am to you all. I love each and every one of you very much.

To one of the greatest English teachers I know, Nettie H. Prim, thank you so much for your assistance in the editing process. Your feedback, suggestions and words of encouragement were greatly appreciated. I love you.

To the gorgeous book cover models, thank you so very much for saying yes without hesitation. Tambria Hunt, Misty Mack, Joshua Richardson, Tiffany Sandifer, Garrett Sudds and

Darline Villanueva, you all are awesome. If it weren't for you, there would be no cover. You all are extremely talented and did an exceptional job. You all are very much loved and appreciated.

To my classmate and friend, Mary Craig, thank you so much for providing me with such a beautiful setting for the book cover. Your kindness and your words of encouragement are greatly appreciated. I am so thankful for you and you are very much loved.

To my friend and book cover photographer, Jazmin Jernigan-Coleman, with Aesthetic Innovations Studios, you are one of the greatest photographers I know. Thank you so very much for making this book cover happen, a beautiful job well done. Your insight was most helpful and your work was immaculate. You are truly awesome and you are loved and appreciated.

To everyone who has purchased this book and is taking out the time to read it, thank you so very much for your love and support. It is my prayer that it blesses you greatly and touches your life in a powerful and positive way. I hope you enjoy reading it just as much as I enjoyed writing it. This is only the beginning and there is so much more in store. I'm excited about where God is leading me and I plan to enjoy the journey. I hope that you will take this journey with me as you continue to support me as I continue to embrace the vision that God has given me. Love you all.

And last but not least. To all of my nay sayers, I thank you as well. You, too, help me to keep pressing toward the mark of the high calling, and for that, I love you.

This storyline was written in June of 2011, and was published and released in December 2011. When I decided to republish, I also decided to give the readers more. I thank you all so much for your love and support. I love you all and this addition is for you . . . Enjoy!

"Evidence is not just a story written on pages. It is a remarkable experience and a journey worth taking." ~ Terri T. Thrash.

Grace and peace be unto you all,

"Now Faith is the substance of things hoped for, the
EVIDENCE of things not seen." Hebrews 11:1 (NKJV)

"Some men's sins are clearly evident, preceding them to
judgment, but those of some men follow later. Likewise, the
good works of some are clearly evident, and those that are
otherwise cannot be hidden." 1Timothy 5:24-25 (NKJV)

Faith is...

EVIDENCE

The Evidence Journey

What happens when a life-altering act results in a deadly consequence and threatens to destroy everything you've built?

Chapter One

As Taylor rolled over in bed she did not feel her husband lying next to her. She looked at her alarm clock which read: 6:07 a.m.

"Good morning, baby. How's my beautiful wife?" Keith asked as he brought her breakfast in bed.

"After last night, I couldn't be better," she answered. "Then you bring me this delicious looking breakfast and your delicious looking body on this bright and sunny morning. Wow, I love all of this wonderful treatment . . . Everything looks good, babe, but how about you be my breakfast in bed?" She smiled and threw her arms around her husband's neck, kissing him softly.

He kissed her, and then pulled her arms from around his neck. "Now let's not get anything started that we can't finish," he said.

"Oh, baby, now that's a good one." Taylor kissed him softly. "Let's not play games here. You know that whatever I start, I finish," she said, continuing to kiss him.

"Tay, baby, I'm serious. I have to get ready to meet with Jeff this morning on this case we have together. This is a pretty big case and I don't need any distractions."

"Oh, I see. So, now I'm a distraction?"

"Tay, you know I didn't mean that."

"No, Keith, I get it. This is Saturday, and it's supposed to be your day off." She crossed her arms in front of her chest. "So, tell me. When can I get some of your time, Mr. Big Time Attorney? When do you play husband? What day does your wife get?" she asked as tears formed in her eyes.

Gently touching her cheek, "Tay, please, don't give me that look. Check this out. Let me go meet with Jeff, and I won't be long at all. I will come back and cater to my beautiful wife all," kissing her lips, "day," he kissed her lips again, "long," he kissed her lips again, then added, "I promise."

"We never spend time together anymore and I thought that we would be able to spend the day together, but that's fine. Don't make me any more promises. It's always about work with you. So, do what you do best . . . Work! Then you can come home to your second job, being a husband. I know how important your first job is to you."

"Taylor, you know that's not true." Keith reached out and grabbed her arm, but she pulled away and marched towards the bathroom, her red lingerie showing ninety percent of her beautiful flawless caramel complexion.

Keith could not resist getting up to follow her. He ran up behind his wife, pulling her back around to face him. He began kissing her and she couldn't resist kissing him back. He picked her up, and she wrapped her legs around him as he carried her to the bed. He sat her down and as she began to unzip his pants, he began taking off his shirt, his muscles bulging through his beautiful honey-colored skin.

Kissing every inch of her body, he began making love to his wife; she receiving every inch of her husband, enjoying every minute of him inside of her. Her hips propelled with every thrust of his pelvis. Their rhythm as one made perfect harmony. As he climaxed, the shaking of the bed knocked the breakfast tray onto the floor, the sound bringing them back to reality as he lay on top of her, kissing her softly.

He looked into her beautiful eyes and smiled. "You are so beautiful. I never would have thought that I would have pulled a woman like you."

"Now why is that, baby? You were the heartbreaker in high school. You were every girls dream. A track, basketball, and football star. The question should be, how did I a freshman, pull you, a senior."

"Well, it was love at first sight, baby girl," he whispered into her ear as if it were a secret.

Taylor looked at her husband and smiled, unable to speak. Every time he whispered into her ear, it would paralyze her. His voice was so soothing.

He looked at the alarm clock, which now read: 8:46 a.m. "Oh, I have to go. I'm supposed to meet Jeff at nine." He kissed her, grabbed his cell phone off the nightstand, and headed for the bathroom. After calling Jeff to say he was running late, he turned on the shower and jumped in.

The sound of the running water gave Taylor an idea. She made her way into the bathroom, tiptoeing into the shower as Keith washed his face. There, she stood behind him, waiting for him to turn around. She began kissing his back softly, and he turned to face her.

He kissed her from her lips to her waist.

She pulled him back up, and began kissing his lips as the water ran over their bodies.

He picked her up and pressed her into the shower wall as she wrapped her legs around him. Their bodies joined once again, and she received him as if she never gets enough of him.

He ran his fingers through her shoulder-length hair as they now lay in bed. He gently kissed her forehead. "Baby, I really have to go. I want to be able to spend all the time in the world with you, but I have to support us. I'm giving this my all. I need you to understand that, Tay . . . I really do.'' He kissed her nose. "Baby, I gotta go. You have me extremely late. I'll call you as soon as I get to the office.''

"Okay, honey, but make sure you make this meeting quick. We have unfinished business here.'' She winked at him.

He kissed her again and headed for the door.

Chapter Two

The doorbell rang about 4:16 p.m. Taylor looked out of the window and saw her sister's car parked in the driveway.

Taylor opened the door. "Hey, honey bun,'' she said, greeting her sister, Tyra.

"Hey, girl, I had to come and check on my baby sister, since you don't come around anymore,'' Tyra said sarcastically. Tyra was only three years older than Taylor, but people would swear that she was her mother because of how protective of her she is.

Taylor hugged her sister. "Well, you do live five blocks away, Tyra. You are always welcome to come visit me.''

"Yeah, well, I be so busy at the counseling center, you would think that I live there.'' She sighed.

"Yes, girl, I know what you mean. Law school has my mind going in circles, but thank God graduation is right around the corner. Then Keith is so busy at the office, it seems as though he doesn't know where home is.''

"Work, work, work and no play," Tyra sighed, and then yelled with excitement, "Oh, but I do have to go to Shreveport for a month to work with a program at the Juvenile Detention Center! I'm so excited about that. I love Shreveport, great people and great hospitality. I don't have to pay living expenses or anything when I get there. Everything will be taken care of. God is truly awesome. I can't wait to work with the girls at the center. They are really great children, but you know how it is when the world gets to them. They just need a little direction and an extra push, and I'm just the woman for the job." She smiled.

"Awww, Sis, that's great, but I'm going to miss you when you leave, big head." Taylor walked over to Tyra and hugged her.

Tyra embraced her, and then waved her hand in the air. "Yeah, yeah, yeah, save that for the birds." She laughed, and then said, "I'm going to miss you, too, but it's just for a month. We will hang out as soon as I get back." She looked around their spacious home. "Wow, did I ever tell you how beautiful your home is?"

Taylor rolled her eyes. "Yes, Ty, every time you come over, you remind me."

Tyra took a seat on the kitchen barstool. "Well, this house is huge, girl. You and Keith are so blessed. God has really shown you guys favor in spite of yourselves."

"Look, don't start with all of that, Tyra. You talk about it every time you come here; about how we need to go to church, like I don't know that. You know, I'm just really tired of discussing it."

"I'm just saying your house is huge, that's all. I'm not here to preach to you." Tyra put her hands up as if she was surrendering.

"Yeah, it is pretty big, huh?" Taylor giggled as she looked around. Her tone then became solemn, "But it feels as if I have no one to share it with." She stared off in a daze.

"What do you mean, Tay? You and Keith are good, right?" Tyra looked at her a little more closely. "Wait, are you thinking about babies?"

"No, not at all," Taylor said, waving away her words. "Babies are the last thing on my mind, but I can't say the same for Keith. He's ready for babies, or so he thinks. But he can't even stay home long enough to be a husband. So how is he going to be a father and help me raise a baby?" She sighed. "I don't understand why he wants children so badly? It's like he has baby fever or something."

"Ha! Girl, you are crazy, but you know men have a biological clock as well."

"I'm just tired of him not spending enough time with me and I know if a baby comes, he will definitely ignore me. Then I'm trying to get through law school myself. Even the thought of a baby is tiring."

"Tay," Tyra chuckled. "I swear, Mom and Dad spoiled you waaay too much and it's showing up in you right now. You can get anything you want from Keith, but you can't give the man a baby. I mean, you have him wrapped around your finger. Anything you want from him, you get."

"Yes. Everything but time," Taylor snapped.

"Let me tell you something, Tay," Tyra began. "You have a husband who love, supports, and adores you. You don't work. He doesn't even want you to work, just so you can focus on school. He makes sure that you are well-taken care of and that you have the finer things in life. What more do you want? Do you know how many women wish they were in your shoes?" She rested her chin on her hand and looked Taylor in her eyes. "So, you tell me. What's the real problem, because I don't think Keith is it."

"I would like to feel as if I am important to him, not just someone he takes care of financially or comes home and makes love to. Don't get me wrong. It's great and all that he wines and dines me, but what about quality time together? He's always putting his work before me and thinks that if he showers me with gifts, then that's okay. Even when he's here, he's working. I feel so alone sometimes. Maybe you don't know how that feels, but I can assure you that it doesn't feel good."

"Well, how do you think God feels when you put everything before Him? Let's be real. I noticed that when you met Keith, soon after, you started falling off with going to church in order to spend time with him. I haven't seen you in church since you've been married. It's been a long time, Tay. You guys need to get your lives in order, before it's too late; Maybe that's the real reason why you feel the way you feel."

"I know, Tyra. I've tried to talk to Keith about that, but the subject of church always starts an argument. I try not to talk about it as much because of that. He gets so angry about it." Taylor sighed.

"Well, why do you think he feels so strongly about church?"

"I don't know. He never discusses it with me."

"Well I say that you guys need to have a heart-to-heart about it. You need to get to the root of the problem, before it tears your marriage apart. Our parents taught us not to forsake the assembly, and you were raised to know that it is important to keep God first in everything . . . Tay, I've never asked you this before, but . . . is Keith saved?" Tyra asked, approaching the subject with caution.

Taylor was offended by her sister's question, which had been a question of her own for quite some time now. "Ty, let's just drop it. Okay?"

"Drop what?" Keith asked, as he walked into the kitchen.

"Keith, I didn't hear you come in, baby," Taylor said. She walked over to him, quickly grabbed his briefcase, and greeted him with a kiss.

"What did I miss?" he asked, and then glanced over at his sister-in-law. "Tyra, how have you been, Sis?" He walked over and hugged her.

"I've been well. Working at the center, trying to make a difference while getting burned out."

"Don't get burned out. You can't save everybody." Keith chuckled. He walked over to the cabinet to grab a glass.

It struck Tyra when Keith mentioned about saving everybody, and she thought to herself, *What did he mean by that exactly?* Then she said, "Well, I guess I better get going. I need to get some rest. Those girls at the center are trying to wear me out . . . Love y'all." She kissed Keith's cheek, hugged Taylor, and then headed towards the door.

"Wait, I'll walk you out," Taylor said. She walked her sister to her car.

"Look, Tay, I love you, but you really need to have that talk with Keith about what you believe, and vice versa. You were not raised to turn your back on God. There's danger in turning your back on Him and you know that, Taylor. I promise you; once y'all get your lives to line up with the Word and will of God, things will get better in your marriage," Tyra said as she hugged her sister.

"Thank you, Tyra. I will have that talk with him as soon as the time is right."

"Well, the time would have been right when you guys first met. Don't wait any longer. You don't want it to be too late . . . Love you." She kissed her cheek.

"Love you too."

She watched her sister drive off. Then she stood and looked up toward the sky. *God, you know my heart, and I want to make things right with you. I just need your help*, she silently prayed. She was ready to have that heart-to-heart with her husband.

Chapter Three

Taylor went into the kitchen to cut up a tray of fruit. She then headed upstairs to the bathroom to run some bath water. She lit the candles around the tub and turned on some soft music. She listened to the words of Boys II Men as they song, "I'll Make Love to You." She pressed the Repeat button, and then headed to their home office where Keith was working on a case.

She stood in the doorway and watched him for a moment. She then walked over to him and kissed him softly on his neck as she wrapped her arms around him. She whispered softly into his ear, "Baby, don't you think it's time to put the cases away? Come spend some time with your wife." She took him by his hand.

He stood up and kissed her. "You are so right, babe. I've missed you all day." He allowed her to lead him to the bathroom.

When he walked in, he looked around at all of the candles. "Wow, honey, this is beautiful, and that fruit is looking mighty good." He looked at her and licked his lips. "And so are you." He kissed her and gently bit her bottom lip.

Her lips brushed up against his ear, "Take off your clothes," she whispered.

He slowly began taking off his clothes while looking her in her eyes as she watched. Then he got into the warm water.

"Just relax," she whispered. "Don't think about work or anything else. Let's just focus on our time together."

He laid back into the tub and began listening to the words of Boys II Men that continued to play over the stereo.

She sat on the side of the tub, fed him some fruit, then gently kissed him. She began washing his back slowly. She stood, removed her clothes and got into the tub, sitting on top of her husband, facing him.

"How was your day, baby?" she asked, trying to get a feel for how to go into the next part of their conversation.

He pulled her into his strong arms. "It is so much better now that I'm here with you. How was yours?"

"It was wonderful and even better now that my husband is home with me." She gently kissed his lips.

"I guess it's time to complete our unfinished business, huh?" He softly kissed her neck.

"Well, you know that I have something beautiful and creative in mind just for you." She bit her lip, and then smiled. She looked him in his eyes. "But right now, we have something more important to talk about." Now she was a little more nervous.

"What about?   What's on your mind, baby?" Keith kissed her and noticed that she was trembling. "You are shaking, baby.   What's wrong?   Are you cold?" He wrapped her in his arms even tighter.

"No . . ."

"Well, what's wrong?   Are you pregnant?" he asked with hope in his tone.

She rolled her eyes. "No, Keith, that's not it."

"Well, is there someone else?" he asked in a joking manner.

"No, baby, just let me talk for a minute."

"Well, you are making me nervous because it seems pretty serious."

"And it is serious. I just need you to listen to me for a minute."

"Okay, I'm sorry. Talk and I'll listen. You have my undivided attention, baby," he said, kissing her lips. He rested his back on the tub as he prepared himself for what his wife wanted to talk to him about.

She took a deep breath and looked him in his eyes before saying, "I want to go to church tomorrow."

He studied her for a minute, then said, "I've never stopped you from going to church . . . Go, and I'll be here when you get back."

"No, that's the thing, Keith. I want us to go . . . together.''

"No, Tay, that ain't happening. You know how I feel about that.''

"Actually, I don't know how you feel about that, or why you feel the way you feel. I need you to talk to me, Keith. I have been married to you for five years and you have never talked to me about your reasons for not wanting to go to church.''

"You never asked,'' he snapped.

"I have asked you, Keith, on several occasions and you know it. You've just always avoided answering the question.''

"You know what, Tay? I'm tired, and I don't have time for this.'' He got out of the tub and grabbed his towel.

"That's your problem. You never have time. You're always running. It's been more than five years and we have never been to church together. Do you know how that makes me feel?'' She got out the tub, grabbed her towel, and followed him into their bedroom.

She pulled at her husband, but he jerked away. "Don't touch me, Tay. Let's just drop this. I thought we were going to have another wonderful night together, but you fooled me. You with all this nonsense!'' he yelled.

"That's the problem. This is not nonsense. You never want to talk about what it is that bothers you so much about church and you get so defensive. I just want you to tell me . . .

Why?" she yelled back at him.

He abruptly turned to face her. "I loved you, Tay, from the moment I met you. You brought so much light to my life. I didn't feel a need to bring up any of that church foolishness. You showed me so much love. I didn't need God, and I certainly didn't need the church. From that moment on, all I needed was you. Now I'm tired, and I'm going to bed." He turned and walked away.

She got back in his face. "Well, I'm here to tell you that I'm not the only one you need, and I would hate for you to find that out the hard way. You need to reevaluate some things in your life. You say that you love me, then do this for me. Go to church with me tomorrow, just this once, and we'll go from there." She looked deeply into his eyes. "Please, Keith."

Keith just stared back into her eyes as her words tugged at his heart, but then he turned and walked away.

"At least talk to me. Tell me why you feel the way you feel," she demanded.

He turned back towards her and kissed her softly on her neck. He slipped her towel away from her body.

"Keith, we need to finish this," she said, and then moaned at his gentle kisses.

"Umm-hmm, I agree. We do need to finish this," he said, continuing to kiss her. His hands began exploring her body.

"Stop it! I need you to take this seriously."

"Oh, I am,'' he began. "Tell me, Tay. Doesn't the Bible say something about not turning away your husband? Well, your husband wants to make love to his wife.'' He kissed her lips.

"Keith, wait!'' Taylor protested.

He kept kissing her until he got her over to the bed.

She fell back onto the bed, and he climbed on top of her.

Their bodies connected.

His anger came out with each one of his vigorous strokes.

She tried to push him off of her as each one of his strokes pained her.

He kept going as if he was punishing her for bringing up something that he didn't want to discuss.

"Keith . . . Wait,'' she groaned, but he failed to listen to her outcry.

Instead, he continued as he covered her mouth. He looked into her eyes as he climaxed. Breathing heavily, he laid down next to her.

Taylor rolled over to her side, tears in her eyes.

Breathlessly, he said, "I love you, Tay, you know that right?''

Concentrating on holding back the tears that stung her

eyes, she didn't respond.

Chapter Four

Taylor allowed her tears to flow as the shower water ran down her face and body. "God, I need you. Please give me the strength to walk into your house of prayer this morning with or without Keith. I can't go another day without making things right with you, even if I have to do it alone . . ."

Keith opened the bathroom door, walked in, and began washing his face in the sink. "Hey, honey, you are up early this morning. What you got going on?" he asked, drying his face.

Silence . . .

Taylor hopped out the shower and dried off.

Keith looked at her intensely. "Taylor, I asked you a question," he said.

She walked past him and towards the bathroom door.

"Tay," he called to her, now grabbing her arm. "I asked you a question," he repeated more sternly.

She pulled away from his grasp. "I'm getting ready for church. Do you care to join me?"

"Naw, I have some work to do."

"Yeah, I figured you would say that," she said sarcastically.

"I'm about to make breakfast. What are you in the mood for?" he asked, changing the subject. He twisted the cap off of the toothpaste and spread the paste onto his toothbrush.

"When do you plan to go with me, Keith? This is something that I need to know. You know what . . . when we first got together, I just assumed that you were saved, but now, I'm not so sure. So, tell me." She crossed her arms in front of her chest. "Are you?"

Keith ignored her as he brushed his teeth.

She stood in the doorway and waited a minute before saying, "Now I've asked you a question, Keith."

He rinsed out his mouth, and then he looked at her for a while. He smiled and said, "Wow, you look beautiful." He attempted to remove her towel, but she hit his hands away.

"Keith, it's simple. Are you saved, yes, or no?" she asked sternly.

"You are married to me now, Tay, so all this other stuff doesn't even matter. We are stuck together, believe it or not." He chuckled.

"Oh, it matters. So, just tell me. Yes, or no?"

"You know what? This right here is getting old. So why don't you just get to where you are trying to go? It's all about you with your selfish . . ."

"Don't you dare try to turn this around on me," she interrupted. "All you do is work, and I'm the selfish one? Well, I beg to differ on your evaluation. You need to look in the mirror, Mr. 'Focus on My Career'."

"You know what? You have some nerve, Taylor. I'm working to support our family and put you through school, so that you can do something that you enjoy, but I'm selfish? You don't even want to have our children, but I'm selfish?"

"Ha! Is that all you think about? *Babies*? Well, if you think that me not wanting to have *your* babies right now is being selfish, then so be it. I'm done with all of this."

"So, you finally admit it? You don't want to have *my* babies. Wow, Tay, you said a mouth full."

Keith went into the home office, and Taylor went into the bedroom to finish getting ready. She fell to her knees overwhelmed with tears. Her lips parted, "God, my marriage is broken without you . . ."

Chapter Five

Taylor walked into the doors of Holy Temple Ministries and the ushers welcomed her with warm smiles. One of them led her up to the fifth row.

"Good morning, Saints. This is the day that the Lord has made, let us rejoice and be glad in it," the pastor shouted from the pulpit.

Everybody in the congregation began to rejoice.

"Go ahead and praise Him, for He is worthy of all the glory, honor, and praise. He woke you up this morning and started you on your way. He clothed you in your right mind and placed your feet on solid ground. He placed air in your lungs, and the Word tells us, 'let everything that hath breath, praise the Lord.' Praise Him right now in this place . . .''

The congregation shouted out praises all over the building.

Taylor instantly felt back at home, even though the man in the pulpit was different from the one she remembered.

The pastor continued, "Jesus is Lord, and He's worthy to be praised. Go with me in your Bibles to St. Luke, chapter 8, verse 43, and open your hearts to receive a Word from our Lord."

The congregation stood, and recited the Word of God together.

"43. And a woman having an issue of blood twelve years, which has spent all her living upon physicians, neither could be healed of any, 44. Came behind him, and touched the border of his garment: and immediately her issue of blood stanched. 45. And Jesus said, 'Who touched me?' When all denied, Peter and they that were with him said, 'Master, the multitude throng thee and press thee, and sayest thou, Who touched me?' 46. And Jesus said, 'Somebody hath touched me: for I perceive that virtue is gone out of me.' 47. And when the woman saw that she was not hid, she came trembling, and falling down before him, she declared unto him before all the people for what cause she had touched him, and how she was healed immediately. 48. And he said unto her, 'Daughter, be of good comfort: thy faith hath made thee whole; go in peace'."

The congregation sat after reading the Word.

The pastor continued, "Press your way through. This woman came to Jesus with an issue. She traveled going from physician to physician looking for healing, but no one had such power. But when she heard of this man named Jesus. The one who healed the sick, opened blind eyes and set captives free, she knew that if she could just press her way to Jesus, she would be made whole." He took a sip of water before continuing, "This was a woman of great faith. Her issue was her blood flow. Your issue or issues may be your finances, your job, your health, your children, or even your marriage. It doesn't matter what your issue may be, if you just press your way through to Jesus, He will make you whole. Give your issues to Him, the one who can handle them. Press your way through and He will heal and deliver you. He is Jehovah Raphé, y'all. He is God and He is God all by himself. He just wants you to let go and He will handle your situation and circumstances."

The congregation shouted, and many were brought to tears.

He continued, "He is Jehovah Jireh. Whatever you need, my God will supply, but you have to trust Him. Trust Him with your life, your marriage, and your children. Trust Him with your all. 'If I may touch but His hem, I shall be made whole.' That's called faith y'all. This woman knew that if she could just get to Jesus, He was all she needed."

The woman sitting next to Taylor broke down in tears and began hollering out the name of Jesus.

The pastor continued, "I don't know what you may be going through, but my God is a healer and a deliverer. Come on and just press your way through to Jesus today. The doors of the church are open." He looked around the congregation. "Whatever you are going through, bring it to Jesus for He is a healer. He is able to deliver you from any situation or circumstance that you may be going through, but you have to step out in faith and trust Him. The God we serve is an awesome God. He is able to take your wrong and make you right. Bring your lives to Him, He can work it out. I'm a witness. Someone out there has walked away from God and your heart is heavy right now. Today, this Word has pierced your heart and you are ready to give your life back to Him. He's waiting for you. He has never left you. He's right there. God hears your prayer.''

Taylor began to squirm in her seat. She felt as though this man was speaking to her all throughout the message. As the choir song *I'll Trust You* by James Fortune & Fiya, tears began to swell in her eyes and before she knew it, she had pressed her way to the altar.

The pastor began whispering into her ear and into her spirit, "Your faith has been strengthened today. Your broken marriage is being repaired today. There is something that you need to discuss with your husband, something that you have been holding back. It's time to let it go. There are some things that you are about go through, but you have to have faith to get through it. You have to stand on the very promises of God and do not be moved by the traps of the enemy. You've fallen off in your worship and prayer life, but you made this choice today, right here, right now, to get it right with Him. You have to be the example for your husband. You have to stand as God allows you to go through this process in your marriage. He's building it. Get prepared for stormy weather, but don't forget the sun is going to shine. No matter how your situation may look, my child, continue to press your way through to Jesus.'' He began praying and speaking over her in tongues.

Taylor fell to her knees and worshipped God like never before.

After church, Tyra walked up to her and said, "Taylor, oh, my God.'' She wrapped her in her arms and hugged her tightly. "God, I love you,'' she whispered into her ear.

Taylor was still in tears as she embraced her sister. She saw her parents who came rushing to her side, hugging her.

"Baby, I'm so proud of you. I had been so worried about you," her mother, Barbra, admitted as she cried tears of her own.

"Oh, Barbra," Taylor's father, Carter, began, "I knew God was going to bring her back to this point. There was no need to worry. He said in His Word that as long as we train our children up in His Word, when they are old, they will not depart from it." He raised his hands in praise, then added, "Praise God." He kissed Taylor's cheek. "It was only a matter of time."

This handsome dark-skinned man walked over. "Taylor? It has been a long time. How have you been?" he asked. He came closer to hug her.

Taylor looked at him for a minute before saying, "Oh, my God. Michael? It has been what, six years or so since I've seen you?" she said, and then hugged him. She and Michael had grown up together and were the best of friends. They went to the same schools, elementary through high school and when he went off to college, they lost touch.

"That sounds about right. You look so beautiful," he said as he admired her. He then looked over at her parents. "Mr. and Mrs. Livingston, how are you doing?"

"Oh, we are fine, Son. It's really good to see you," Carter said. He shook Michael's hand, then looked at Taylor and asked, "Taylor, are you going to stop by the house later?"

"Yes, Daddy," Taylor kissed her parents, hugged Tyra, and then watched them walk to the car together.

"Well, Mrs. Taylor Davenport. I was about to head to

lunch; would you like to join me?'' Michael asked.

"Wow, Mike, you look great," Taylor said as if she couldn't believe her eyes.

"Well, thank you. You look quite gorgeous yourself, ma'am; now, how about that lunch?'' He looked at her and was amazed at how beautiful she was.

"Yes, lunch sounds great. It gives us a chance to catch up . . .''

Chapter Six

Keith gently kissed Taylor's forehead. "I'm about to head to the office. I'll see you later," he said, and then headed for the door.

They haven't exchanged many words since Sunday morning. After Taylor came back from lunch with Michael, she and Keith had small talk, but it was obvious to her that he didn't want to engage in conversation.

Taylor lay in bed and began to think about Michael. She really enjoyed catching up with him, and she couldn't believe how much he'd grown spiritually. She was impressed with the man he'd become. He had just moved back home a couple of months ago. He was already a well-known architect who had started his own company in New Orleans, which is doing quite well. Then he decided to branch out and bring the company to his home town, Baton Rouge, Louisiana. Taylor couldn't believe how handsome he'd become and even more so, she couldn't believe that he was single with no children. After catching up, they agreed to meet up again for lunch and for some reason, she couldn't wait . . .

***

Keith knocked on Kimbrailee Whitmore's office door. He and Kim had been really good friends since their freshman year in high school. He also helped her to get hired as one of the law firm's paralegals. He walked into her office to ask about one of the cases he was working on, but then he saw that her eyes were red and puffy. As he came closer, he saw the bruise under her left eye that she tried her best to cover with make-up.

He walked back over to the door, closed it, and then walked over to her desk. "Kim, what's up? What's going on?" he asked.

"Nothing much, trying to look up some information on this Gary case. What can I do for you, Keith?" she asked without looking up, attempting to hide her black eye.

"No, Kim, you know what I'm talking about."

"I've been working like crazy, and I haven't had any sleep. That's all," she said, continuing to work on her case.

"Kim ... Has Trey been hitting you?"

"Look, I know what this may look like but, Keith, Trey loves me and it's okay. I'm okay ... Believe me when I say, we are good ... He ... loves ... me. He really does ... I don't doubt that," she said as if trying to convince herself. She paused for a while as her thoughts reverted to her husband's verbal and physical abuse towards her the night before and she burst into tears.

Keith pulled her up from her chair and hugged her.

"Kim, this is not okay, and that's not love. No man has the right to put his hands on you." He looked closely at her black eye before saying, "You deserve better." He gently kissed her forehead.

"I know, but he will get better, and things will get better for us." She looked deeply into his eyes. "He said that he won't do it again, so we are good. We'll be fine just please, don't say anything."

"We have been friends for too long, Kim. Why haven't you come to me? I've noticed the bruises that were on your wrist, and the one that was on your arm once and I didn't say anything, but this man has hit you in your face." He shook his head in disbelief. "I can't just sit back and act as if I don't know anything."

"Please, Keith, don't say anything. I'm okay, and he won't do it again," she repeated, disregarding everything else he said.

"You can't be so sure of that, and what if it's worst next time. What if he puts you in the hospital or if it ends in the death of you? How long has this been going on?"

She looked at him as if he should have known. Then she slowly answered, "Since our first date in high school."

He thought back and remembered that she did have bruises on her that he ignored back then. More like him turning a blind eye to what his former best friend, Treyvionne, was doing even though he didn't agree with it. "He's been doing this the whole time?" he asked, surprised.

Kim slowly nodded.

Keith looked at her eye once again in disbelief, and then said, "I just can't believe that he had the nerve to hit you in your face. You are too beautiful for that. What in the hell is wrong with Trey?" He pushed her hair away from her face.

She smiled at his words. "Taylor is so lucky to have you. You are an amazing man."

"If only she knew," he responded.

"You say that as though something is wrong. You two okay?"

"I'm not going to get into all that right now. It'll work itself out."

Knock, knock, knock . . .

Startled, Kim pulled away from Keith's embrace.

Treyvionne Whitmore walked into the office without an invite. His eyes darted between the two of them. "Hey, I thought we could do lunch today," he said to Kim, now looking at her intensely.

"Yes . . . Yeah, of course. Sounds good," she rambled. "That'll be great, Trey. Keith just came in to grab this file to work on." She reached on her desk to grab a file to hand to Keith. She looked into Keith's eyes, and her eyes begged him not to say anything as she handed him the folder.

Trey looked over at Keith. "Keith, my man, how's it going? How you liking this white collar job; working for the white man?'' he asked, being sarcastic.

"Well, brother, if you haven't noticed the title on the building, I've been partner for quite a while now . . . the youngest to make partner actually. Oh, and in record time might I add. By the way, how's your knee? When do you plan to get back out there on that field?'' Keith shot right back, clenching his jaw.

Keith and Treyvionne use to be the best of friends in high school and all throughout college. Keith began working towards his career and Trey was drafted into the NFL his sophomore year of college. As they went in separate directions, they grew apart. Trey played all the way up to the first championship game. He injured his knee during that game and he was never the same. He always had anger issues and he was always aggressive, but Keith didn't know that he was aggressive on and off the field. Trey's alcoholism had become worse soon after his injury and he became even more angry and aggressive. He was even more abusive towards Kim. He became envious of Keith when he found out from Kim how well he was doing in the office and how closely they worked together.

"Well, Keith,'' Kim chimed in. "I guess I'm going to head to lunch with my husband, but when I get back I will finish up on that case for you.'' She tried to rush him out the door before he said anything else that would upset Trey. She knew that anytime that football field was mentioned to Trey, it angered him.

"I'll catch you later, Trey,'' Keith said to him, but his eyes were fixed on Kim's.

"Yeah, you sure will, my boy,'' Trey responded.

After getting in the car, Trey asked Kim, "What was that about?" He started the car and drove out of the parking lot.

"What are you talking about?" Kim asked.

He grabbed her by her arm. "Don't play with me, Kim. It looks like something else was going on in that office besides work," he said angrily.

"Trey, you are hurting me. I told you he came in to ask about a case."

"Ask about a case or to get that file? Seems like you doing a lot of lying, and you know I can't stand it when you try to manipulate me . . . You sleeping with him?" he asked. He began speeding down the street.

Kim began coughing uncontrollably before saying, "Trey, you need to slow down. You are going to get us killed!" She held on to her seat.

"Is that what you want? You want me to kill you, is that it?" he yelled, now going 95 mph in a 60. "If I find out you sleeping with him or anyone else, that's what I will do," he threatened. "You got me?" He took his eyes off of the road to look her in hers. He wanted to make sure that he put fear in her.

Her voice trembled with fear, "I got you, Trey, now would you please slow down? There's nothing going on with me and Keith, I promise. I wouldn't do that to you."

He looked into her eyes. "We understand each other then?"

She nodded, her words caught inside of her throat. She felt a shortness of breath as she started coughing again.

They walked into the restaurant and were seated immediately. The waitress took their orders and they sat silently and waited until their food arrived.

"I noticed you didn't come home last night," Kim said with caution, then she added, "where did you spend your night?" her voice was low as she looked down at her salad. She mustered up the nerve to ask him this since they were in public. She knew that he wouldn't be as aggressive with her out in the open as he was with her behind closed doors.

"I don't see how that's any of your business," he said; his tone cold.

"I am your wife and I consider you not being home at night, a part of my business. I've been a good wife to you, haven't I? I don't deserve this treatment from you."

"What? Did Keith tell you that? Does he make you feel like a woman and that you deserve more?"

"What happened to you? We use to be happy, or at least okay. You haven't told me that you love me in what seems like forever. Just tell me. What have I done to you to make you so unhappy and to make you treat me this way?"

He banged his fist on the table and Kim jumped. "You think you better than me because you some paralegal?"

Everyone in the restaurant looked over at them.

"Trey, calm down; you are embarrassing me," Kim whispered loudly.

"Oh, I'm an embarrassment now. When I was pro, I wasn't an embarrassment, was I? You looked at me differently then. I was your meal ticket then, huh? Well, I tell you what, *Kimbrailee*, since I'm so much of an embarrassment to you, I'll leave. You pay the meal ticket and find your way back to your high paying office job," he said. He cleaned the corners of his mouth with his napkin and threw it down on the table before getting up to leave.

"Trey," Kim called out to him, her voice in a whisper. "Trey," she called out to him again before she watched him disappear around the corner.

Trey left out the door without looking back.

Kim pulled out her cell phone and made a call to Keith...

"I don't understand, Kim. What is going on with Trey?" Keith asked as he opened the car door for her. He then walked around to the driver's side and got in.

Kim answered, "I don't know. He was always arrogant and angry. Yeah, he may have hit me a few times when we were in school, but it was never this bad. Yes, I know. He may have cheated and everything in the book, but believe it or not, I did love him and I felt as though he would one day grow to really love me." She sighed. "You just wouldn't understand. I saw the best in him, Keith."

"Well, if he loves you, he has a terrible way of showing it," he said. Not understanding her view, he frowned. "You are worth so much more than that."

"You are not going to tell anyone else about this, right? I don't want to embarrass him or mess up his good name."

Keith frowned even more. "Is that what this is about, his good name?"

"You wouldn't understand, Keith. He needs me. Ever since he got injured, he's been feeling really down. I mean, he drinks like crazy and I know that's a part of why he treats me that way. When he's not drunk, he can be the best man in the world," she explained.

"Really, so he was drunk? That's why he clowned you so badly today?"

She sat in silence and stared out of the window. Keith had just put something on her mind to think about because today, Trey was fully sober. This time she couldn't use drinking as an excuse for his behavior.

They rode silently the rest of the way back to the office...

Chapter Seven

Taylor met Keith at the door. "Hey, honey," gently kissing his lips, "late day?" she asked. She took his briefcase and sat it down next to the couch.

Keith took off his suit coat and laid it over the back of the couch.

She untied his tie, and then kissed his lips once again.

He sighed deeply before saying, "Yeah, had a lot going on today." He inhaled and took in the smell of the food. "Something smells great. What are you in here cooking?"

"Your favorite, you should know," she said. "Keith, I was thinking. We have been upset with each other for too long and I'm ready to bury it." Her lips now softly brushed his ear as she whispered, "I want to make love to my husband tonight." She now looked into his eyes and giggled like a schoolgirl.

He kissed her lips. "Sounds great to me. So, let's skip dinner," he said laughing. He lifted her up into his arms.

"No, let's have dinner first, and then I'll be your desert," she said as he put her down. She walked into the kitchen, fixed their plates and set them on the dinner table.

"You will not believe the day that I had at the office," Keith began. "We have so many cases that we are working on. You would think that we are the only law firm in Baton Rouge." He put a fork full of spaghetti into his mouth.

"Well, babe, I can't wait till I get that law degree, and we can start our own practice together. That will be great. We'll focus on family law." She laughed.

"Yeah, I can't wait until you get that degree either, because it's costing me a fortune." He chuckled.

Taylor leaned over the table and hit his arm. "You punk," she said playfully.

His mind reverted to Kim and Trey. He looked Taylor in her eyes. "I love you so much, Tay, and I would never put my hands on you. I would never abuse you in any way. Always remember that," he told her.

Taylor's smile slowly faded. She became a little confused with his last statement . . .

***

Taylor pulled back the covers and got in bed next to Keith. "What was that about earlier?" she asked.

He looked at her strangely. He had no idea what she was talking about, so he asked, "What?"

"At dinner, you said that you would never put your hands on me, or abuse me in any way . . . Sooo, what was that about?"

"Oh, yeah, I was just thinking about what all happened today."

"Well, tell me about it . . . What all happened today?" She ran her hand down his arm.

"Trey came into the office tripping. I didn't realize that he and Kim had so many issues."

"What do you mean, tripping? Keith, you knew that Trey was a fool when we were all in school together," she said with resolution.

"Yeah, but I don't think it was as bad as it is now."

"What do you mean?"

"He beats her, Tay. She came to work today with a black eye. Do you know this man came to the office to take her to lunch today? Then they got into an argument and he left her there, in the restaurant. She had to call me for a ride back to the office. Can you believe that?"

"Yes, I can believe that. He beat her while we were in school. You know she had bruises on her all the time. I tried to talk her out of marrying him, but you see that didn't work." Taylor sighed. "I really don't know what she saw in him anyway. I understand he was handsome with great skills on the field, but I wouldn't have married someone who beat the crap out of me. Then, not only that, he cheated on her like crazy."

Keith looked at her. "Was it really that bad?"

"Yes. It was really that bad."

His mind reverted to his senior year, and then he said, "I guess I saw a few bruises on her back in the day but, wow, I wouldn't have ever expected this. We all were the best of friends, but now he acts like he can't stand me and hates her. I can't even begin to comprehend it. I don't understand where it all took a turn. She opened up a little to me today and told me that things got worst with his anger and his drinking after he was injured." His face showed his concern for his friend. "I feel so bad for her. You should have seen her today."

"Well, we were all pretty close. So I can definitely understand your concern. I really don't know why we all grew so far apart. I know it must have been hard for the both of them after he got injured. I was never that fond of Trey because he was always so arrogant, but I would never wish anything bad on him." She thought for a minute before saying, "I have an idea, baby. Since this is bothering you so much, how about we invite them over for dinner? We can all talk, play catch-up and have a good time. You know, get back close like we use to be. It'll be a dinner party so to speak." Her tone became a little more jovial when she said, "Oh, and we can invite Mike, and he can bring a date."

Keith frowned. "Mike?"

"Yes, Michael Bradberry. I meant to tell you that I saw him Sunday after church. He came back here to do architecture work. He has his own business and seems to be doing pretty well. I figured we can just invite all of our old friends over for dinner and play catch-up, that's all." She picked the brush up from the nightstand to brush her hair.

　　Keith thought for a minute. "Oh, yeah, Michael, I remember him, but we were never that close. Seems like you guys already did some catching up, so much so until you forgot to tell me about it," he said with question in his tone.

　　"No, when I came home Sunday, you seemed very short with me and I forgot to tell you. That's all," continuing to brush her hair . . .

People were walking all around the hospital and every nurse seemed to be wearing purple and red . . . Taylor was called back to the room to see the doctor. As she waited, she looked around the room at the white walls. One of the walls had a beautiful drawing of a woman holding a baby girl. Taylor felt her stomach move, and she wasn't sure why. She kept looking around, and then she saw a Bible on the desk.

　　Wow! This place seems so different, she thought.

　　The nurse entered the room to take her vitals and Taylor noticed that she did not say a word.

　　These people are so rude. You can't even get a hello when they enter the room. Does anyone talk around here? Why am I even here? Taylor thought to herself.

The doctor entered the room and walked over to Taylor. He touched her shoulder and his touch felt so familiar to her. "Taylor, there's something you need to speak with your husband about," he said to her. Even his voice sounded familiar to her, but she didn't recognize his face.

"What do you mean, Doctor? Is something wrong with me?" Taylor asked.

"There's something your husband needs to know. Doesn't he deserve to know the truth, Taylor?"

"What are you talking about? He needs to know what?" she asked as she became irritable.

"If you don't tell him, I will have to show him," the doctor said calmly, now touching her hand.

"What are you talking about, and who told you to call me Taylor? It's Mrs. Davenport to you. I don't know you like that," Taylor said, now becoming angry.

"You know me, you just refuse to listen to me . . ." he said, and that's when she saw the blood . . .

Taylor woke up screaming. She sat up in the bed and

threw back the covers.

Keith was awakened from his sleep as he heard her screaming hysterically. "Baby, what's wrong?" He looked down and saw the blood on the sheet between her legs.

Taylor got up and rushed to the bathroom.

He ran in behind her. "Tay, what's wrong?" he asked again. "Are you in pain or something?"

"No, I'm sorry I screamed. I just had a bad dream, and then my cycle came," she said, still shocked from her dream and now shocked about her cycle.

"But you just had your cycle two weeks ago. Is it normal for you to be having it again this soon?" he asked, confused.

"Yes, Keith, it is normal. Some women have cycles twice a month, silly. You didn't learn that in sex ed?" she said, laughing nervously.

Still very confused, "No, I never heard that," he said.

"Go back to bed, honey. I'm fine. Oh, and would you mind changing the sheets for me please?" She kissed his lips, hoping he wouldn't ask any more questions. "Thanks, babe," she added, then she gently pushed him out of the door.

"Tay, are you sure that you are okay? You are making me really nervous, baby." He was worried at this point.

"Keith, I'm fine. I promise," she told him. "Now, go, so I can clean up."

Taylor hadn't had a cycle in years, but as far as she was concerned, that wasn't for Keith to know.

What was that dream all about? She wondered to herself.

Chapter Eight

Keith sat in the car and called his younger sister, Candis.

"Hey, Candi, how are you?" he asked, calling her by the nickname he gave her when they were younger.

"Everything's good, Keith. What's up?" she asked.

"I have a female question to ask you."

Candis laughed. "Okay . . . Hit me."

"I figured since you're a nurse, you would know . . . Is it possible for a woman to have two cycles in one month?"

She paused and thought for a minute before saying, "Two in one month? Yes, it's possible, but I can't really say that it is necessarily normal. It has been many women that have come to the hospital when it comes to their cycles," she explained. "Why, Keith, what's going on?" she asked, now concerned.

"Well, Taylor woke up last night and was bleeding. She said that it was her cycle, but she had her cycle two weeks ago."

"Well," Candis began. "There was a woman who came in before who thought she was having a cycle about two weeks after she had her first cycle, but it ended up not being a cycle. She found out that she had a miscarriage. The lady didn't even know she was fifteen weeks pregnant because she continued to have a regular cycle. Cycles can be tricky sometimes. You just have to know your body. Maybe Taylor should see the doctor because some women have miscarriages, and don't even realize it sometimes. I know that y'all have been trying to have a baby, so, just to be sure, I believe she should see the doctor."

"Okay, thanks so much, Candi," Keith said, now even more concerned about his wife. He got out of the car and rushed back through the front door after making a few more calls. "Babe," he yelled to Taylor. "Let's go in to see Dr. Morris today. I called while I was in the car and made you an appointment. He said he has room for you this morning."

Taylor's eyes were wide with surprise. "What are you talking about? I thought you were headed to work."

"No, I'm not going in. This is more important. I want to make sure that you are okay. Candi was saying . . ." he began to explain.

Taylor held up her hand, interjecting, "Wait . . . You called Candis? Keith, why did you do that? I told you I was fine," she protested. She was even more concerned that he involved his sister . . . a nurse.

"I just want you to be sure. Let's just go in to see Dr. Morris, and then I will have some kind of peace knowing that you are really okay." He shook his head. "I can't take not knowing whether we lost a baby, and I sure wouldn't want any harm done to your body . . . You need to make sure that you didn't have a miscarriage last night.''

She crossed her arms in front of her chest. "Really, Keith? A miscarriage? I wasn't pregnant, honey. Trust me on this. You are overreacting . . . I'm fine,'' she said, trying to convince him.

He wasn't pleased with her response, and he was far from convinced. "I can't take anything happening to you, Taylor, and you and I both know that last night was not normal,'' he said sternly, letting Taylor know that he wasn't going to let up on the issue.

"Okay, Keith, go to work and I'll go in myself to see the doctor, but I can assure you that I'm fine.'' She kissed his lips. "No worries. I will tell you all the details as soon as I leave the doctor's office.'' She led him back to the front door.

"I'm going with you to that doctor,'' he said, looking into her eyes, allowing her to see his seriousness. "I'm your husband, and I am concerned about you. We're going to that doctor together. Period.''

She swallowed hard. "Okay, well, let me go get ready, babe,'' she said, hoping he didn't hear the trembling in her voice. As soon as she made it to the bathroom she closed the door and locked it. She waited a minute as she thought to herself, *What am I going to do now?* She decided to take her time in the bathroom, hoping that Keith would decide to go to work instead of trying to accompany her to the doctor.

Keith knocked on the bathroom door and twisted the knob, but it remained locked. "Tay, you are taking a long time in there. You've been in there thirty minutes. Dr. Morris said to bring you in as soon as possible, so that he can fit you in. Otherwise, he said to just take you in to the hospital.'' He tapped on the door. "What are you doing in there? You never lock the door.''

"Give me a minute!'' she yelled through the door.

"Is everything okay?''

"Yes, everything is fine. I was just taking a shower . . . Everything's good!'' she yelled. In her mind she was trying to figure things out.

"You just took a shower when you woke up in the middle of the night bleeding, Tay,'' he said as if to remind her. His tone told her that he was suspicious.

Silence . . .

Taylor opened the bathroom door after thirty more minutes and was surprised to see Keith still standing there. Now with his eyes, he told her that he was suspicious.

"I didn't hear any water,'' he said, continuing to look at her intensely.

Taylor just looked at him as she tried to figure out what to say. She then thought to herself, *How could I be so stupid? I didn't even think to run the water.*

"I'm going to work,'' he said. Without waiting for a response he walked out of the door.

Taylor was in shock because she knew her husband and,

what he just did was not normal. She knew he was no longer worried . . . He had become suspicious.

***

While Keith was sitting in his office his mind was everywhere. Something about this situation did not feel right to him. He knew his wife, and something was going on with her whether she wanted to admit it or not. He didn't know what else to do, so he pulled out his cell phone and called his father, John.

"Hi, Dad, how are you?" he asked.

"I'm good, Son, how are you? Your sister called me earlier saying that Taylor was sick. How is she?" he asked. His dad always viewed Taylor as his daughter, and when Candis told him that she was sick, he was concerned by the news.

"Well, that's the thing, Dad, I don't really know. I feel like something's not right, like there's something that she's not telling me. Then, when I get prepared to take her to the doctor this morning, she started acting funny. She was stalling and I can't figure out why," Keith said. He had been trying to figure it out since he left home. "She can't be sure that she didn't have a miscarriage last night. So why wouldn't she want to see a doctor just to be sure?" He sighed heavily. "Sometimes I don't understand Taylor."

"Well, Son, it's not that strange that she didn't want to go to the doctor. Sometimes people are so afraid of what they may find out. She may be scared to find out that something may be wrong with her body or that she could have possibly lost a child. That could be devastating to a mother, you know?" He tried to give him reason.

"Yeah . . . Yeah, maybe you are right. Maybe she is scared. That makes sense," he said, thankful that he had the chance to talk to his father. He made him feel so much at ease about the situation.

"Son, you need to pray," John added.

"Okay, Dad. It was good talking to you, but I gotta get back to this case," Keith said, attempting to rush him off the phone.

"I love you, Son."

"I love you too, Dad. I gotta go."

Keith called to check on Taylor, and then he finished up on his case.

Knock, knock, knock . . .

Kim walked into his office. "Hey, Keith, I'm done with the Gary case," she said, handing him the file.

"Kim, do you have a minute?" he asked.

"Of course."

"I want to ask you something, but it's kind of a personal question," his tone a little lower.

"Oookay . . . I don't mind, Keith. You can ask me anything," she assured him.

"How do you think you would feel if you had a miscarriage?"

Kim slowly sat down in the chair in front of his desk. "Wow, when you said personal, I didn't really think *personal*." She paused before continuing, "It's kind of difficult to say. I would feel scared and maybe hurt . . . Why do you ask?" She was now curious.

"I'm not sure, but I'm thinking that Tay could have possibly had one last night, but she doesn't want to see a doctor. My dad was saying that she may be scared to find out and I thought that made sense, but I don't really know." He paused when he saw her posture change. Her shoulders that were once upright, now hung a little lower. "What do you think?"

"I'm sorry to hear that, Keith, but maybe I should stay out of it."

"No, Kim. I would like to know a woman's perspective. Your point of view is important to me," he said, reassuring her.

"Well," she began. "I believe she should go to a doctor and get her body checked out just in case she really did have a miscarriage. I know it did a lot of damage to my . . ." She stopped in midsentence, realizing what she was saying.

Keith waited for her to finish her statement.

She looked at her watch, trying to find a way out of finishing the conversation they were having. "I better go. I hope everything turns out okay," she said. She got up from her seat and rushed toward the door.

"Kim, wait!" he called to her before she was able to walk out.

She slowly turned around, hoping that he wasn't about to ask her to finish her statement.

"Taylor mentioned about having a dinner party tomorrow night and we want you and Trey to come,'' he informed her.

"Thanks, but I'm afraid I must turn down your invite. It was a sweet gesture, but you and Taylor seem to have a lot going on, and you guys need to just take some time to yourselves. She's probably not even thinking about a dinner party after what took place last night.''

He sat and thought for a minute before saying, "Yeah, you are probably right. I'll push it back to a later date. I will discuss it with Tay, and I'll get back with you on the date that we come up with, but go ahead and talk it over with Trey and get back with me.''

"Okay, I will. You talk everything over with Taylor.'' She smiled and headed out the door.

Chapter Nine

Taylor went into Dr. Allen's office and was waiting to be seen.

The nurse called her to the back. "Hi, Mrs. Davenport, what can we do for you today?" she asked with Taylor's chart in her hand.

"Well, my body is going through some changes with my cycle, so I wanted to know should I be concerned. I've been taking my birth-control pills consistently for about four years now, and I have not had a cycle in three years, but last night I woke up with blood all over my sheets. I just need to know that everything is okay with my body," Taylor explained with concern, her dream from last night still in the forefront of her mind.

"Okay, Mrs. Davenport. We will get the doctor in to answer all of your questions and concerns, but in the meantime, I need to take your vitals," the nurse said. She took her blood pressure and temperature. "Okay, Dr. Allen will be right in," she said, and then she quickly exited the room.

The doctor came in with Taylor's chart in her hand. She

stood and looked over the notes that the nurse wrote in it. She looked up at Taylor. "Mrs. Davenport, tell me what's going on."

"Well, I haven't had a cycle in three years, and I would like to know if it is normal for me to have one out of the blue considering that I've been taking my pills consistently. It came in the middle of the night and I mean it literally scared me. I thought something was wrong," she explained.

"Well, Mrs. Davenport, yes, it is normal for you to have a cycle after not having one for three years. Sometimes the body reacts differently when you are on the pill and women tend to have cycles at different times while on the pill. Have you been having any pains or anything?" Dr. Allen asked.

"No, I feel fine, I guess. That just scared me and my husband, that's all," Taylor explained.

"Well, we will take some blood from you and run some tests to make sure everything is okay . . . Sounds good?" she asked. She left the room without even waiting for a response.

After her blood was taken, Taylor went to the front desk to set up her next appointment.

"Taylor?" Keith's sister, Candis, walked up to the counter and looked at her with confusion. "I thought that was you. What are you doing here? Keith said that you guys were going in to see Dr. Morris today. I didn't realize that you were coming to see Dr. Allen. She's a great doctor, though. Is this your first visit with her?"

"Candi, um . . ." Taylor paused, trying to figure out what to say. "Yes, this is my first visit with her. Dr. Morris was pretty full today, so he sent me here,'' she lied.

"Wow, really? He never seems to do that. My friend Samantha works for him,'' Candis said as she pointed to the olive-skinned girl standing next to her. "We just came here to pick up our girl, Jessica, for lunch,'' she explained further, now pointing to the girl behind the desk who was setting up Taylor's appointment.

"Oh, okay. Well, I guess I better get going,'' Taylor said, rushing toward the door.

Jessica yelled from behind the desk, "Wait, Mrs. Davenport, you forgot your appointment card!''

Candis took the card from Jessica's hand and walked over to Taylor with it. She squint her eyes and asked, "Are you sure you're okay, Taylor?'' She held the card out to her.

Taylor grabbed the card. "Yes, I'm fine. Thanks, Candis.'' She left out the door without looking back.

"Ooookay, she was acting really strange,'' Candis said to Samantha and Jessica as they got in the car.

"I agree. She did start acting very strange when she saw you. Y'all related or something?'' Jessica asked. She thought about the fact that Taylor lied, and it made her say, "Oh, and, girl, she lied to you. She has been Dr. Allen's patient for a good four years or so,'' she informed her.

Candis mouth dropped, "Are you sure, Jessica?''

"Yes, girl, I am sure. I know all of Dr. Allen's patients,

and I'm always at the office when Mrs. Davenport comes in, but I'm trying to figure out why she would lie to you about it.''

"Yeah, got me wondering the same thing,'' Candis thought aloud.

***

Taylor walked in her front door trying to figure out what to do next. *God, I pray that Candis does not say anything to Keith about this. I would never be able to explain this to him*, she thought. She put away her paper work from the doctor's office in a box in the top of her walk-in closet, and then went to the bathroom to get cleaned up so that she could prepare dinner.

She allowed the shower water to run over her body as the dream she had last night, began to unfold. Fearful, she began to pray . . . "God, give me time. I will tell him when the time is right, I promise. I just need time.'' She prayed, but Taylor was not planning to tell Keith anything anytime soon, if ever . . .

***

Once Candis dropped Jessica and Samantha back off, she pulled out her cell phone and called Keith. "Keith, I thought you said that you and Taylor were going to Dr. Morris's office today?''

"Yes, we were supposed to, but Taylor acted like she didn't want to go, so I wasn't going to force her into going. I figured she needed time, so I came on in to work. Why? Did she call you? Is everything okay with her?'' He became concerned all over again.

"I'm not sure. Did you know that she has another

doctor? I saw her today in Dr. Allen's office, and she lied to me about it being her first visit. According to records, she's been seeing this doctor for about four years. I wouldn't have come to you with this, Keith, but I feel like something is not right with this picture and you are my brother, so I want you to be aware,'' Candis explained with caution.

"Candi, are you sure? Maybe this is a special doctor and she went there for a second opinion. We've been trying to have babies for a while now, and she's been having complications with getting pregnant, that's what we were both seeing Dr. Morris about. Maybe she just desires a second opinion, and I don't blame her," Keith said with a little doubt of his own in his voice.

"Okay, Keith; that could be true. I just want you to be aware of what's going on. I love you and Tay, and I just thought she was acting out of the norm today,'' she explained.

"Thanks, Candi; and you know I love you too. I know you are concerned, but I'm sure everything is okay. She may not have wanted me to know about this other doctor or something,'' he replied, then thought to himself, *But why wouldn't she want me to know? I am her husband. We should have no secrets.*

Candis cut into his thoughts with her next statement, "You are probably right, Keith. I'm sure everything is fine. Don't worry about mentioning it to her, maybe she is a little embarrassed by it or something and that may be the reason why she hasn't told you yet. I'm sure that's why she started acting strangely when she saw me there. There's probably nothing to worry about.''

"Yeah, I'm sure that's what it is. I won't mention it,

baby girl,'' he assured her.

***

Keith walked in the door. "Tay, babe, where you at?'' he yelled over Boys II Men singing, "Can You Stand the Rain,'' through the stereo.

"Hey, I'm in the kitchen, honey!'' Taylor yelled.

Keith walked into the living room to turn down the stereo before heading to the kitchen. He saw Taylor standing at the stove, cooking. "You didn't have to cook, Tay. I was going to do all that. You should be resting, baby,'' he said, and then kissed her forehead. "How are you feeling? Did you get you some rest today?'' He took the fork out of her hand and began finishing up the cooking for her.

"I'm fine, and I've been resting all day. Nothing is wrong, Keith. Trust me.'' She was hoping that he didn't know anything further than what she was telling him.

"Well, I just want to make sure you are okay. I want you off your feet until we see Dr. Morris.'' He waited a minute to see what her reaction would be. "You didn't make it in to see the doctor today, right?''

She shook her head.

He continued, "So how about you stay off your feet until you are able to be seen by the doctor because I don't want anything happening to you,'' he said, trying not to sound as if he knew anything. He began fixing their plates.

"Yeah, I wasn't able to go in today, but I will try to go in next week," she lied. She walked over to the candle lit table, and sat down as she watched her husband at the stove.

"Okay, that's good," he said. He turned and looked at her. "But, Tay, what makes you so sure that everything is okay with you?"

She responded, "I prayed about it." With that response, she knew he would now change the subject.

He brought her plate to the table. "Well, great! We will be able to start our family in no time then," he said, looking into her eyes.

"Yeah." She became uncomfortable and looked away. "We should be able to before we know it."

Keith knew then that something was different. Anytime he mentioned starting a family, Taylor would jump down his throat every time. Taylor and Keith ate silently together as both of their minds began to wonder . . .

The doctor brought a beautiful baby girl into the room and placed her in Taylor's arms. The baby girl grabbed Taylor's finger and began to smile as she wiggled in her arms. Taylor looked down at the beautiful baby girl that she held and realized that she was smiling back at her. But then her smile quickly faded once she noticed that the doctor had left the room.

"Wait . . . doctor . . . come back! This baby isn't mine! Somebody, please! Come get this baby . . . Somebody, help me! Come get this baby! Hey . . . somebody!" Taylor yelled at the top of her lungs, and the baby began to cry just as loud . . .

After tossing and turning all night, Taylor jumped up out of her sleep once again screaming.

Keith jumped up out of his sleep from her piercing scream. "Baby, what's wrong?" he asked as he grabbed her to calm her down.

She was crying hysterically.

"What's wrong, Tay? Talk to me, baby. Tell me what's going on." He hugged her, attempting to calm her down.

Taylor continued to cry. "I . . . had . . . a . . . bad . . . dream . . ." she managed to get out in between sobs.

"Tell me about it. What's going on in these bad dreams that you've been having lately?"

Taylor looked into his eyes and said, "I . . . I . . . think... I've . . . killed . . . someone . . ."

Chapter Ten

Taylor and Keith contacted their friends to come over for the dinner party that they had planned for that evening. She and Keith had been preparing for this all day. As Taylor stood at the stove, Keith walked up behind her, wrapping his arms around her waist. As she felt him breathing down her neck, she got chill bumps.

Kissing her neck softly, "I love you so much and right now I think you should come upstairs with me, so I can show you how much," he said, then turned her around to face him.

"Keith, the food is almost done and everyone should be arriving really soon. We don't have time to do what's on your mind," she said, running her finger down the bridge of his nose. She kissed his lips.

"It will only take a minute," Keith promised her.

Taylor looked at him with a smirk on her face as if she knew that it wasn't going to take him a minute.

"Please, Tay." He kissed her lips. "Just one minute," he

begged. He picked her up and sat her on the counter.

She looked into his eyes, and then kissed him passionately, letting him know that she was giving in to his plea. She reached inside his pants and touched him in his most personal place. Breathing heavily, she whispered into his ear, "You are a very persuasive man." She kissed his lips.

He nodded. "Umm-hmm, you know that's what I do." He kissed her lips, taking her bottom lip into his mouth, biting it softly.

The doorbell rang.

"Dang," Keith said as he looked at Taylor with disappointment. He quickly fixed his pants. "We will definitely finish this later, or do you just want me to tell them to leave?"

She laughed. "We are going to finish this later, and I will make it well-worth your wait."

He smiled. "You promise?"

"With all my heart," she promised, then sealed it with a kiss.

The doorbell rang once more.

Taylor pulled back from their kiss and laughed. "Go get the door, baby. We can't keep our guest waiting."

He helped her down from the counter, kissing her one last time before going to answer the door.

Taylor washed her hands in the sink and finished up

dinner.

Keith finally opened the door. "Hey. Mike, Right? How've you been?" he asked. He firmly shook his hand.

"Yeah, that's me. I've been well . . . It has been a really long time since we've seen each other. How have you been?" Michael asked.

"Tay and I are really good," Keith made it a point to say. "Thanks for asking. I'm glad you could make it. Come on in and make yourself at home. The food should be ready in no time." He pointed to the living room. He looked confused when he saw the gorgeous Latino who now walked up and stood beside Michael.

After catching his look, Michael said, "Oh, I'm sorry, Keith. Where are my manners? This is Silvia Martinez. She works for me. Silvia, this is Keith, one of my classmates from high school."

Silvia reached out her hand to Keith. "Mucha gusto, Keith." Silvia looked at him from his head to his toes as if he were her prey. She bit her bottom lip as their hands met.

Keith thought her Spanish accent was beautiful, and he responded, "Pleased to meet you as well." He then pulled his hand away from her grasp.

About fifteen minutes later, Trey and Kim showed up.

Michael said grace and everyone sat at the dinner table, enjoying their meals while they reminisced on their high school years and caught up on the present.

"So, Michael," Trey began, arrogantly. "What's been up with you? I remember when you weren't nothing but a lil' nerd, more like a lil' punk. Now you looking all GQ and done pulled yourself a supermodel. What's up with that?" He then looked at Silvia. "How he pulled you, baby doll, with yo' sexy self? I bet he paid you to be his date, didn't he? Tell the truth and shame the devil." He laughed a haughty laugh, then took another sip of his beer.

"No. We are just really good friends, and by the way, me llamo is Silvia," she said with an attitude as if she were offended by his statement.

"Well, *Silvia*, where yo' man at and why he let you come out with this low budget?" Trey asked.

Michael just shook his head and chuckled as he finished his dinner. He wasn't willing to respond to ignorance.

"Well, *Trey*, Michael is far from low budget." Silvia winked at Michael, and then returned her focus back to Trey. "And I don't have a man." She tilted her head and focused her attention solely on him. "Me, personally, I enjoy rocking the title."

Trey leaned forward in his seat. "And what title might that be?" he asked curiously.

"Bachelorette . . . Being single, I have no one to answer to, and I love being free to do *whatever* it is I want to do," she said to him, then took a sip of her Moscato. She looked at Trey over the rim of her glass.

Trey looked her in her eyes and knew exactly what she

was insinuating. "Well, what is it that you want to do, sexy?" He picked up his beer and took another sip.

"Okay, Trey," Kim whispered to him, "I think you've had enough." She attempted to take the beer from his hand.

Trey viciously grabbed her hand. "You know not to ever do that! You slow, stupid, or dumb? Don't you *ever* grab *anything* from me!" he yelled.

"Hey, Trey!" Keith hollered at him. "I think you need to calm down, and don't you ever grab her like that again!"

Taylor looked at her husband, shocked at how he responded.

Trey took another sip of his beer. "Or what you gon' do playboy besides get knocked down? What, you a mighty big man now, huh, Keith?"

"Look, I'm not trying to be with all that, Trey. I just want you to calm down and respect my house and *everyone* in it," Keith shot back in a tone that let him know that he wasn't playing and neither was he afraid.

Silvia leaned over and whispered into Taylor's ear, "Do you have some coffee? If you can just fix him a cup, I'll take him outside to get some fresh air. I can help him to calm down."

Taylor looked at Silvia with question.

After seeing the look of question on Taylor's face, she continued, "Oh, I've dealt with his kind before. I used to work for Alcoholics Anonymous, and I can tell that he's an alcoholic,'' she informed her, continuing to whisper the information into her ear.

Taylor got up from the table to get her that cup of coffee. Once she got into the kitchen she prayed silently, *Please, God, get that man out of my house*, she referred to Trey, then she thought to herself, *Inviting them here was a mistake, I can feel it.* After fixing the cup of coffee, she came back to the table and handed it to Silvia. "Here you go.'' She continued to look at her with doubt.

"Gracious.'' She touched Taylor's hand while grabbing the cup from her, making Taylor feel uncomfortable.

"You are welcome,'' Taylor said.

Silvia got up and went over to Trey. She leaned over his shoulder. "Here's some coffee for you.'' She handed him the cup. "Would you like to join me outside for some fresh air?''

Trey didn't say a word as he looked into her eyes. The look in her eyes told him that it was more to this than just going outside to get some fresh air. So he quickly got up and followed her outside to the porch.

Everyone at the table looked around at each other silently.

When Taylor saw the look of embarrassment on Kim's face, she said, "Oh, um . . . Don't worry.'' She waved her hand in the air. "She knows a little bit about alcoholism. She said she used to work for Alcoholics Anonymous,'' she further explained, sensing the tension in the room.

Michael thought to himself, *No she didn't. God, what is she up to?*   He knew that Silvia never worked for Alcoholics Anonymous and the fact that she lied to Taylor about it made him suspicious.

"I'm sorry you guys." Kim cried. "I just . . . I just don't know what to do anymore."

Michael reached over and touched her hand. "Look, God does not intend for you to be hurting at the hands of your husband. I believe that God can fix any marriage no matter how rough the marriage may be, and if you desire for Him to fix yours, He will. But you have to trust Him to do so. Just go to Him in prayer and He will hear you," he gently explained.

"What makes you so sure that God can fix her marriage or anything for that matter?" Keith asked him, his tone hostile.

"I have seen God work in the lives of many people. I've seen cancer bow down at the name of Jesus, and I have seen people who were dying be raised up and healed by the blood of Jesus. I am more than sure that He can fix her marriage if she truly trusts Him with it. The key is giving God your marriage and allowing Him to help you work on your marriage. He can and will turn things around for you. God is an awesome God and His power is real. He is faithful and He will fulfill every one of His promises. We just need to trust Him," Michael further explained.

Keith shook his head and laughed . . .

***

Silvia sat extremely close to Trey while sitting on the porch step.

"So, what can I do to help you calm down?" she asked.

Trey didn't respond. She began to look very familiar to him, but he just couldn't place her face.

"What do you want me to do to calm you down?" she asked again. She reached over and touched him in a place that let him know that she wasn't talking about calming him down with no coffee or fresh air.

He looked down to where her hand rested. "You know what you're doing?" he asked.

"Sí, I know exactly what I'm doing, and I'll prove it to you if you let me," she said, assuring him.

Trey sat down his cup of coffee and grabbed her by her arm. He pulled her to his car that was parked on the street in front of the house. He pushed her into the backseat and got in behind her. They were like wild animals trying to attack one another as they kissed wildly.

She unzipped his pants and straddled him. She kissed him on his neck. "Do you want me?" she asked. She bit his ear, then kissed his neck once again.

No response . . .

She lowered herself down onto his manhood, and then traced his lips with her tongue. He could not believe that this woman approached him the way she did, and here he was having sex with yet another stranger. He pulled her long dark-brown hair and held her head to where he could look into her big brown eyes as he began to climax, but Silvia looked away . . .

After Kim and Michael finished their conversation, she decided to walk outside to look for Trey so that they could go home. It was getting late and she had become extremely tired all of a sudden. When she got outside, she saw the shadow in the car. She walked over to the car thinking that Trey had fallen to sleep drunk.

As she got closer she gasped at what she saw. Silvia was on top of her husband, pleasing him. She knew that her husband had cheated on her several times before, but never had she caught him in the act. She turned and quickly ran back up the porch steps and through the front door. She ran right into Michael as he was on his way out.

"I'm sorry . . . I didn't mean to run into you. Oh, my God. . . I'm so sorry," she said, crying hysterically.

"What's wrong, Kim?" Michael asked.

"I need someone to take me home. I don't feel so good," she said, holding her stomach.

Keith walked up behind them. "Trey left?" he asked.

"No, somebody just take me home . . . *Please!*" she yelled.

Michael touched her shoulder to calm her down. "I'll take you."

Keith walked outside and saw Trey getting out of the car with Silvia. "What is this?" he asked, looking Trey in his eyes.

"Oh," Trey laughed, "I'm sober now," he said, zipping

up his pants.

Everybody was now outside trying to piece everything together.

"I'll take you home, Kim, and, Michael, you can take Silvia home," Taylor said, looking Michael in his eyes as she nodded, making sure he understood.

Silvia looked at Kim and her lips turned up into a smirk.

Tears continued to fall from Kim's eyes. This woman showed no remorse for what she had done to Kim's heart at that moment.

"Yeah, we better get going, Silvia. It's late," Michael said firmly, disapproval in his tone.

Trey saw Kim walk away with Taylor. "Wait, where you going?" he yelled to her.

Kim kept walking without looking back.

"I'm talking to you, you . . ."

Michael quickly walked up to Trey. "Watch your mouth," he said, interrupting him. "You are a coward, and you will reap what you sow," he declared.

Trey looked at him and didn't say a word.

Kim left with Taylor, and Silvia left with Michael.

Keith stared at Trey for a moment and shook his head before saying, "You can get out my yard." He went up the steps and back into the house.

Trey walked through the door behind him. "What, you think you better than me?''

"As a matter of fact, I do.'' Keith scowled. "I would never put my hands on a woman, and then you have the nerve to come here and have sex with some other woman in your car right under your wife's nose.'' He shook his head, disturbed by the situation. "You are so stupid, Trey.''

"You don't know what I was doing in that car; but if you want to know, all you have to do is ask. Yeah, I had sex with her.'' He shrugged. "What can I say, you saw that woman. Then the sex was good, so I have no complaints. Maybe you should try hooking up with someone else other than your wife and maybe you'll get that chip off your shoulder,'' Trey shot back.

"You are sick, man,'' said Keith with disgust.

"Well, maybe, but I only have one life to live and I'm going to live my life to the fullest.''

"What the hell happened to you? You use to be better than this. You had so much going for you and now this. You have a beautiful wife who loves you and you have the nerve to treat her the way you do, yet she is still beside you. I just don't understand.''

"You want to know what happened to me, Keith; life happened and it just came in and ambushed me without warning. I had it all, then boom! Everything . . . gone. My hopes and dreams, my career . . . gone. I lost everything, and I'm just trying to figure out why is that woman still here,'' he yelled angrily, pointing towards the door as if Kim was standing there. "You know what I think? I think you want my wife. I see the way you look at her and how you talk to her. Yeah, you seem to have forgotten about that day I walked into the office on the two of you. I felt that energy between you two. But I guarantee you this. You had better . . . not . . . touch her, if you know what's good for you," he said, looking Keith in his eyes.

Keith without thinking stepped to Trey, and there they stood face-to-face, toe-to-toe, mano a mano. "Are you really threatening me, man? You sure you want to do that? Get out my house right now before I do something that I'll regret, because obviously you have lost . . . your . . . mind," he said firmly, meaning every word.

Trey walked out the door and to his car. There, he sat for a moment. *You will reap what you sow.* The words of Michael played over and over in his mind like a broken record. He started the engine and sped off.

***

Taylor looked back and forth between Kim and the road. "I'm so sorry, Kim, but why do you put up with that?" she asked.

"Taylor," Kim began, "I would like you to drop me at my parent's house. I just . . . I can't deal with what I saw tonight. That woman was on top of my husband having sex with him right out in the open . . . I just don't know what to do anymore. I love him, I can't leave him. I would be a disgrace to my family." She spoke aloud, but it was as if she was talking to herself.

"Kim, don't worry about disgracing your family. Maybe

if you told them what you are going through with Trey, they would understand your reason for needing to leave him.''

Kim just looked at Taylor, and her eyes told her that she no longer wanted to discuss it.

"Okay, I will take you to your parents. Are you gonna be okay?''

Kim nodded. "Yes.''

They rode silently the rest of the way.

***

"Did you have sex with him?'' Michael asked Silvia.

"What? I don't have sex with married men . . . I can't believe you have the nerve to ask me that,'' she responded as if she were offended.

"I can't believe you had the nerve to have sex with that married man outside while his wife was right there in the house,'' he shot back, not believing a word she just told him.

"What? You have no proof that I had sex with anyone. I don't even know that man, and I am not a whore like you are trying to make me out to be.''

Michael pulled into her apartment complex and parked the car.

"Look, Silvia. You are right. I don't know what you did in that car with that man; but whatever it was that man's wife thought she saw, really disturbed her.''

"I'm sorry, Michael, for whatever y'all *thought*, but like I said, it wasn't what you thought." She paused and looked at him, then touched his hand. "So, would you like to come up for a minute?"

He moved his hand away from hers and replied, "No, but I'll watch you walk up."

"Please, Mike, just for a second. I promise I will make it worth your time." She leaned over and kissed him softly on his lips, then ran her hand down his inner thigh.

Gently pushing her away from him, "What are you doing, Silvia?" he asked. "I said that I wasn't coming up, so you need to get out of my car." He reached over her to open her door.

"I believe you really want to come up. I can feel it in my... what do you call it . . . spirit," she said sarcastically, then laughed out loud.

"Goodnight, Silvia." The look on his face let her know that he was serious.

She rolled her eyes. "Buenas noches." She got out of the car and walked up the stairs.

Michael, in dismay, watched her enter her apartment. He sighed deeply, and then drove off.

Chapter Eleven

Taylor had been having disturbing dreams since the first Sunday that she had decided to return to church for the first time in years. The dreams were becoming more and more frequent and started to feel more and more real. Keith often woke up to her screaming in the middle of the night and tried to console her.

Taylor was beginning to understand her dreams more and more as they continued to haunt her. She had a feeling that Pandora's Box was about to be opened soon enough, and she was not prepared for that. She had to figure out how to tell her husband everything that he needed to know. She just knew that he wouldn't be able to handle the secret she kept . . .

Keith walked into the room and kissed her forehead. "Are you feeling better, sweetie? You are really beginning to scare me with these dreams that you've been waking up from. What's wrong, Tay? Talk to me, and let me know what's going on." He took her hand into his. "There's a reason for these dreams, babe, and maybe if you talk to me I can help you face them."

"I'm okay, Keith, and it's nothing to worry about. I'm fine. Trust me," she said, holding back her tears.

He hugged her. "Tay, I love you, and you can talk to me about anything, you know this. I feel like you are trying to hide something, and I just need you to talk to me, baby. Whatever is on your mind I promise I'll understand, and we can get through it together," he assured her.

Taylor's tears escaped her eyes, and Keith kissed them away. She smiled and took a deep breath. "I'm fine, honey. Trust me." She kissed his nose. "No worries." She looked deeper into his eyes. "I'm about to take me a shower." She smiled, then asked, "Would you like to join me?"

"You go ahead." He kissed her once again. "I have to get prepared for a deposition this morning."

Taylor hopped in the shower, hoping to shake the feeling of fear and anxiety that had come over her. She felt as if her life was about to change with the blinking of an eye. "God, please help me shake this feeling," she prayed aloud. She allowed the water and the scent of lavender to soothe her shaking body.

Taylor's cell phone began ringing.

Keith yelled through the bathroom door, "Tay, your phone is ringing!"

"Grab it for me! It's in my purse on the dresser!" she yelled over the sound of the shower water.

Keith hurried and grabbed her purse, but once he reached it, her cell phone stopped ringing . . . and what he discovered in her purse really disturbed him.

"Did you get it, Keith?" Taylor yelled after moments of silence.

Keith stormed through the bathroom door. "No, I didn't... but I got this!" Furiously, he pulled open the shower door. "What in the hell is this, Tay?"

"Keith, what are you talking about?" she asked, trying to wipe the water from her face, so that she could see clearer. "Oh, my God! Keith, baby, I can explain," she said after seeing what he was holding up.

"Explain what, Tay?" He threw her birth-control pills across the room.

As they flew past Taylor, they hit the wall and splattered everywhere. She had never seen her husband so angry. Shocked, she wasn't able to say a word.

"Explain what?" Keith repeated. "You got me sitting around like a fool, thinking that something was wrong with you or me when it came to us trying to have children, and all this time it was because of you! You were deliberately trying not to have children when you knew that I was trying to have a family!" He walked out of the bathroom, and Taylor hopped out the shower to follow.

"Keith, please wait. Let me explain," she kept saying, but she really didn't know how she could explain it to him with him being in a rage. She watched as he pulled out his luggage.

Keith began packing some of his clothes.

Taylor grabbed his arm. "Keith, please," she begged.

He pulled away and jumped at her, but caught himself. Trying to control himself, he turned his back to her, continuing to pack.

"Keith, just listen to me, baby," she began. "All that talk about children, and you knew how I felt about that. I knew you wanted children, and I didn't want to hurt you; but the truth is; you wanted them, not me. You felt as though you were ready to start a family, but I wasn't ready. I was trying to start my life. Keith, I was not ready to have children. That's why I aborted the first one," she blurted out. She covered her mouth in shock, realizing what she had just revealed.

Keith instantly stopped packing. Slapping her to the floor, "What did you just say?"

Holding the side of her face, she cried hysterically as she looked up at him.

Shocked by her words and his own actions, tears filled his eyes as he realized what he had done. He didn't say another word. He left his bag of clothes behind and headed for his car. There, he sat and cried as he thought about everything that had just transpired. It was all surreal and he couldn't believe it. He was hurt like never before. He began looking back on all the evidence of what Taylor had just revealed. The fact that about five months after they married, Taylor was going through mood swings, and then at one point, she would not allow him to have sex with her for a while. Then, there were the times when she would say that she was on her cycle, but the dates would be all mixed up. He wanted to trust his wife. He couldn't believe that Taylor would do that to him . . . to his unborn child . . . to their family.

Taylor cried out, "Oh, my God!" She remained in the same place where Keith left her.

She knew that she had really messed up with Keith, and at this point, she was not so sure about her marriage. She knew that Keith was hurt by the information that he had just received, and there was nothing she could do to fix it. He had never been so angry with her in his life, and he had never placed his hands on her in that manner until now. She could not believe all that had just taken place. *What am I gonna do to fix this*? She thought, but the real question was, *what will happen next?*

***

After riding around for hours, Keith pulled into the parking lot of his office well after five o'clock. There was not a car in sight. He walked into his office and sat at his desk as he continued to reflect on what had taken place with Taylor.

Kim walked past his office and was surprised to see him. "Oh, my God, Keith, you scared me!" she said, grabbing her chest. "I didn't know anyone else was here."

"I'm sorry. I didn't mean to scare you. What are you still doing here? I didn't see your car in the lot."

"Well, I took a cab. I got a pretty late start today." She walked in closer to him. "Keith, is something wrong?"

The bruise around her neck caught his attention. "Oh, my God, Kim." He released a sigh as he shook his head. "Why do you keep allowing him to do this to you?"

This time she didn't even attempt to cover the bruise with make-up. That was one of the reasons why she waited until everyone had left the office before she came in. She didn't feel like covering her skin with all that make-up, and she didn't want to be interrogated about her bruises. "I . . . don't know." Quickly changing the subject and her tone, "I was about to get out of here and get a drink at Casie's Bar and Grill. I could really use one, and it seems as though you need to join me."

"I don't know. I've had a rough day. I haven't gotten any work done and I have a lot to do . . . I forgot." He shook his head as he realized. "I missed a deposition this morning."

"Well, just use this as a 'take a break day.' It really sounds like you could use one, and I'm sure you could use a drink as well." She smiled.

"Maybe you are right." He finally gave in. "Let's go get that drink."

Keith and Kim walked into Casie's Bar and Grill. Tonight it wasn't a big crowd, and they loved it whenever it was like that. They picked out a table and ordered their drinks.

Kim studied her friend as she saw the disturbed look on his face. "Keith, what's wrong?" She looked at him closely. "I've known you for years, and you are not your usual self. It's definitely not like you to miss work, let alone, a deposition," she said.

"I never would have thought that my marriage would come to this," he began. "All I ever wanted was to make Taylor happy and to start a family . . . I can't believe her, that she would be so selfish," he said, forgetting that he was talking to someone.

Kim watched him with concern. "What happened?"

"She was taking birth-control pills, Kim." He now looked up at her. "All this time she was deceiving me. I thought something was wrong with the way one of our bodies was functioning or something, but it was her with her lying, selfish, deceitful . . ."

"Keith, maybe she was afraid to be a mother. Maybe she wasn't ready," Kim interjected, trying to make light of the situation.

"She had an abortion, Kim. She aborted our child. How could she be so selfish?" He shook his head. "I didn't even know." The thought made him furious. "I don't know what to do. I can't even trust her anymore. I can't believe that she was deceiving me all this time. I really don't know what I should do." He was hoping for Kim to give him some advice on what she thinks he should do next.

The waitress brought them their drinks, three shots of vodka for Keith, and two Coronas for Kim.

Keith downed his three shots, and Kim drank her first Corona and half of the second.

She looked up at him, and she couldn't help but say, "Keith, I'm so sorry. I can understand what you are going through. I, too, lost a child." She empathized with him, her eyes now filled with tears.

"What? I'm sorry. I didn't know." His focus was now

on her.

"No, that's okay. I was twelve," she began. "My dad had left me and my mom to go do what he called, 'a job.' He left us under high surveillance, so that we would be safe, but he didn't know that he left us in harm's way. He left us in the hands of trouble and he didn't even know it." She shook her head as she remembered the past. She turned up her Corona, finishing it off before she continued, "It was three of my daddy's 'business men' as he called them. My mom had been so sick, and they were supposed to take care of her while he was away. They put something in her drink one night, and it knocked her out cold. She . . . she couldn't even . . . she couldn't even hear my screams." She sobbed.

Keith reached across the table and grabbed her hand.

She continued, "Those men came in and raped me, and she couldn't even hear my screams. I . . . I screamed so loud, but she couldn't hear me . . . Blood was everywhere. I tried to wash my clothes, my sheets, and I tried to scrub away their scents, but I could still smell them. I swear I tried to wash it away. I was twelve years old . . . I was just a baby." She cried hysterically as her thoughts took her back to that very night.

"Is everything okay here?" the waitress asked as she brought their second round of drinks. Two shots of vodka were placed on the table in front of them.

"Everything is okay," Keith said to the waitress, but his eyes were fixed on Kim's eyes.

Kim downed one of the shots as her eyes stayed on Keith's eyes.

The waitress glanced at both of them, then walked away.

Kim continued, "It was about eight weeks later, and I tried to cover it up, but then the blood came . . . then the baby... There was so much blood. My mother screamed when she saw all of the blood and what she called that 'alien' on the floor. My father came in and all he could say was, 'who did this,' and I told him, 'I tried to fight them daddy, I promise I did.' He went and found the surveillance tape from that night and those men have been missing ever since. A finger from each one of them was sent to each of their families. My parents had taken me to a doctor, and he said that it was too much damage done. I will never be able to carry a child again." At this point Kim was hysterical.

Keith moved his chair closer to her and held her. She waited a minute before standing to go to the restroom. She stumbled.

Keith caught her by her arm. "I think you've had too much. Let me call you a cab," he said as he helped her to steady herself.

"No, I want you to take me home . . . no cabs. I came here with you. I'm leaving with you," she said. At this point it was as if she didn't trust anyone but Keith.

"Okay, let me take care of the bill, and I'll take you home. Okay?" He tried to comfort her. He downed his last shot, hoping that it would comfort him.

***

Keith walked Kim inside her two-story home and made sure that she was okay.

"Let me get you a drink," she said as she headed to her kitchen.

"Kim, I don't think I need any more to drink. I don't know how I did it, but I'm just glad I got us here safely . . . Are you gonna be okay here?" he asked.

Before he knew it, Kim had fixed their drinks and had them in her hands as she walked back over to him. She handed him a glass, then walked over and sat on the couch. "Please, sit with me." She patted the couch beside her.

Keith hesitated for a minute, and then sat down beside her.

"What I shared with you tonight, I've never shared with anyone, and I didn't realize how much it hurt. You just don't understand what it feels like to feel caged all your life. All this time I've felt like a prisoner caged by fear." She began to whisper as if someone who didn't need to know this secret could hear her, "Believe it or not, my dad killed those men. I know he did. You see, my father is Italian, and my mother is Filipino. My family is Catholic, and my dad was a part of the Mafia. Even though he tried his best to hide it from me, I knew. If my dad knew how Trey treated me, he would kill him, and I can't divorce. I would shame my family. They don't believe in divorce, so I am in a dead end situation. I don't want Trey dead, and I don't want to shame my family," she explained as she continued to drink.

Keith listened to her as he drank the rest of his drink. He leaned forward to set his empty glass down on the table.

Kim reached out and touched his hand as he set the glass down.   Their eyes met. "Keith, I have loved you since high school. I just hid those feelings because you were with Taylor, and I was with Trey, but the whole time I wanted to be with you," she confessed. "But I understand, you never saw me the way that I saw you." She turned up her glass, now finishing her drink. She set the glass down on the table next to his.

"I've always cared for you, Kim.   Nothing will ever change that, but I've always loved Tay," Keith gently explained.

Kim looked into his eyes. "Thank you so much for always being a friend." She leaned over and brushed his lips with hers.

He kissed her deeply as her hand slipped inside his pants.

She then unzipped them and climbed on top of him.

"Kim, wait. I can't do this. We can't do this," he said. He gently moved her off of him, fixed his pant and headed for the door.

Kim was right behind him. "Keith, wait. Trey is out of town." She chuckled and rolled her eyes at the thought of what he was doing out of town. "He's always out of town, and I . . . I just don't want to be alone tonight," she said with tears now running down her face. "Please . . . don't go."

Her words stopping him in his tracks, he turned around, walked up to her and began kissing her passionately.   They kissed all the way up the stairs and to her bedroom. They ripped each other's clothes off all the way there.

Once their bodies made contact, it was as if she hadn't made love to anyone in years. Keith released all of his stress and anger as she grabbed him tighter. He pleased her, and he enjoyed every minute of her touching and kissing him. She longed for him, and he fulfilled her every desire. She had never been touched like that by her husband; and at that moment, Keith gave her what she thought she had been missing in her marriage all these years. Keith made her feel wanted and loved every minute of him being inside of her. Her arms wrapped tightly around his neck as he climaxed.

As Kim looked into his eyes, Keith snapped back into reality. "Oh, my God, Kim, I'm sorry. I shouldn't have . . . I'm so sorry." He sobered up quickly as he realized what he had done. He began grabbing his clothes.

"Wait, Keith." She grabbed his arm. "Don't leave me here alone. Please, stay with me. Just for tonight, and you can leave in the morning," she begged, tears in her eyes. "No one will ever find out about this. I promise, just please."

"Kim, I'm so sorry, but I can't. Knowing what just happened is enough . . . I have to go."

When she saw the tears form in his eyes, she let go of his arm.

He kissed her forehead and got up to leave.

Her tears fell as she watched him walk away.

Chapter Twelve

*K*eith pulled into Mi Amore Hotel, one of the most luxurious hotels in Baton Rouge. He checked in and went to the bar area. He ordered two beers and a shot of Grey Goose Vodka. He was thinking about everything that had just taken place. He sat and rubbed his temples as he waited for his drinks. The bartender set the drinks down in front of him, and Keith turned each one of them up the minute he got them.

"Looks like you could use some company, papi," a soft voice said, as a hand was placed on his shoulder. "Keith, right?" she asked.

Keith looked up and saw this beautiful Latino woman.

"Yes," he answered. "Silvia?" he asked, getting confirmation.

Silvia sat on the bar stool next to him. "Wow, you remembered." She leaned into him, grabbed his inner thigh and allowed her lips to brush his ear as she whispered, "I have that kind of effect on men." She looked into his eyes, and he looked back into hers. His eyes narrowed as he began to study hers.

Then she asked, "What brings you here?" She was so close to him, he could smell the liquor on her breath.

"I'm just here. What about you?" he asked, changing the focus from him to her.

"Well, the bartender makes the best drinks ever." She winked at the bartender, and then returned her focus back to Keith. "I always come here when I want to let down my hair, relax, and have some fun if you know what I mean." She bit her bottom lip and allowed her eyes to trace his body. Then her eyes met his.

Un-thinkable by Alicia Keys began to play over the speakers.

"Oooo, I love this song . . . Come dance with me," Silvia said, grabbing his hand.

He looked at her and said, "No, I don't think that's a good idea."

"It's just a dance. It's not like I'm asking to have yo' baby." She laughed out loud.

Keith clenched his jaw together as the thought of what happened earlier with Taylor angered him all over again.

Silvia took him by his hand and walked him to the dance floor. She and Keith danced, and then she began throwing some of her Latin dance in as Keith watched. She turned her back to him and rubbed her body up against his, moving her body like a snake. She smiled as she felt him become erect. Her sex appeal had him in a complete trance as he watched her. She moved her body so fluently, and he began having transient thoughts about being intimate with this woman.

"Wow, okay. I think I will go get another drink," he said, gently pushing her away from him.

Her lips touched him as she whispered into his ear, "What? You don't want to do the un-thinkable tonight, papi?"

Keith thought that her Spanish accent was simply beautiful, and it drove him crazy. He looked at her, then walked away. He went back over to the bar and took a seat.

Silvia came and sat on the bar stool next to him. "Bartender! Let me get a Hypnotic and get him three more of whatever he had," she yelled over the music.

"You know what, Silvia," Keith began. "I've changed my mind. I've had enough, but thanks."

"What? You afraid you can't handle your liquor? What is one, or two more drinks, Keith? You can handle that, can't you?" she asked as if it were a dare.

The bartender concocted a few more drinks, then brought their drinks over to them.

Keith guzzled down each one of them.

Silvia laughed. "Easy there now, papi. You act as though you are trying to wash away your problems." She touched his hand as she leaned over, allowing her cleavage to show a little more. She traced his ear lobe with her tongue, then whispered to him, "I can help you get rid of them for at least a few hours.''

Keith's eyes fell on her neck, then down to her cleavage, then down to her legs. His eyes lingered there for a moment. Her legs were so beautiful and inviting to him and he desired to have them wrapped around him tightly. It took every bit of him to look away. He tried his best to shake the thoughts that ran through his mind.

While he was in deep thought, Silvia ordered two more Hypnotics for herself and two more shots of Grey Goose Vodka for him.

The bartender brought them over, and Keith downed those as well.

"So what are you getting into tonight, papi? Please say me.'' Silvia threw her head back and laughed out loud. She then sucked her teeth and looked into his eyes.

Keith couldn't take his eyes off of her. Her beautiful brown eyes magnetized him and for a minute he got lost in them. He looked at her from her head to her toes. She had on a beautiful vintage, Pink Lucy dress designed by T'Shemise, and she looked stunning in it. This woman was absolutely beautiful to him, and her stimulating attractiveness was so intriguing. Keith licked his lips as his eyes scanned her body once more, then he quickly looked away, trying to control his inappropriate thoughts.

What the hell am I thinking? He thought to himself. "I gotta go,'' he said to her. He put down two-hundred dollars for the bill and left.

Silvia bit her lip as she watched him walk away. She didn't say a word, but she smirked at the very thought of what she had planned next.

Keith felt like throwing up. He could barely make it up to his room without falling over. He knew that he had way too many drinks, and it showed up in his walk. He staggered all the way up to his room. He just wanted to get rid of every thought that he had as he now lay on the bed. There were six knocks on the door. Keith got up and opened it without asking any questions.

"I can help you relax," Silvia said. She began kissing him all the way over to the bed.

Everything was going so fast, and Keith felt as though he didn't know what was happening. She pushed him onto the bed and unzipped his pants, his manhood now completely revealed. After seeing him fully exposed, she smiled, showing her approval.

"Wait a minute. What are you doing?" His words slurred. He tried to push her hands away as he sat up on his forearms. Everything around him began to get dark.

"Wait what?" She kissed his lips. "It's no secret, Keith. I can tell by the look in your eyes that you want me, so I'm just giving you what you want. Just relax. I'll take care of you," she said, pushing him back down on the bed. She was aggressive as she took full control of the situation and climbed on top of him...

***

Knock, knock, knock . . .

"Housekeeping!'' the maid exclaimed.

The knocks at the door woke Keith up, and his head was pounding. Even when the knocks had stopped he felt as if he was still hearing them. He looked around the room for his clothes. His pants and shirt were on the floor next to the bed.

"Hold on for a second!'' he yelled. He tried to put on his pants as quickly as he could. He sat back down on the bed trying to gather his thoughts, but then he heard the toilet flush.

The bathroom door swung open, and Silvia came out wrapped in a towel. Her hair was soaked, body glistening.

Keith slowly stood up. "What are you doing here?'' he hissed.

Silvia didn't say a word as she stood still. She just stared at him with her signature smirk on her face.

Keith walked over to the door and cracked it. "Look,'' he said to the maid. "I'm kinda busy in here.'' He tried to clear the nervousness from his throat. "If you don't mind, could you come back in a few minutes? I would appreciate it,'' his voice trembled.

"Not a problem, sir, but is everything okay?'' the maid asked.

He swallowed, then answered, "Yes, thank you.'' He was fearful of the real answer to that question. He closed the door and turned back to face Silvia. "I'm going to ask you again; what are you doing here? What happened last night?'' he asked firmly.

Silvia smiled and walked over to him. "Anoche," she began as she licked her lips. "Sí, last night was amazing, papi." She walked a little closer. "Don't worry. Nothing happened that you didn't want to happen. I can promise you that." She smirked. She looked down below his waistline, then said, "Looks like we have company again." She moved in a little closer, now closing in the space between them.

He closed his eyes as he took in her peaches and cream scent. "Look, Silvia, you need to leave," he said, then pushed her away.

She came closer. "Look, papi, why are you tripping? I told you nothing happened, but we can make something happen right now if you would like to. Look like he's ready," she said, then touched his manhood. "Oh, yeah." She chuckled. "He's most definitely ready." She now grabbed his manhood. "And so am I."

Keith hit her hand away. "Get out now!" he screamed at her as he pointed to the door.

"You want me to leave?" She stepped back and held her arms out away from her sides, then added, "With just a towel on?"

Keith looked at her in that towel and sighed deeply. "Okay, you stay here. I'll go." He grabbed his shirt, and headed for the door.

Keith turned in his room key and informed the desk clerk that he needed another room. The clerk told him the room number and handed him the key. He headed to the elevator. When he got to the room, he looked at his cell phone, then checked his messages. He had forty missed calls and six voice messages. Taylor, Kim, Candis, his father and his co-worker, Jeff, had been calling. Keith took off his clothes and hopped in the shower which he allowed to be ice cold.

He allowed the water to run over his body as he tried to remember what all had taken place last night. As much as he tried to, he could honestly say that he couldn't remember at the moment. He felt extremely guilty for the situation that had taken place with Kim, but now he felt guilty for what may have taken place with Silvia. He could feel that something wasn't right, and he wasn't so sure that he really wanted to know what that something was, or the reality of what all had taken place last night . . .

Chapter Thirteen

Taylor walked up and banged on Michael's door.

"Taylor, what's wrong?" he asked after inviting her in.

"I've been calling him all night, and he won't answer. I called his dad and his sister. Nobody knows where he is. He won't answer his phone, Mike," Taylor said without taking a breath.

"Slow down, and explain to me who and what you are talking about," Michael said. He led her into the living room to sit down.

"Keith found out about the abortion," she squealed.

"Oh, my God, Taylor," Michael said as he now held her. "You had an abortion?"

"Yes, I did. It's not something I'm proud of. It was within our first year of marriage, and I feel so bad. Keith was so hurt when he found out." Taylor shook her head as if trying to shake away the memory of how angry he was. "He's never reacted that way before. You should have seen him. He was fuming."

"How did he find out?"

"I told him while we were arguing about children. He found my birth-control pills. Then about the abortion, and then there were the dreams that I was having. That doctor in my dream told me that I needed to tell him, but I didn't expect this..." she rambled.

"Wait . . . Slow down, Taylor. You were taking birth-control pills, and he didn't know it? Then you told him about the abortion? You were having dreams about it, or are you saying that this was all a dream? I'm not sure I'm following you," he asked questions for clarity.

"No, I wish this were a dream, but it is far from it. It's a nightmare that has turned into my reality." She covered her mouth as she gasped, "Oh, my God. What if he never forgives me for this? What if he decides he wants a divorce? I can't live without him in my life. He means everything to me," she said, still in tears.

"Taylor, everything will be okay. Just take it to God in prayer. There will be no divorce, and everything will work out for your good and for the good of your marriage." He hugged her tightly.

She gently pushed away from his embrace. "Everyone keeps saying that!" she yelled. "Pray, have faith, go to church, and keep God first. Soon as I decide that I want to go back to church and give God back His rightful place in my life, all hell breaks loose; but I'm supposed to trust God. Look at my marriage, Mike,'' she said. "Look what it has come to. I can't even find out where my husband is. My marriage could be over as far as I know!'' Taylor yelled angrily.

"You sound like you are trying to blame God for your marriage falling apart. Taylor, God didn't tell you to deceive your husband, nor did He tell you to have an abortion. You made those choices on your own. So many of us create our own messes, then we want to blame God for them. Life is about choices, Taylor, and *you* made *those* choices. What I will say is that God can take your wrong and make things right in your life if you trust Him. God is more than enough, so attach your hope to your faith. All will work out. It takes much prayer, and you have to have faith that God can work it out,'' Michael explained with loving-kindness.

"Well, I've made a mess, Mike, and I don't know where to begin to fix it.'' She cried.

"I just told you, Taylor. You are not going to fix it on your own, give it to God, and trust Him with it. You can't keep trying to solve this thing yourself because this is bigger than you. Trust me. You need to strengthen your faith, and trust Him. Without faith, it is impossible to please God.'' He gently grabbed her hand. "Before you leave here, I will pray with you, and it is up to you to remain in prayer. You need to go into worship. Worship is what's going to bring you out of this in victory. You want your marriage to work, then faith in God's Word will make that happen. If you think you will need marriage counseling, Pastor Matthews and his wife are great partners in that area,'' he informed her. "You should think about that.''

"Mike, do you really believe that Keith will forgive me? I know this is going to be so hard for him. He was really big on having a family of his own, and I know that he feels as though I destroyed his. I can feel it." She looked down at the floor and shook her head. "I don't know if God can fix this."

Michael pulled her head up and looked into her eyes. "If you just have faith, He will. God has always shown me that He will work it out. We sometimes get so caught up in our situations and circumstances that we began looking at what we are in instead of looking to God, the one who holds us and our circumstances in the palm of His hand. He is able to carry us through and bring us out in victory," he assured her. His words encouraged her.

Michael quoted some scriptures into her hearing, and they prayed together. He prayed that her faith increases and that it fails not . . .

***

Keith walked into his father's house and sat down at the kitchen table.

"Son, I have been expecting you. Is everything okay?" John asked. He grabbed them some bottled waters from the refrigerator and sat with Keith at the table. He then placed one of the bottles in front him.

"No, I'm afraid not." Keith answered as he stared off into space.

"Tell me what's going on."

Taylor had come to John earlier looking for Keith, but when she found out that he wasn't there, she stayed and talked with him for a while. She didn't go into complete details, but he knew part of what Keith was dealing with.

Keith took a deep breath, then began, "Dad, I'm not so sure that Taylor and I are going to work out."

"What do you mean, son? Tell me why you feel that way."

"Taylor has been lying to me basically since the beginning of our marriage, and I just can't trust her anymore. It's like I'm questioning everything now."

"Well, what has Taylor lied about?"

Keith rubbed his temples and answered, "Almost everything. She was taking birth-control pills throughout our marriage, and she had us going to fertility clinics when I thought that we were just having problems conceiving children."

"I know that you are hurt, son, but your marriage can survive this," John said to him with confidence.

"She had an abortion, Dad," Keith blurted out with tears now in his eyes.

John was jarred by the news he had just received. This was something that Taylor did not inform her father-in-law of when she had come by earlier. He reached over the table and touched his son's hand. He sincerely said, "I'm so sorry, son."

"Dad, she killed my baby! She was pregnant and didn't

even care to inform me. I was going to be a father, but she took that away from me. Now tell me, Dad. How can my marriage survive that? She didn't allow my baby a chance to survive!'' he yelled out in anger as his tears began to flow. "This woman, whom I loved, killed my baby. So, tell me, Dad. How can I get past that?''

"You have to forgive her, son, just like God forgives. You can't allow that to hinder you from moving forward in your marriage.''

Keith became angry at the mention of God. "What? Did you forgive Mom, or better yet, did God forgive her?'' he countered.

"Yes, I have forgiven your mother; and if she has asked God for forgiveness, He has forgiven her as well.''

"If God is so big on my marriage surviving how come He didn't allow yours to survive?'' Keith asked. His father could hear the anger in his tone.

"Your mother left me. I didn't leave her. I was all for making our marriage work, but she chose to leave the marriage. You have the choice to stay in your marriage and to fight for it. Taylor loves you, and she's willing to fight for this marriage. Go home to your wife, Keith, and talk this through.''

"Wait, are you telling me that you have talked to Taylor? Did she tell you about this?'' Keith asked, and then he began clenching his jaw.

"No, she didn't go into any details, but she came by to see if you were here. She talked to me for a little while.'' He paused. "Keith, go back home to your wife; she loves you.''

Keith got up and walked out without saying another word to his father. It angered him that his dad had already talked to Taylor and seemed to side with her. And all that God stuff, he was not trying to hear.

Keith got into his car and drove off into the night. His cell phone rang, and he answered it.

Jeff cleared his throat on the other end of the receiver. "Hey, man. What is going on with you? You haven't been at work or answering your phone. We were trying to get some information on this McCallister case, and some more evidence has emerged. You know we'll be going to trial in no time. Kim missed work also and we really needed the both of you,'' he said. He waited for some answers, but there was only silence on the other end. "Hellooo? Keith, are you there, man?''

"I'm sorry, Jeff. I was out sick, and I'm going through a lot right now. Um, I should be back in the morning,'' Keith informed him.

Jeff paused. "Okay cool. We've been worried because we know it's not like you to miss work and not call. Kim, she called to let us know that she was sick. All that coughing she was doing over the phone, I'm glad she didn't come in. You probably got what she has. I hope you feel better, man.''

"Thanks, I'm sure I will.'' He paused, changing his tone, "Hey, Jeff, you said Kim is real sick?''

"Yeah, man, she sounded terrible when I talked to her. Coughing and crying," Jeff informed him.

They finished their conversation and hung up.

Keith pulled into Kim's driveway and got out of his car. He went up to her front door and knocked.

No answer . . .

He began ringing the bell.

Kim finally opened the door.

"Hey, Kim, how are you?" Keith asked, inviting himself in.

"Not that great, probably a bug I caught. Trey had been real sick last week walking around here coughing and stuff. He probably passed me his cold unfortunately," Kim told him. She went and sat down on the couch, out of breath.

"What are you taking for it?" he asked out of concern.

Kim was very pale and seemed to be extremely weak. "I took some Nyquil, and I should be out like a light soon," she said, snapping her fingers. "Keith, I tried calling you many times last night. I'm so sorry for what happened, and I promise to keep this between us. I feel so bad about this. Trey was the first man that I had given myself to voluntarily, and I've never cheated on him," she said sincerely with tears in her eyes.

Keith hugged her tightly. "I know that you were a faithful wife to him and I'm sorry. I feel like it's my fault, I should have stopped us last night. I've never been unfaithful to Taylor, but we can't change the past. Like you said, we will keep it between us." He looked into her eyes. "I just came to make sure that you were okay and to make sure that you didn't need anything,'' he said, changing the subject back to her present situation.

"I'm okay.'' She coughed some more before saying, "Thank you so much for checking on me.'' She looked up at him. "Thank you for everything. You are such a great friend, and I could never thank you enough for what you did last night. I needed you, Keith. I needed that. You showed me what I have been looking for my whole life. Trey was never as gentle and loving as you were last night.''

Keith choked back his tears and didn't say a word. He kissed her forehead and headed out the door. Even though he and Trey were no longer the best of friends, he felt as though he betrayed him. He never meant for this to happen and his tears came from the thought of being unfaithful to his wife.

Chapter Fourteen

Taylor was in her bedroom and was thinking about everything that Mike had told her. His words of encouragement and his prayer gave her comfort. Even though Keith hasn't come home, she still believes that God will save her marriage. She fell onto her knees and began to pray and worship God. She cried and prayed, cried and prayed for hours. She felt a great comfort as she lay before God, communing with Him. She cried out to Him and He comforted her. She decided to hop into the shower, and she continued to pray and sing songs unto her Heavenly Father. When she got out of the shower, she heard His voice say, "GO DOWN STAIRS." She threw on her robe and headed down the stairs.

She was headed into the kitchen to get a glass of water, but she stopped in her tracks when she saw the shadow of someone sitting in the dark living room. "Keith?" she called out his name as she slowly walked into the living room. She got closer to the dark shadow. She reached for the lamp and turned it on. She saw the tears running down Keith's face as he sat on the couch in silence. "Oh, my God, I'm so glad you are home," she said. She began approaching him with caution. "Keith, I'm so sorry. I really am." She waited for him to speak, but after he stayed silent, she continued, "Please, just talk to me. Tell me what you are feeling." She now sat on the other end of the couch, fearful that if she got too close, he might leave again.

"Taylor, just tell me why. How could you do that? How could you not tell me that you were pregnant?" he asked, looking at the wall straight ahead.

Taylor swallowed hard and took a deep breath. "I'm so sorry, Keith. There is no excuse for what I did, but please believe me when I say, I am truly sorry for hurting you," she said sincerely with tears now running down her face.

Keith continued, "That was our baby, our gift. All I ever wanted was a family and I feel as though you took that from me, and you did it without my consent. I was your husband and having a baby was more important to me than life itself, but you were so selfish, you took that from me." He shook his head in disbelief. "The little bit of hope that I had of having a family, you snatched it away." His tears were flowing steadily.

"You said 'was my husband,' what do you mean by that? Keith, I want to save our marriage. I want us to work." Again, she waited for him to respond, but when he didn't, she continued, "I want us to start a family. I am off the pill, and we can still start that family that you've always wanted. Please, Keith, just give us a chance," Taylor begged her husband as she now held him in her arms. He cried like she'd never seen him cry before.

***

Hours had passed, and Keith woke up lying beside Taylor on the couch. He realized that he had cried himself to sleep, and Taylor obviously held him until she had fallen asleep as well. He looked at her as she slept, and she was definitely the most beautiful woman in the world to him. He untied her robe and ran his fingers down her stomach to her navel. Even though he desired to go further than that, he refrained.

Still asleep, Taylor squirmed from the cool air against her skin, and he closed her robe back up. He continued to look at her a while longer as he sat in deep thought. He was not only hurt by what Taylor had done to their family, he was hurt by what he had now done to their family. He kissed her forehead, eased himself away from her and headed to the shower. When he got out, Taylor was standing in the doorway.

"Why didn't you wake me, baby?" she asked as she moved in closer.

He reached around her and grabbed his towel, not saying a word. He dried off and walked out of the bathroom.

She followed. "Keith, we are going to have to talk. We can't be like this forever."

He grabbed a suit from the closet and started getting dressed. "I have to go to work. I've missed two days already, and I'm running late." He paused, stopping to look at her. "Oh, where did you say Mike work?"

Taylor stood and studied her husband before saying, "Bradberry and Company, off of McNeil Drive." She paused. "Why do you ask?" Suspicion was in her tone.

He turned away from her and looked into the mirror as he buttoned down his shirt. "I thought you said he had his own company, and I overheard the guys talking about it at work. I just wanted to make sure I didn't have it confused with another company," he lied. "I have to go, Tay," he said, continuing to quickly put on his clothes.

"Okay, well, can we talk later? Maybe go to dinner?" she asked with hope now in her tone.

He put on his Stacy Adams shoes, completing his look. "No," he said, and headed for the door.

Once Keith got into his car, he entered Bradberry and Company into his GPS system, then backed out of his driveway. He rode around until he pulled up in the parking lot of Bradberry and Company.

The receptionist at the front desk smiled when Keith walked through the door. "Hello, sir, how may I help you today?" she asked.

"Yes, I'm looking for Silvia Martinez," Keith informed her.

"Wow, another one," she said out loud to herself, giggling.

"What do you mean by that?" he asked, disturbed by her comment.

She smiled, sat up a little straighter and quickly said, "Nothing at all, sir. Her office is right down the hall, first door to your left." She pointed down the hall.

Keith headed to Silvia's office and walked in without an invite.

Silvia looked up from her work. "Keith! What gives me the pleasure of doing you, I mean, seeing you today? You miss me already?" she asked as she stood up.

Keith got straight to the point. "Silvia, I need to know what happened the other night?"

She looked him over. "Wow. I already told you. Nothing happened that you didn't want to happen," she said. She bit her lip and moved in closer. "Do we have company again?" she asked as she looked down below his waistline.

"Look, Silvia, I don't have time to play your little games. Now you tell me what happened, and you tell me the truth," he said. He now grabbed her by her arm.

Michael passed by Silvia's office and saw Keith grabbing her. He was concerned by what he saw. It looked as if things had become heated between the two, so he made sure that he stayed close by.

Silvia looked at Keith's hand around her arm. "Lucky for you," she looked back up at him, "I like it rough." She laughed.

He let go of her arm. "Silvia, I'm not playing with you," he stated firmly.

"Look, I told you nothing happened. Trust me, if anything did, you would have definitely remembered. You can believe that," she replied to him. She could tell by the look on his face that he wasn't satisfied with her answer. She sighed, "Okay, you want to know what happened? You had too many drinks, and you passed out. I got sick from having too many drinks. I went in the bathroom, threw up, came back and crashed beside you. Yes, we slept together, Keith, but we did not have sex." She got even closer to him. "There's no fun in having sex with a passed out man," she looked him up and down, then added, "it doesn't matter how sexy he is." She licked her lips. "Mmmm, and trust me, papi, you are sexy . . . But I'm not a rapist, Keith. I like to feel wanted while I please my men." She rubbed her hands down the breast of his suit.

He pushed her hands away and headed out of her office. This time he believed her when she said that nothing happened.

"Hasta luego, papi." She bit her lip as she watched him walk away. She yelled out Lauren Hill's lyrics to him, "Ready or not, here I come, you can't hide . . . I'm gonna find you and make you want me." She laughed out loud.

Michael had ended his conversation with the receptionist when he saw Keith headed towards the door. "Keith," he said, stopping him. "How's it going, man?"

Keith looked back at him. "Oh, hey, Mike, how's it going?"

He walked up to him, extending his hand, and Keith shook it. "Awesome. I was just about to head to lunch. Join me," Michael said to him, letting Keith know in his tone that he was looking for him to join him without a protest.

"Well, I do have to get to work, Mike, maybe next time."

"I really think now's a good time, Keith. You can ride with me."

"Okay, let me just make a quick call," Keith told him. He pulled out his cell and called his office.

Michael and Keith pulled into the parking lot of Casie's Bar and Grill. "Man, they have some of the best food," Michael said as they took a seat at a table for three.

Keith looked around, preparing himself to be interrogated about being in Michael's place of business today. He now responded to Michael's comment, "Yes, and some of the best drinks. I know I could use one." He signaled for the waitress.

She came over and took their orders.

"So, what brought you to my place of business today?" Michael asked curiously.

Keith chuckled because of his anticipation of the interrogation. He thought to himself, *I knew it*, before saying, "Well, I wanted to check with Silvia about some decoration plans for one of the attorneys I work with. I needed her to quote me some prices," he lied as he continued to look around the restaurant trying not to make eye contact with Michael.

"Well, that's a shock, considering that Silvia strictly deals with floor plans, and she knows absolutely nothing about quoting prices," Michael informed him.

"What is it that you really want to know, Michael?" Keith asked, now frustrated.

"Okay, I'll get straight to the point. You have a wife who loves you, and you don't want to mess up your marriage behind foolishness. I don't know what was going on with you and Silvia, but from the looks of it, it wasn't business related. Silvia can be a snake, Keith, and she can bite, so be careful," Michael explained to him.

"What do you mean by that?" Keith asked, now interested.

"Silvia is the type of woman who has *ulterior motives* when it comes to men. She has destroyed many families. She's about getting what she wants, and she doesn't care about what or who she destroys in the process. I mean, don't get me wrong I hired her because the girl has mad skills. She is very talented at what she does when it comes to her work. She can work miracles with a floor plan, but I'm afraid she has no morals and values. You need to stay far away from her," he warned.

"You seem to know a lot about her," Keith said.

"Well, let me say this. I watch and I listen. I know she has a lot of unresolved issues, but I see the good in her. She could use some moral reconstruction, but I gave her a chance to work for me because I know she has great potential. A lot of men can't handle women like Silvia; you know the type of women who throw themselves at you. But God has given me strength and the heart to deal with her on a different level. I want to try to make a difference in her life and build her up. I will say this though," he paused and looked Keith in his eyes before continuing, "I am sorry that I brought her to your dinner party, real sorry. I didn't mean for any of that to go down."

The waitress served them, and Michael said grace aloud.

He put a forkful of broccoli into his mouth, and then took a sip of his water. Keith downed his Hennessey and Coke that he ordered.

"Man, you need to slow down. Drinking on an empty stomach, can't be good. You know why they call them drinks 'spirits,' huh?'' Michael asked as he cleaned his plate.

Keith watched him finish the rest of his food. "Man, you can eat.'' He chuckled, then continued, "Why do they call the drinks 'spirits,' man?'' he asked as he continued laughing.

"What happens after you drink those spirits? You get drunk, right?'' He paused. "Then you have all kinds of spirits in you,'' Michael explained and they both laughed. "Yeah, man, you laugh, but it's the truth. People get drunk and go left field. They lose their minds. They get to acting all out of the norm. That be those 'spirits' taking over,'' Michael said.

Keith sat in deep thought before saying, "I never thought of it like that.''

"But seriously, Keith, Taylor's a good woman, and I know you are a good man. Marriage goes through its ups and downs, but it's worth holding on to. Don't you agree?'' He watched Keith nod in agreement, and then he continued, "The Bible tells us that 'he who finds a wife finds a good thing and finds favor from the Lord.' It also tells the husband to love his wife. Just because your wife makes a mistake doesn't mean you stop loving her. Whatever is going on with you and Taylor, I know that your love is strong enough to get through it and overcome it,'' Michael said, looking Keith in his eyes.

Michael's talk helped Keith to open his eyes a little

more. "You are right, Mike. I really appreciate this conversation."

For the first time in a long time, Keith did not get angry from someone mentioning the Bible or quoting scripture. He instantly gained much respect for Michael. The waitress brought the bill, and Michael paid.

They pulled back into the parking lot of Bradberry and Co. Keith thanked him again, then got into his car and headed to his office.

Chapter Fifteen

Keith walked into his office and sat down for a minute. He thought about the conversation that he just had with Michael.

Jeff walked in. "Yo', man, where you been? Let's get done with this McCallister case. I'm so tired of this case. I'm starting to want to put him in jail for killing his wife and family, and we supposed to be defending the man. You know what they say, guilty until proven innocent," Jeff said, laughing. He looked at Keith strangely. "What's wrong? You still sick?"

"Naw, man, just thinking . . . What would drive a husband to kill his wife?" he asked. He thought about different scenarios before saying, "Let's get on this case," now back in work mode.

"Hey, do you know what Kim did with that Jones file?" Jeff asked.

Keith shook his head. "No. Is she still out sick?"

"Yeah, man. She called me earlier sounding worse than

she did yesterday. I told her to stay home. She doesn't need to bring that mess up here. I'm not trying to get sick, and I don't want to pass nothing to my wife. Whenever she gets sick she acts like she can't do anything around the house.''

He and Jeff played catch up on their cases and put together the last pieces to the McCallister case. He walked out of his office at 9:05 p.m.

***

Keith walked into his bedroom with flowers in his hands. Taylor was asleep on the bed until he walked over and gently kissed her forehead. She woke up, and he sat on the edge of the bed next to her.

She sat up and hugged her husband. "I thought you weren't going to come back home tonight,'' she admitted.

"I have something for you.'' He handed her the flowers.

She took them and smelled them, her eyes on his eyes the whole time. She laid the flowers on the nightstand by their wedding photo. She continued looking at Keith, studying him.

He sat in place for a while and just stared at her. Then he finally said, "What you told me the other day, Taylor, hurt me to my heart, but it doesn't change the fact that I love you. I want to move forward with you, but I can't lie, it still hurts. I realize that I have to let that go in order to move forward. I love you too much, and I don't want to lose you.'' He then began thinking about the abortion, and it made him get angry all over again. "You could have just told me that you were pregnant, Tay. I wish you would have told me to just use condoms before it even got to that point. I can't stand the thought of you killing our baby.'' Tears swelled in his eyes.

His words, "killing our baby,'' really pricked her heart, so she said, "Keith, I'm so sorry. I want us to get past this, I really do. Let's try again. Let's have our baby, Keith.'' Tears filled her eyes as she empathized with her husband.

Keith looked at her for a good minute before his own guilt set in again. "I think I will sleep in the guestroom tonight.'' He got up and headed across the hall.

Taylor cried for hours until she finally fell asleep.

Keith couldn't help but toss and turn as he began to mourn the death of his unborn child. He tried his best to rest, but his mind wouldn't let him. His heart was so heavy with anger, hurt and guilt, all at the same time. He loved Taylor and there was no doubt in his mind that he wanted to make his marriage work. Tonight, he brought her those flowers out of guilt from the mess that he made. He wanted to tell her that he, too, messed up. The thought of it weighed heavily on him. He knew in his heart that his marriage was damaged goods. He was feeling so burdened that his head began to ache from all of the pressure, but finally he fell asleep.

Taylor woke up in the middle of the night and tip-toed into the guest room. She got into bed with Keith and began kissing him on his neck and back as she ran her hand down his muscular arm.

He stirred and woke up. He looked into her eyes.

"I can't sleep,'' she said. She continued to kiss on him.

Keith kissed her lips gently as he pulled her into his strong arms and held her close.

She felt comforted as he continued to kiss her. "I'm sorry, Keith," her lips brushed his ear, "I'll make it up to you," her lips now brushed his neck, "I promise," she said, now gently kissing his lips.

Keith removed her robe and revealed her nakedness. He kissed her, and then stopped.

She looked him in his eyes, confused at first, but then she gently kissed his lips once again.

He ran his fingers softly down her side as he passionately kissed her lips back.

She moaned loudly at his touch, drunk with anticipation.

Keith traced every inch of her body with his mouth and the moment they made one, a tear ran down her cheek. When he looked into her eyes, tears formed in his. The guilt he was feeling was strong and it became overwhelming. He stopped in the middle of making love to her and got up, which was something that he had never done before when making love to his wife. "I'm sorry, Tay. I just can't," he said, and then headed to the guest bathroom to take a cold shower.

"Keith, what's wrong?" Taylor cried out to him, but he didn't answer. She knew that her marriage was in a mess that was too big for her to fix. Tears fell down her face. She now covered herself, attempting to hide her nakedness. Making love to her husband didn't feel the same. He had never turned her away before and for him to do what he just did left her in fear.

Chapter Sixteen

Trey walked into the house of his mistress, Keisha Fullerton, who he met at a strip club in Dallas while he was playing pro ball. He has cheated on Kim with numerous women, and still does, but Keisha is one of the only women who he has ever had an ongoing affair with. She was seated on the couch in the living room reading a book when he walked over to her and kissed the top of her head.

Startled, she screamed out, "Trey, you scared me! I know you have a key, but it would be nice if you call to let me know when you are coming by." She wrapped one arm around his neck as he leaned over the back of the couch. She kissed his lips. "You and the wife into it again?"

"Nope, I just wanted to come by and check on my family. What you cooked?" he asked her and headed for the kitchen.

She got up and followed. "Nope, I'm your dinner tonight." She kissed him.

He grabbed her hair as their tongues met. He then

grabbed her up, and she wrapped her legs around him as he carried her back over to the couch.

She sat on top of him and they continued to kiss passionately. She moved around on top of him until she felt him become erect. She took off his pants, his manhood now exposed through his boxers. She lowered herself onto him while kissing his neck, then his lips. She looked into his eyes.

He moaned as she continued to move her hips around on him. After eleven minutes, he climaxed. "I should have gotten you to give me a lap dance first, then maybe I would have lasted longer." He chuckled, then he smacked her on her butt.

"You always last long enough for me, baby. But I can still give you that dance. You know how I love to dance for you, babe." She licked his neck, then kissed it softly.

"Where's the baby?" he asked.

"Sleep."

"Well, let's go to the room and make that dance happen." He took her by the hand and led her to the bedroom.

She smiled and allowed him to lead the way.

Once they got there, she went to the bathroom and changed into her black lingerie and her special black stilettos that Trey loved so much. She came out covered in the red robe that he bought her for her birthday. He sat down in his favorite chair that he enjoyed his lap dances in. He looked at her and licked his lips.

She dropped her robe and began to dance around the X-Pole that he had put up in her bedroom for his pleasure.

She began dancing on Trey's lap and his hands traced her beautiful, curvaceous, caramel complexioned body.

He looked into her eyes as she danced to one of her favorite songs, *Cater to U,* by Destiny's Child.

That was one thing that he loved about Keisha. She catered to him with no questions asked. She made him feel wanted, and he loved the look of respect that she had in her eyes for him. Whenever he looked into his wife's eyes, he always thought he saw a look of disapproval and disrespect; as if she no longer viewed him as a man. But Keisha did everything he liked and, because of that, he took care of her. He paid all of her bills from what he had left in his savings account, one that Kim had no knowledge of. He did very little for his home where he and his wife resided. After he got injured playing pro ball, Kim began taking care of all the bills. From that point on, she took on the provider role. He felt hopeless whenever he was home with her. But here, he felt like a king. This was one of the reasons why he stayed away from his home often to spend time at what he called his, "real home."

Keisha gave Trey the lap dance that he wanted and he stood at attention. He enjoyed it whenever she danced for him. When he met her, she was eighteen and stripping in a Dallas nightclub. At the time she had a thugged out boyfriend who she had fallen in love with until he began treating her terribly after he moved her away from her family. She felt as though Trey had rescued her after moving her away from Dallas and closer to him. Young and naive, once again, she fell in love. Ever since they met, he has taken care of her, so now this was her way to show her appreciation. She felt like she owed him. When it came to sex, whatever Trey asked from her, he got it, and she always made sure that she satisfied him. When he asked her to stop stripping at the club, she did. He had her full attention, and she made sure she performed everything well for him.

She began performing what he enjoyed most. He grabbed her long hair as she continued doing what she loved to do to please him. He pulled her hair harder as culmination took place. He pulled her back up, and she kissed him with passion.

"My wife would never do any of the things you do for me," he said, now out of breath.

She smiled, taking it as a compliment. "Well, why did you marry her, Trey?"

"Because she was my high school sweetheart. Don't get me wrong, I love Kim. I fell in love with her in high school. She has always been the subservient type and that's what I loved most about her. But when it comes to the bedroom, I have to make her do things. In high school every dude up there wanted her, but I was the one who got her. She is still just as beautiful as she was back then, and the men still look at her in amazement. I must admit, she is a bad woman, maybe too much of a woman at times. Even though she doesn't say anything, she looks at me with disrespect, and then I have to smack her back down to size," he explained.

"You shouldn't hit her, Trey. Just leave her."

"You think I'm going to leave that woman. I told you I love her. I'm not leaving her," he said firmly.

"Have you told her yet about . . ."

"No! I will tell her when I'm good and ready," he interrupted her question.

"Trey! You say that every time, but you never tell her. She needs to know. You have to tell her. It's not right to keep that from her. You aren't even giving her a chance to live with it, just like my ex didn't give me a chance." She paused as she thought about her ex, then she continued, "She has to know, Trey. She just has to," Keisha said with a look of sadness.

"I said, I will tell her when I'm good and ready, Keisha…"

"And what if it's too late then?" she interrupted.

"Really, I think it's none of your business. What is it to you? You are taken care of. You and I are both getting what we need."

"You are wrong, Trey, and I won't be a part of this. If you don't tell her, I will," she said, now tears in her eyes.

"You won't tell her anything unless you want to check out a little earlier than you already are." He grabbed her arm and looked into her eyes. "I'm done with this conversation, and I'm done with you for tonight." He pushed her onto the bed and left.

***

After Trey left Keisha's, he stopped to visit a popular strip club, one of his favorite places to go to relax. He got a few drinks and had sex in the VIP room with two of the well-known strippers who he had sex with regularly. When he arrived home, he hopped in the shower to wash away the scents of the other women that he was just with. He got out of the shower and slipped into bed with Kim. He began kissing on her.

Kim woke up. "Trey, what are you doing?" she asked groggily, moving away from him.

He pulled her back to him and continued kissing on her. "About to have sex with my wife if that's okay with you."

She smelled the liquor that lingered on his breath. "Trey, have you been drinking?"

"What about it?" he asked, breathing his breath into her face.

She turned her face away from him. "I don't feel well. I've had this cold for a while, and I've been waking up drenched in sweat. So, please, Trey, not tonight." She coughed a deep dry cough that made her throat feel sore.

He grabbed her by her throat. "Yeah, so what? You can still make love to your husband, right?" he growled.

"Trey . . . I . . . I'm serious, I don't . . . feel well. Please . . . I . . . can't breathe," she tried to get her words out as his hand squeezed tighter around her throat.

Trey got on top of his wife and began having sex with her without her consent. After a minute, he stopped. "Who in the hell have you been with, Kim?" he yelled, now looking into her eyes.

"What are you talking about? You're drunk," she said, trying to pull away.

He pulled her closer. "It's a simple question."

Kim pulled away from him and ran over to the wall, now crying out of fear.

Trey jumped up and ran behind her. He began choking her with one hand as he reached down and fondled her with the other. "Who have you been with?" he asked again, hitting the wall, busting a hole in it beside her head.

"Nobody, Trey, I swear." She cried at the top of her lungs, now terrified. She'd never seen that look in his eyes before.

"You are lying, and I know it," he said, slapping her to the floor. He kicked her several times in her ribs and stomach. He then grabbed her up by her neck, raising her up off the floor. "Are you going to tell me now, or do I have to beat it out of you?" he threatened.

"Trey, please!" She paused, trying to catch her breath but couldn't. She patted his chest attempting to calm him down. "Don't do this, baby. Please . . . I'm sorry," she screamed.

He squint his eyes. "Oh, now you sorry? You sorry all right, and I'm about to show you just how sorry you are. Who have you been with?" he continued to ask with both hands now around her throat as he held her up against the wall, her feet not touching the floor.

Kim's face turned completely red and he dropped her

onto the floor. She began coughing and crying uncontrollably. She felt as if she could not catch her breath as she lay on the floor, her vision now blurred. Her ribs ached from him kicking her, and her throat felt as though his hands were still around it.

Trey sat on the edge of the bed holding his now bruised and bloody hand from hitting the wall. He watched Kim as she grabbed her stomach. She tried to crawl her way into the bathroom to get away from him, but he got up and grabbed her by her ankles.

"Where are you going you lying piece of trash? You are going to tell me what I want to know, or you gon' die tonight,'' he said as he dragged her closer to the bed.

"Trey, please, stop! I haven't been with anyone,'' she cried out, now kicking her feet trying to get away.

He drew back his fist, but then the doorbell rang.

Trey looked at the window and saw the flashing police lights shining through the curtains. "You say one word, and I swear I will kill you,'' he said, dragging her into the bathroom. "Run you some bath water and clean yourself up."

Kim was relieved when she saw those lights. She felt as if tonight would have been the night that he would have killed her, even though this was not his first time threatening to do so.

Trey went downstairs and opened the door. There, stood two officers, Officer Townsend and Officer Bennett. "How may I help you, officers?'' he asked.

"Yes, one of your neighbors called and said they heard

some loud noises over here, and they were a bit concerned . . . Is your wife home?'' Officer Bennett asked.

"Yes, she's taking a bath. Would you like me to go get her?'' he asked calmly.

Officer Townsend looked at him with suspicion. "A bath at two o'clock in the morning?'' He paused. "May we step in for a minute?'' he asked as he continued to pay close attention to Trey.

"Sure, would you like some donuts and coffee as well?'' Trey asked, being sarcastic.

Officer Townsend looked at Trey's hand, then asked, "What happened to your hand?''

"I hit it hard on the nightstand while my wife was performing . . . Well, you know, it was just that good.'' Trey chuckled.

"If you don't mind, we would like to speak with your wife,'' Townsend said firmly, then added, "make sure everything is okay. You know?''

"Yeah, let me go get her for you,'' Trey said. He turned to go upstairs.

He stopped when he heard, "Wait, I knew that I recognized you. You are Treyvionne Whitmore, Saints running back,'' Officer Bennett said to him.

He turned around. "Yeah, I *was* a Saints running back.''

"Yeah, you were pretty good, too, until you messed up

that knee. I wish you would have gotten back out there. You were a joy to watch. Man, I tell you, you worked miracles on that field.''

Trey looked down at the floor, then said, "Yeah. I miss being out there.'' That was the only place he felt like he was worth something.

Officer Townsend cleared his throat, interrupting them, "Your wife, Mr. Whitmore,'' he said to Trey, then looked at Officer Bennett as if to remind him of what they were there for.

Trey went up the stairs and once he got in the bathroom, he told Kim to quickly fix her face and to come downstairs. She got out of the tub and quickly put some make-up on her face and neck to hide her bruises. She walked down the stairs slowly as she felt the pain in her ribs with every move she made.

"Hi, officers, is there something wrong?'' she asked, while trying to appear as if there was nothing wrong in her home.

Officer Townsend studied Kim, then looked around to see if anything gave him a sign that she was being abused. He walked up closer to her, and her eyes told him everything.

Trey began to get impatient as he watched this man stare into his wife's eyes. "Officer, the neighbors probably heard my wife and I having sex. I'm sorry if we get a lil' too rough, and I'm sorry that our neighbors could hear us. What can I say? She likes it rough,'' he said. He hugged Kim around her waist tightly, warning her to keep her mouth shut.

She began to cough badly.

"Wow, ma'am, that cough sounds pretty bad, " Officer Townsend said with concern. "Are you okay here?" he asked, but it was not in regards to her cough. He walked closely up to her, looking her in her eyes once again. All she had to do was say what he already knew, and show him that she wanted out, and he was going to get her out.

"She's fine," Trey said. "I'm taking her to the doc in the morning, but if you don't mind, I would like to get back to our sex life." He walked towards the door, letting them know that he was ready for them to leave.

Officer Bennett became a little impatient himself. "Okay, well, sorry to bother you. You two just try to keep the noise level down." He reached out and shook Trey's hand. "It was a pleasure meeting you, Mr. Whitmore. Enjoy the rest of your night."

Trey nodded to him, then he left out the door, leaving Officer Townsend behind.

Townsend looked at Kim and with his eyes he told her that she deserved better. Then he, too, left her in her misery.

After Trey closed the door he turned and slowly walked up to Kim.

She held her breath, bracing herself.

He slapped her so hard, her face instantly turned red. "What? Did you really think that I was going to kill you?" He paused, and then whispered into her ear, "I killed you a long time ago," his voice cold. He walked up the stairs to their bedroom.

Kim fell to the floor coughing uncontrollably, and that is where she stayed for the rest of the night.

Chapter Seventeen

*K*im walked into her office extremely sore. She didn't want to miss another day because she had missed enough days already. She made herself come in even though she felt extremely tired and she even seemed to have a fever. She sat at her desk as she looked into her compact mirror. She noticed that she had started bruising more easily. She could still see the bruises around her neck even though she put make-up on them. She really did not feel like coming in at all and, after last night, she definitely didn't feel like being questioned.

Keith knocked on her door and walked in. "Hey, Kim, you feeling better?" he asked, handing her a file.

Quickly closing her compact mirror, "I'm okay," she said, then began coughing.

"Are you sure you're okay? That cough sounds terrible. You want me to get you a bottle of water or something?" He looked at her with concern. He could see it in her face that she had lost a lot of weight since the last time he saw her.

She shook her head and began coughing again.

"Kim, you don't look well, and that cough definitely doesn't sound good." He walked over to her and touched her face. "You are burning up. Have you been to the doctor?"

"No . . . I'm good. I just . . . I just need to go to the restroom," she said in between coughs, barely able to really speak. Every time she coughed her ribs ached. She stood up and took a few steps toward the door, and then blacked out.

Keith ran over to her. "Someone, call an ambulance!" he yelled out for help.

***

Kim woke up and looked around this unfamiliar place where she lay. She looked over at Keith who was sitting at her side. "What happened?" she asked.

"You passed out and had to be rushed to the hospital. They wanted you to stay for a while, so they can run some tests to see what's going on. I told them about your bad cough and your weight loss. They checked your vitals and your fever was extremely high and your blood count is extremely low. They said that you are anemic and that may have been why you passed out; not enough iron. Have you been eating properly?" he asked.

"Yes, I've been eating fine," she said as she tried to sit up. She groaned from the pain she still felt from her ribs.

"What's wrong? Are you hurting or something?" Keith asked. He opened her blouse to see. "Oh, my God!" He saw the bruises on her. "This looks terrible. Did Trey do this?"

She just looked at him without saying a word.

"Kim, you could have a set of broken ribs from the looks of this," he said, gently touching her bruises.

She groaned from the pain of his touch.

"You need to let them x-ray you," he said. "You don't know if you have any internal bleeding, or anything. You have to tell them about this."

"No, Keith, I'm fine," she said, with fear in her eyes. "They will not know about this. Just let them give me some medicine for this cold and send me on my way . . . I'll be fine."

Keith dropped his head and said, "You really need to leave him before he kills you."

Kim nodded and tears formed in her eyes.

The doctor came back into the room and began questioning her about her symptoms. Everything became overwhelming to her and she began crying. Keith held her hand and squeezed it gently, attempting to comfort her. The doctor informed her that he will do some more testing to see what could be the problem.

The nurse came in and took more blood. "I don't want to get too much from you because your iron level is so low. Your husband has been a great help with telling us about your symptoms." The nurse looked over at Keith and smiled.

"Oh, no, I'm not her husband. We are just really good friends," Keith quickly informed her.

She apologized and left out with the blood for testing.

"Wow," Kim said. "That was so easy for you to say. You wanted to make sure that you cleared that up quick. What? Does the thought of you being my husband disturb you or something?"

"No, it's not that at all, but I'm not your husband, Kim. Simple as that. I just didn't want her to give any misinformation," he told her as he looked deeply into her eyes. "We are great friends and nothing will ever change that. I will always be here for you, and you know that."

After about an hour the doctor returned and informed her that she had a flu-like virus and that she needed to eat healthy meals, get plenty of rest and stay hydrated. He wanted her to be on bed rest for the next couple of days. He prescribed her some antibiotics and released her from their care. Keith helped her to his car and took her home.

"Keith, I really need to be at the office. We have so much work to do, and I need to be there. I've missed several days already. They are going to fire me . . . Just take me back to work with you," Kim said.

"No, you need to be in bed. We understand that you are sick, and trust me they are not going to fire you. We need you too much and, right now, you need rest." Keith helped her into her house, and then into bed.

"Thank you so much. You really don't understand how much I appreciate your friendship." She hugged him. She groaned loudly as his strong embrace hurt her ribs.

Keith loosened his embrace. "Oh, I'm sorry." He gently grabbed her hand. "I want you to get away from him before it's too late, and he kills you. I can't live with that. I will feel as if your blood is on my hands, and I can't take that. You need to leave him before he takes your life."

"I know, but he needs me right now. Maybe one day I will get the nerve to leave."

"Okay, but I can't stress that enough. I don't want anything to happen to you." He pushed her hair away from her face before asking, "Do you need anything before I leave?"

She smiled at how caring and loving he is. "No, I'm fine, just go back to work."

"Okay. I'll be checking on you." He kissed her forehead and headed for the door.

***

Keith walked into his office about fifteen minutes later. Some people were packing up to go home after finishing a day of hard work.

"Hey, Keith, Mr. McCallister is waiting in your office. He wants to talk to you about the case," Jeff informed him. When Keith looked at him with question, he shrugged.

"Okay, thanks, man. How long has he been waiting here?" Keith asked, while on his way to his office.

"Not long, about five minutes."

Mark McCallister is one of the firm's highest paying

clients. His case was a case of great magnitude. If McCallister is found guilty, he could spend the rest of his life in prison or possibly get the death penalty, which is what the prosecutors are seeking. McCallister is accused of killing his wife and children, and Keith is lead counsel on the case. He had been married for twenty-five years and seemed to love his wife and children dearly.

It has been rumored that McCallister's wife was having an affair and that he just lost his mind after finding out about it, which lead him to kill his entire family. McCallister is a well-known psychologist who is also heir to his father's wealth. So, the question is, would an affair really drive him to kill his entire family?

McCallister had been cool, calm and collected while in the public eye, but the truth is, behind closed doors he grieved the death of his family. All of the evidence pointed to him, and it was a big chance that Keith and the other associates could lose this case. Keith knew the chances of that, but he stood strong, that's why McCallister chose him. He knew that Keith was one of the best, and he was giving him a chance to prove just how excellent of an attorney he really is.

"Mr. McCallister, good to see you. What can I do for you, sir?" Keith asked as he walked into his office and saw Mr. McCallister sitting in one of the chairs in front of his desk. McCallister stood, and Keith walked over and shook his hand.

"Well, son, I know that the trial is coming up soon and I was just wanting to check on you to see how you are doing." He took a deep breath. "Keith, I know this is a stressful case, and everything is pointing to me, but I can assure you that I didn't kill my family no matter how it looks. I loved my wife and children dearly. No way would I have killed them. I am a man of faith, and I trust God for the truth to be revealed. I've been praying and I mean praying hard. I trust that God is about to do something with this case. There is a reason why I am here in this position.'' Tears formed in his eyes, but they didn't fall.

This was the first time that Keith saw McCallister show any emotion during this entire case. "A man of faith?'' Keith chuckled. "Well, I have it under control, sir. We are piecing everything together and we believe all will turn out well. We have our private investigative team on it, and we are going to review everything that they have on the case. I'm sure everything will work out in your favor," he assured him.

"I'm sure it will, son, but please understand, you are not the one in control, God is,'' he said. He looked at Keith for a moment, then headed for the door.

"Mr. McCallister, what makes your faith in God so strong?'' Keith asked curiously.

McCallister turned around to face Keith, and he looked him square in his eyes and said, "Because God has proven Himself to be God all my life. Why would He stop now?'' He then turned and walked out of the office.

Keith sat down in his seat and was in deep thought, *Because God has proven Himself to be God all my life. Why would He stop now?* The words of Mr. McCallister played over and over in his mind.

Jeff knocked on Keith's door, breaking him away from his thoughts. He came in and asked, "What was that all about? What did he want?'' He had a look of concern. "He only wanted to talk to you for some reason. When he got here I told him that you had stepped out, but he was determined to wait and talk to only you.''

"Well, I'm not really sure exactly. He came in to see how I was doing on the case, then he went to a different level.'' Keith stared off into space as the words of McCallister continued to play in his mind, *Because God has proven Himself to be God all my life. Why would He stop now?*

Jeff cut into his thoughts once again, "Hey, how is Kim? Everyone has been concerned. Man, she has lost a lot of weight since we last saw her. I mean, that weight loss was rapid,'' he said, snapping his fingers. "All that from a cold . . . What did the doc say?''

"Well, she will be out a little while longer. He put her on bed rest. It's not a cold, she has a flu-like virus,'' Keith informed him.

"Wow, I didn't know it do you like that. Glad she didn't spread it, then everybody would have been out sick, and you know we can't have that,'' Jeff said, shaking his head. "We have way too many cases for everybody to be getting sick.''

"Yeah, Jeff, you are right about that. I think I'm going to go ahead and wrap it up. I'm feeling a little tired, and I need get some rest myself,'' Keith told him. He began packing his files into his brief case.

"Yeah, I understand. You are looking a little flushed. Get you some water. Hopefully Kim didn't pass you that flu-like virus. Go get you some rest, so you can be ready to finish this case out,'' Jeff said. He left out of Keith's office. He planned on staying at the office a while longer to work on a few cases.

***

Keith walked into his house and was surprised to see a big brown box sitting in the middle of his living room floor. He was hoping that Taylor was not planning to move out. Of course, he was upset about the abortion, but he wanted his marriage without a doubt. He went over to the refrigerator to get some water, and then he turned up the air conditioner. He felt like he was burning up.

The doorbell rang several times, so he hurried to get the door and when he did, he was surprised to see who was there. "Janice? What in hell are you doing here?" he asked, appalled by her presence.

"I just want to talk to you, son. May I come in?" his mother asked.

Keith walked away, but the door remained opened. He went back into the kitchen to grab his glass of water.

His mother followed. "I know you feel as though it is too late for me to say this, but I'm sorry for all of the pain that I've caused this family. I love you so much." She attempted to hug him, but he backed away from her, bumping into the counter.

He pushed away from her embrace. "You love me? Really, Janice? You left us, but now you love me?" Keith said, now raising his voice. "How did you find me?"

Janice answered, "I've talked with your father, and he told me where to find you. I want to make things right, Keith."

He set his glass down on the counter. "Ha! Now that's funny. Make things right? What the hell? There's no making things right. You are a hypocrite, but you want to make things right? I'll tell you how you can make things right. You can go to hell," he said sternly.

Hurt by his words, tears formed in her eyes. She rubbed his head. "You have grown into such a handsome young man." She smiled. "I heard you got married, and I want to wish you nothing but happiness. I'm sorry that I haven't been a part of your life, and I know that I can't make up all the time I've missed, but I do love you, son. Time apart didn't change that." Her tears now fell from her eyes.

"You wish *me* happiness? Well, I wish you death, Janice." Keith was shocked by his own words.

"I am dying, Keith. I have liver cancer, and it has spread to my pancreas. Your wish has already come true. I'm suffering, yet I'm fighting for my life." She cried. "Believe me when I say, I'm paying for all of the things that I've done wrong."

Keith now embraced his mother and held her in his arms as he shed tears of his own. "I'm so sorry," he whispered to her. His heart ached for his mother and at that very moment, he forgave her. They spent hours catching up, and when she got ready to leave, he gave her an open invitation to come over or call at any time.

Chapter Eighteen

Taylor walked in the front door and saw Keith sitting in the living room with his head laid back on the sofa looking off into space as *Lonely* by Brian McKnight, played on the stereo. He had been giving her the silent treatment, so she didn't really know how to approach him, but she could tell by the look on his face that something was wrong. "Keith, is everything okay?" she asked, approaching him with caution.

Keith got up and pulled her into his arms and embraced her tightly. "I'm so sorry, Tay. I don't want you to leave me, baby. You are the most important person in my life. I need you," he said as he continued to embrace her.

Confused, she looked at him. "I'm not leaving you . . . What would make you think that?"

"Well, I saw this box sitting here in the middle of the floor, and I was afraid to open it. I thought it was some of your things. I thought you were packing to leave."

After seeing the tears in his eyes, she said, "No, Keith, I

am not leaving you. That box has my graduation stuff in it.''
She looked him in his eyes to make sure he understood. "You
know; my cap and gown? I picked it up from Southern today. I
will be graduating soon, top of my class, remember?'' She
reminded him.

Keith closed his eyes and nodded. "Yes, I remember.
There has been so much on my mind, and we haven't really been
talking. I've just been a bit bothered by all that has happened.''
He kissed her forehead. "I'm tired of this silence between us, and
I'm ready to work on saving our marriage. Life is too short, and
I don't want to live mine without you in it.''

Taylor was so relieved to hear those words from him.

He embraced her tightly, and she was comforted.

She gently kissed his lips. "I want to make love to my
husband.''

He picked her up, and she wrapped her legs around him.
He carried her upstairs to their bedroom as he continued to kiss
her with passion. He laid her on the bed and removed her
clothes. He kissed every inch of her body, running his tongue,
then his fingers against her soft skin. She moaned at his
gentleness. He removed his clothes as Taylor watched and
waited. He looked into her eyes, and she smiled. She had been
waiting for the moment that her husband would make passionate
love to her again, and she was thankful that the moment had
finally come. Keith reached into the nightstand and pulled out a
condom.

Taylor looked at him. Confused, she asked, "What is
that? What are you doing?''

"I picked up some condoms the other day just in case…"

She shook her head. "Just in case what?" she asked, interrupting his sentence.

"Taylor, I know that you do not want to have children, and I don't want to take any chances. I don't want you to get pregnant, then you decide that it's too much for you," he said, putting on the condom. "I'm respecting your wishes," he said sincerely.

"I can't believe you, Keith. We have never used protection, and we are not going to start now. I want to give you what you've always wanted. I want to start our family now," she said as she pulled off the condom for him.

Keith smiled at her words. As soon as the two joined, Taylor moaned from every stroke of husband's pelvis, and Keith enjoyed every minute of being intimate with her. He forgot all about his worries and his infidelity. All that was on his mind was his love for his wife.

Taylor rested on Keith's chest, kissing it softly. "That was breathtaking. I've missed these moments with you," she said, then gently kissed his lips. "I know that I hurt you, and I am so sorry. I love you so much, and I will never do anything to hurt you again. I know that my choice has had an effect on you… Maybe we should go through counseling together for the sake of our marriage." She paused. "I have been seeing Pastor Matthew's wife for counseling, and she's truly amazing. I have been blessed while sitting up under her wise counsel. She has really made it plain to me about my position as a wife. I haven't discussed with her about the," she hesitated, then swallowed hard before continuing, "abortion, but I told her that we were

going through a rough patch in our marriage.'' Once again she
hesitated with her next statement as she felt him tense up. She
continued, "She mentioned about us going to church together as
husband and wife, and she talked about how God will truly bless
our covenant. Baby, I believe her. I know how this subject
bothers you, but you never told me why. This is something that
has been weighing heavily on me, and I think we should go
together,'' Taylor said, looking into Keith's teary eyes.

He sat in silence as he looked back into her eyes.

Taylor continued, "Keith, please, baby. We need this.''
Tears now formed in her eyes as she watched the tears in his
begin to fall.

"My mother came by earlier,'' he began.

Taylor was completely shocked, and he had her full
attention. She had never met his mother, and he had never really
spoken of her. She didn't even know if she was dead or alive.

Keith continued, "She told me she's dying. Can you
believe that? She came by to tell me that. I hadn't seen this
woman since I was a teenager, and she came by to tell me she is
dying.'' His tears continued to flow even more. "What am I
supposed to do with that news? She's my mother.''

Taylor didn't say a word. She just embraced him and
listened.

"My father was a great husband and a great father. I'm
talking about a devout Christian, a great man of God,'' said
Keith, with admiration. "You talk about the church so much,
Tay, but let me tell you about the church.'' He took a deep

breath as though it was difficult for him when he pulled from his past. "The pastor of our church preached the word all right. He preached my mother right out of her home . . . Church secretary... yeah, right, pastor's mistress more like it." He began getting angry. "My mother was an alcoholic and the whore of a pastor. This man tried to make the Word fit his lifestyle. Speaking false prophecy and the whole works. He tried to get every dime out of that congregation and he did. He was so influential, yet a hypocrite. The Devil's Advocate is what I knew him to be." Keith shook his head. "I saw right through him, and I was just a child . . . He had sex with young girls, Tay, and my sister was one of them. I overhead my sister when she told my mother that he had taken advantage of her, and my mother called her the 'devil', which she said to be the 'father of lies.' She didn't see that the pastor was the devil himself leading a church. He was sick and so was she. You see, Taylor, my sister, too, had an abortion . . . My mother took her to abort that man's baby!" he yelled.

Taylor's mouth dropped and she was completely shocked at all of the information she had just received. He had never once told her this.

Tears ran down Keith's face as he continued to think back to his past. "You think the church will save you? Well, some churches will destroy your faith and leave you for dead. It will drain the very life out of you till you are left with nothing. My dad was a deacon, the pastor's right hand man, and he wanted to trust him. He wanted to trust that he was doing right by his wife, but the whole time he was sleeping with his wife. Late nights doing secretary work for a church, come on now. I knew that was a lie. All that time I was wondering why my father couldn't see this, and I became angry with him. Then, as I grew older, I realized that he knew the whole time. He wanted to protect me and Candi . . . his family. What did he really protect us from? The truth? He wanted us to believe that the church was good, but in reality it was poison. I have felt this way for the longest time and was angry at my dad, and I hated my mother. When she came by here today, we talked like never before. She told me how in life, you reap what you sow, and she said that God has made that evident in her life. She lost everything, and now she's losing her life." He cried even more.

Taylor continued to embrace him, attempting to comfort him.

He continued, "She told me that ain't nothing new under the sun and ain't nothing hid that won't be revealed. What's done in the dark, will always come to the light. God will repay you for all you have done in this life. She told me that the world is filled with two kinds of people, God's people and workers of iniquity. That pastor was later killed. Someone shot him, two bullets to the heart and one to the head. Who did it? It was the father of a young girl who he had taken advantage of. To every action there's a consequence. After death comes judgment. Today my mother told me that people will be people. Not everyone who says that they are a child of God is. You have to be careful, she says, 'be mindful of the wolves in sheep's clothing,'" he chuckled, and then continued, "Taylor, for a long time I blamed the church for breaking my family apart, and I even blamed God. I was so angry at Him. I never wanted to see the inside of a church ever again. It was because of my mother's transgressions that I turned my back on God, but now I have realized that God has never turned His back on me. She said that she has repented and has surrendered to the will of God. She came here to ask for my forgiveness and, today, I forgave her with everything in me." He cried.

Taylor wrapped him tighter in her arms as she cried with him, now understanding his position.

He looked into her eyes as he continued to cry. "I asked God for forgiveness and, now, I'm asking for yours. Forgive me, Taylor, for not being the husband that God has called me to be. I have done wrong by you and I am so sorry," Keith begged for her forgiveness, but little did she know about the depths of his begging of forgiveness.

"I forgive you, Keith, and we're going to be okay. Will you forgive me for not being the wife that God has called me to be and for my selfishness throughout this marriage?" she asked as she continued to embrace him.

"Yes, baby, I forgive you. I am willing to go to church with you, and I am willing to go to counseling. Whatever it takes, I am more than willing. I want us to move on from here, and I want God to bless our marriage. God has blessed me with an angel, and I want to do right by you. I Love you so much."

She smiled, assuring him that God will save their marriage.

"Promise me, Tay, that no matter what happens, we will make our marriage work. We will stay in this marriage for better and for worse, until death do us part."

Taylor sincerely looked into Keith's eyes and replied, "I promise, Keith. I promise with my whole heart." She kissed him passionately, and they began to make love all over again.

Chapter Nineteen

Another Sunday had finally come and Keith was awake, getting prepared for church before Taylor had awakened. This was his third Sunday accompanying her to church. He met the pastor and immediately felt in his spirit that he was a true man of God, a man who is after God's own heart. The first Sunday that Keith went to Holy Temple Ministries, Pastor Matthews preached about the prodigal son and how God has a way of bringing those who have strayed, back to Him. That Sunday, Keith was moved by the Holy Spirit and he went down, and rededicated his life to Christ. Pastor Matthews prophesied over him, and it really touched him. Keith had never experienced worship like that. He felt as though God had revealed so many things about his life to Pastor Matthews, and it gave him confirmation about a lot of things in his life. After that, he and Taylor had gone to a couple of counseling sessions with the pastor and his wife, and he truly believed that this man and his wife were anointed.

Keith sat and watched Taylor as she slept peacefully. He thought about how they had been making love like newlyweds ever since the night he poured his heart out to her. He leaned over, kissing her forehead softly.

Taylor stirred in her sleep and woke up to Keith staring at her. "What are you doing, Keith?" she asked while smiling at him.

"I'm getting ready to accompany my wife to church, but I was wondering if you wanted to show God how much we love each other before we get there." He chuckled. He sat on the edge of the bed with nothing but a towel on. He leaned over and brushed his lips against hers. He pulled back the red satin sheet that covered her, and then traced her navel with the tips of his fingers.

As the tips of his fingers tickled her, she giggled. "Tempting . . . I must admit, but we don't have time for all that."

"I'll be quick, I promise. It'll only take a minute," he assured her.

"Keith, you and I both know that you definitely can't be quick. Quick is not your style, honey. Let's get ready to go, and I'll make it up to you tonight." She kissed him again and rubbed his chest, then his biceps.

"Okay, it's your loss." He got up, took off his towel, looked back, smiled and winked at her, then headed to their walk-in closet.

Taylor's eyes followed his naked body and she laughed, then shook her head. Her husband knew exactly what he was doing and she wanted him right then and there, but she knew that he would have them late, so she passed. She said her prayers and thanked God that her husband was now a man after His very heart. Keith had been reading his Bible daily and talking to Michael about different things he wanted to know about the Bible. He and Michael had become rather close, almost like brothers. Michael was someone that Keith looked up to as a man of God. He truly trusted him to be Christian and he knew it by his lifestyle, something he rarely saw in people who called themselves Christians. Keith was serious about surrendering his all to God and Taylor smiled at the thought. She now was truly happy with her marriage. He was spending more time at home with her and being a husband. Work no longer came first in his life. It is now God first, then his family.

After church, Keith, Taylor and Michael went to lunch at Raymond's, a very well-known Italian restaurant.

"Man," Michael began. "Church was awesome. Pastor Matthews knows how to deliver a good Word." He shook his head. "I tell you, that man is gifted," he said, finishing his salad.

Keith's attention had been drawn to the corner table where Silvia sat with one of her friends.

Silvia made eye contact with him and gave him a discreet wave with a smirk on her face.

Keith gave a disgusted look as he shook his head.

Taylor caught the look on Keith's face. "Everything okay?" she asked him, confused by his facial expression.

"I'm good, baby." He dropped his fork onto his plate. "Do you mind if we get some to go plates and get out of here? I'm really not that hungry now," he said to her and Michael.

Michael looked at Keith strangely, then at Taylor, then back at him. "We just got our entrees but, of course," he nodded, then added, "we can do that."

Taylor cleaned the corners of her mouth with her napkin, then placed it on the table. "Well, just let me run to the restroom. I've been holding it since we left church," she said.

As Silvia watched Taylor head for the restroom she thought to herself, *Time to mess up his world.* She waited a few seconds, and then headed for the restroom herself.

Keith watched as Silvia went into the restroom and he prayed to God that it didn't mean trouble. After a minute he started to sweat.

"You okay, Keith?" Michael asked him, concerned by his behavior.

"I'm fine . . . I think." Keith was very concerned because he had a feeling that something was about to go down, but he was hoping for Taylor to just hurry and come out, so they can move on with their lives without any interruptions from Silvia. Seconds seemed like forever to him. *Hurry up Taylor. Just come on out of there and let's go.* He thought to himself as he looked at his watch.

Silvia stood at the sink washing her hands as she looked into the mirror at the stall behind her, waiting for Taylor to come out of it. When she heard the toilet flush, she smiled, anticipating what was next.

Taylor walked over to the sink and began washing her hands.

Silvia's eyes turned into slits, and she turned to face Taylor. "Don't I know you?'' she asked.

Taylor looked up and took a good look at Silvia's face. "Yes, I believe we've met before.''

Silvia's tone changed, "Yes, we have. How's your husband? Keith, right?'' she asked as if she didn't remember.

"He's doing well. As a matter of fact, we were just finishing up our lunch,'' Taylor informed her. Her intuition told her that something wasn't right about this woman, and then she thought to herself, *Why is she asking about my husband*?

Silvia bit her bottom lip before saying, "Wow, I was just thinking about him . . . Mmmm, mami, I bet your husband is a great lover. I mean, I didn't have the opportunity to really find out the last time he and I were together, but I was able to . . . umm.'' She slowly licked her lips. "Well, let's just say, I bet he's great at what he does . . . I was thinking, maybe the three of us could maybe one day get together. You know, maybe experiment a bit? You don't mind sharing your husband, do you?'' She grabbed Taylor's hand and put it up to her mouth, kissing the back of it softly.

Taylor snatched her hand out of her grasp. "Are you crazy? What the hell are you talking about? What do you mean, the last time you and him were together?''

Silvia looked at her and smiled. She slowly walked up closer to her and allowed her smile to fade. "How 'bout you ask your husband about that?''

Taylor looked at her in disbelief. She backed away from

her, then stormed out of the restroom and back to the table where Keith and Michael waited for her. "We need to leave . . . *Now!*" she yelled with tears in her eyes.

Keith stood up and looked at her. "What's wrong, Tay? Talk to me, just tell me what happened." At this point he was filled with concern. He knew that whatever it was that Taylor was upset about had to do with Silvia.

Michael signaled the waitress for the check, and then said, "Okay, Taylor, calm down. We will leave now." He pulled out his wallet to pay for their meals.

Taylor left out of the restaurant and headed to the car.

Walking fast, Keith was halfway to the restroom when Silvia had opened the door. He caught her by surprise as he pushed her back through the door and up against the restroom wall. "What did you say to my wife?" he yelled.

Silvia laughed as she panted.

Keith grabbed her face. "What did you say to her, Silvia?" his tone a little firmer now.

One of the waitresses yelled in at him, "Sir, you can't be in there."

Keith looked Silvia in her eyes. "I'm not playing with you, Silvia. This is not a game, this is my life!" he yelled as tears now filled his eyes.

Silvia giggled. "I told you that I was going to find you, Keith. What, you didn't believe me, papi?"

"What did you tell her? Silvia, she's my wife!'' Keith said, now feeling exhausted.

"I told her what happened between us.'' She licked his lips and he turned his head. She continued, "I just thought she should know.'' She rubbed her hands down the breast of his coat.

He pushed her hands away. "Nothing happened between us,'' he said through clenched teeth.

"How do you know? What makes you so sure about that? You don't know what really happened. You only know what I told you, and that could have been a lie, Keith. Maybe we did make love. Maybe that night you thought I *was* your wife,'' she said with her signature smirk on her face.

Keith grunted loudly as he picked her up by her shoulders and headed to the stall not knowing what he was capable of next. His anger was at a whole new level that he wasn't familiar with and he wanted her to feel his wrath.

Michael came in right on time and grabbed Keith, pulling him away from her. "You need to think about it, Keith,'' he said in a calm voice. "Calm down, and let's go get some fresh air.'' He walked Keith out the door, then looked back at Silvia with her smirk still planted on her face.

She fixed her clothes, then winked at him.

Michael gave her a look of disgust as he shook his head. He didn't know what that was all about, but he knew that there was something behind the scene that had just taken place in this five-star restaurant.

***

Taylor and Keith drove home without a word spoken and when they arrived, silence greeted them at the front door. Taylor walked to the kitchen and grabbed a bottle of water from the refrigerator. Keith watched her in silence, not knowing what to say. He didn't know what Silvia had told her in that restroom and he feared the thought.

Taylor's voice cut through the cold silence, "Did you sleep with her, Keith?'' she asked with her back still turned to him, terrified of his answer.

"What did she say to you, Tay?'' he asked, avoiding the question.

Taylor quickly turned to face him. "I asked you, did you sleep with her?'' she asked again firmly, now looking him dead in his eyes.

"I did not have sex with that woman,'' he responded as he looked away.

She grabbed his face and looked into his eyes deeper, reading them. "No, Keith. I want you to look me in my eyes and tell me that you didn't sleep with her.''

"I do not believe that I had sex with her,'' he said now looking her dead center in her eyes. He couldn't remember that night clearly, but he believed with all his heart that he didn't have sex with Silvia.

"What does that mean exactly? You don't *believe* you had sex with her? You know whether or not you had sex with her, Keith.''

"No, Taylor. I don't believe we had sex.''

She chuckled. "There goes that word again. What do you mean? *Believe?* That leaves it open for question. You say that like you don't know, like there's some uncertainty there. How could you not know if you had sex with her or not? And don't you *dare* lie to me." The look on her face let him know that she wanted the truth and nothing less.

Keith sighed deeply and silently prayed before saying, "It was the day you told me about the abortion. I ended up renting a room that night. I went to the hotel's bar and I had a lot to drink. I wasn't feeling well, so I went up to my room. Before I knew it, she was at my door. I tried to get her to leave, but I ended up passing out. I don't know exactly what happened, but I do not believe that we had sex. I promise you that with everything in me. I wouldn't do that to you . . . with her, Tay?! Come on, give me some credit. I am a better man than that.''

"Really, Keith, right now I'm not so sure that you are. Why would you even allow her into your room? You know what kind of woman she is. I mean, look at what she did to Kim and Trey. So, tell me. What reason would she possibly have to be in your room?'' Taylor asked, waiting for him to further explain.

"We had a few drinks, and then I went up to my room, *alone*. I left her there at the bar. Next thing I know, she knocks on my door, I open it, and she bomb rushes me. I passed out on the bed,'' he looked at the grim look on Taylor's face before adding, "I did not have sex with her. Taylor, please trust me when I say that.''

"Did you kiss her?''

"She kissed me . . . I pushed her away,'' he replied.

"Hmmm.'' She rubbed her temples. "Okay, I'm tired, and I'm going to bed . . . in the guestroom,'' she said as she headed for the stairs, but then she turned back around to face him. "I am disappointed in you, Keith, but I believe you when you say that you did not have sex with her. All you had to do was tell me about the situation in the first place and all of this could have been avoided.''

"I'm so sorry, baby. I promise you that it won't happen again.'' He walked over to her and hugged her. "No guestroom. Sleep with me tonight.'' He kissed her forehead.

She looked him deeply into his eyes and took his hand, then led him to their bedroom where they enjoyed the rest of their night . . . together.

Chapter Twenty

Keith, his associates, and the investigative team pulled the McCallister case together and everything was looking good for the day. This was their third day at trial. A lot of evidence pointed to McCallister; but late yesterday, a very significant piece of evidence came through, and today would be the day that they would present it.

Keith sat and waited for cross examination as the prosecutors questioned one of their witnesses. When they finished, Keith got up and began cross examining. While questioning the witness he began to feel extremely hot and out of breath. He started to perspire profusely. His stature abruptly changed, and he needed to sit down for a minute.

The judge stared at him for a moment. "Mr. Davenport, are you okay?" she asked with a look of concern.

"Your, Honor, may we take a five minute recess?" he asked, grabbing his chest as it began to feel tight.

"Yes, we will take a five minute recess," she said, then banged her gavel.

Keith rushed out of the courtroom and to the water fountain.

Jeff was right on his heels. "You okay, man?" he asked.

Keith sat on the bench in the hall and tried to catch his breath. "It's hot in there, huh?" He took a look around as if things now looked different to him. "I felt like I was going to pass out," he said, still out of breath.

"It feels good in there to me. Maybe you are just a little nervous. Get you some more water and maybe that will help," Jeff responded.

Keith said a little prayer, got some more water, and was headed back to the courtroom until he heard Mr. McCallister call his name. "Yes sir, I'm fine. No need to worry," he said before McCallister could ask any questions.

"Son, I am concerned about you. Are you sure you are okay? Today you have been sitting in that courtroom doing a lot of coughing and sweating a river. It doesn't sound or look good. Maybe you should see a doctor if you haven't already," McCallister said to him out of concern.

"I'm sure I'm fine, sir; now let's go win this case," Keith said. He patted him on the back, and they went back into the courtroom together.

The defense called a few witnesses to the stand, and then they presented that one significant piece of evidence. It turns out that the neighbor's house next door to the McCallister's had surveillance. Mr. McCallister's neighbors never even thought about looking at the tape until something weighed heavily on their hearts to review the tape from the night that his family was murdered. Fortunately, they didn't record over it before they had the chance to review it. They knew that it was God who put it on their hearts to view the tape. When they saw what was on it, they immediately took it to Keith's office. It was last minute, but it was a major piece of evidence that they needed in order to prove this man's innocence.

The video showed that someone else had entered the McCallister's home unannounced right before the estimated time of the murder, and the same individual left the home in a rush a short time later. The neighbors had seen the man on the surveillance several times before, but he was always with Mrs. McCallister. Mrs. McCallister told her neighbors that the young man was doing work on their house, but it was rumored by others in the neighborhood that he was her lover.

After questioning one of Mrs. McCallister's best friends, she revealed that Mrs. McCallister was indeed having an affair with the young man shown on the tape. Mrs. McCallister told her lover that she wanted to end the affair and make things right with her family. When she informed the young man of this, he threatened to kill her and her entire family. Mrs. McCallister had shared that information with her best friend in confidence and begged her to keep quiet about it until she figured out what to do. Her friend promised not to say anything, and that she would give her time to tell Mr. McCallister about her affair, so that they could go to the police together. Her friend sat on the bench and cried, now regretting that she ever made that promise to keep quiet.

After questioning the best friend, they called Mr. McCallister to the witness stand for questioning, and he gave his testimony of that night. He was in the shower the night his family was murdered, and when he heard the gun fire he immediately got out and rushed into his children's bedroom, but they had already died from their gunshot wounds to the head. Then, he ran through the house to look for his wife and he found her on the kitchen floor in fetal position as she suffered from her gunshot wound to the stomach. Now in shock, he watched as blood flowed from her mouth and wound. He kneeled down beside her and applied pressure to her wound, attempting to stop the bleeding, but when looking into her eyes he could see that she was dying. Tears flowed from her eyes as she touched his chest and begged for forgiveness. When she died in his arms it brought him back to reality, and he immediately called 911. Mr. McCallister sat on the stand filled with emotions after he told the story of that horrible night.

After the defense presented their witnesses, their evidence, and rested their case, Mr. McCallister was proven to be innocent. Friends and neighbors of Mr. McCallister celebrated his innocence, and everyone congratulated Keith and his team.

Mr. McCallister walked over to Keith and shook his hand on a job well done. He said to Keith, "Son, there is nothing hid that won't be revealed. God is a just God." He thanked him and his associates again and walked away. Those words stuck with Keith, remembering that his mother had once said the same thing. Keith was relieved that this case was over, and he thanked God for the outcome.

***

Keith went back to his office after forgetting a case file that he was planning to work on at home. He decided to call Kim to check on her and to tell her how the case turned out since she had been out sick for a while now. When he called he didn't get an answer, so he decided to stop by her place. He walked up to the door and knocked on it.

No answer . . .

He decided to ring the bell several times.

Kim finally answered the door. "Keith, what are you doing here? How is the trial going?'' she asked. She began coughing.

"He was proven innocent today, but how are you, Kim? I mean, really. I've been concerned about you,'' Keith said, not even giving her time to rejoice about the case outcome.

"Keith, I'm fine, just trying to shake this cold, virus or whatever the doctor said it was. I've been having a little fever here and there, but I'm good. No need to worry. I'm glad everything turned out well with the McCallister case and hopefully I will feel well enough to come back to work in a couple more days.'' She looked at him for a moment. "You don't look so well yourself. Are you feeling okay?" she asked with concern.

"I'm good, just been tired and stressed from this case, that's all,'' he replied. Keith looked at her as she walked away from the door. "Wow, Kim, you have lost a lot of weight. Have you been taking your antibiotics and eating right?''

"Yes and no. The antibiotics seem to make me sick. I keep throwing up and stuff. So I don't take it as often as he told me to take it. I haven't had much of an appetite . . . Keith, I'm scared,'' she admitted.

"Scared of what?''

"I want to do something different in my life. I feel like God is trying to tell me something. I mean, I use to go to Mass with my parents when I was young, but I can't really say that I believed. I pretended to understand, but I never really did. Then, when I went off to school I didn't believe in too much of anything,'' she revealed her truth to him. "My Dad was a cold-hearted killer, and I was supposed to believe in what he believed? How could I believe in anything? I have lived a nightmare my whole life.''

Keith gently replied, "Well, Kim, you don't have to live that nightmare any longer. You have to believe in something. You know the funny thing is that Taylor and I have been going to church, and I must admit; our marriage is so much better. I feel like God has been trying to get me to this point for a long time and if you feel Him calling you into repentance, then don't ignore that call.'' He took her hand into his. "I hope that you can forgive me for my part in all of this.'' He pulled her into his arms and hugged her.

"I've already forgiven you,'' she told him as she continued to embrace him.

Kim heard the keys rattle at the door, and she pulled away from Keith's embrace.

Trey walked in and looked at the both of them without saying a word.

Keith's voice broke into the awkward silence, "How's it

going, man?''

Trey studied Keith for a minute before answering him, "Everything's good. You look like you losing weight, man. You okay?'' he asked coldly as he looked at him, then back at Kim.

"Yeah, I'm good, just been exhausted from this case," he responded.

"Naw, I'm afraid it may not be that case. You may need to see the doc. Get it checked out. You feel me? You may have another case that you need to be worried about." Trey looked at him intensely before heading to the kitchen to get a beer.

Keith gave a confused look.

There was so much tension in the room as Trey watched Keith and Kim from the Kitchen barstool. At that moment he knew that Keith was the one who had been with his wife. He could feel it and even see it.

"Well, I guess I better go. Get better, Kim.'' Keith looked directly into her eyes letting her know that he was serious before saying, "If he even acts like he's going to try to lay a hand on you, I want you to call me. I mean it.''

"I will, I promise," she responded, then walked him to the door.

She stood in the doorway and watched him drive off, then she closed the door and walked back over to the couch to sit down for a minute. She felt as if she was fighting to breathe as she began coughing.

Trey walked over to her. "What was that about?" he asked.

"Nothing. He just came to check on me. People in the office had been concerned about me, that's all," she said. She continued coughing as she tried to catch her breath.

"Well, what do you think is wrong with you?" he asked calmly. He was so calm that it bothered her. She knew that it was not like her husband to be as mellow as he was now, especially after seeing another man in his home.

"Remember, I told you the doctor said I had a flu-like virus a while ago." She coughed. "Now I have this cold that's hard to shake." She began sweating profusely.

Trey chuckled lightly. "I tell you, those doctors always get it confused with a flu-like virus. If you are not specific, they won't even test you for certain things." He shook his head before saying, "Sad, I tell you."

"What are you talking about, Trey?"

"You don't have a cold, Kim, or flu-like virus . . . You have AIDS," he informed her.

"Wh-what?" she asked in mid-cough.

"I didn't stutter. You heard me correctly. You are sick, period. A cold you can get rid of, this, you can't. It is as simple as that. Get tested," he coldly stated.

"What are you saying?" she asked in disbelief.

"Put it this way. He gave it to her, she gave it to me, I

gave it to you and you gave it to Keith," he said it with absolute, then headed for the door without looking back.

Kim fell to her knees and began to groan loudly. She felt an excruciating pain as if she had just been shot in her heart and left for dead. Her thoughts went to Keith and Taylor, saddened by the thought that she may have destroyed their family with the unknown. The news that she had just received from her husband left her aghast.

***

Keith arrived home feeling really sick and was drenched in sweat. He took off his suit jacket as soon as he came through the front door.

"Hey, baby, what's wrong?" Taylor asked. She walked up to him and wiped the sweat from his forehead. She untied his tie and walked with him over to the couch.

"I don't know. Today was really rough to get through, but we did finish the trial, and we came out on top." He smiled.

"I knew that you would, babe. That's no surprise to me, but I am concerned about you though. Let me fix you some green tea or something. Maybe that will help you feel a tad bit better." She kissed him and went into the kitchen to fix his tea.

Keith sat on the couch and watched his wife. He felt extremely exhausted, but he wanted to take her in his arms and make love to her.

Taylor walked back over to him. "Here you go, baby," she said, handing him the tea.

He took the cup from her and set it on the end table. "Thanks, but I bet a dose of you would make me feel a whole lot better," he said, pulling her into his arms.

"Oh, really," she kissed his neck, "well, let's take this to the bedroom," she said. She pulled him up, and they headed to their bedroom. She catered to her husband all night long.

Chapter Twenty-One

Friday had come and gone and Taylor made it through graduation. All of her family, her in-laws and Michael attended. She had graduated from Southern University Law Center of Baton Rouge, Louisiana. Taylor had so much support and she was ecstatic to finally be finished with law school. Now her plan is to take the bar exam, pass it and open up a law office with her husband. After graduation, Taylor's family and friends surprised her with a graduation dinner that they had catered by Raymond's. Everything turned out beautifully, and Taylor was overjoyed. That night she showed Keith every bit of her appreciation by catering to him and making passionate love to him all night long.

***

Monday had come, and Taylor woke up feeling extremely sick. She ran to the bathroom and threw up.

Keith awakened from his sleep after feeling her abrupt movement. "Taylor. Are you okay?'' he asked after running in behind her. He rubbed her back as she hung over the toilet.

"I don't feel so well. My stomach is killing me," she told him.

"It may be some kind of virus going around. Everyone seems to be getting sick all of a sudden. Maybe you should see the doctor this morning. You need me to get you something, call and make you an appointment or anything?" he asked concerned as he watched her continue to throw up.

"No, I could use something to eat though." She threw up a little more.

"Okay, I'll go fix you something to eat," he said. After she finished throwing up, he helped her to the sink to brush her teeth and wash out her mouth. He made sure that she was okay before he kissed her forehead and headed downstairs to prepare her breakfast.

The doorbell rang and Keith answered the door.

"Hey, brother-in-law!" Tyra exclaimed. "How's everything with you?" She kissed his cheek.

"Everything's good, just finishing up breakfast. Have a seat and join us if you have some time."

Tyra walked over to the kitchen table where Taylor sat. "I think I will take you up on that offer," she said. She took her seat next to Taylor. "Hey, Sis, you okay?" she asked, looking at Taylor's disheveled appearance.

"A bit sick today, but it's all good. I got my husband to cook for me," Taylor said as she laughed, knowing that Keith cooked for her quite often, whether she was sick or not.

"I see," Tyra said. "I wish I could find a man half as good as Keith, huh, brother-in-law?" They both looked at Keith and laughed like little schoolgirls.

He looked at the both of them, shook his head and smiled. "Breakfast is served," he said as he placed their plates down on the table.

Taylor ran to the bathroom with one hand over her mouth and the other holding her stomach.

Tyra and Keith ran into the bathroom behind her.

"You okay, Tay?" Tyra asked.

Taylor replied, "Yes. The smell of the food just made me sick, but I'm okay."

Keith pulled her hair back for her as she continued to throw up into the toilet. He kissed the back of her neck, and then left out of the bathroom to get her a glass of water.

Tyra closed the bathroom door behind him. "Tay, are you pregnant?" she asked in a loud whisper.

Tears formed in Taylor's eyes. She nodded. "I think so." She looked up at Tyra, then added, "I'm so scared."

Tyra kneeled down beside her and hugged her. "There's no need to be scared, Taylor. You have a great support system. Everything will be fine. I'm so happy for you!" she exclaimed. "It has been a long time coming. Does Keith know?"

"No. I'm not even for sure if I am or not. I don't want to tell him anything right now. I want to at least wait until I know for sure,'' Taylor explained.

"Well, Tay, try to see a doctor as soon as possible. It is very important for the health of the baby that you find out soon," she touched her stomach, and added, "and we want a healthy baby, don't we?'' She smiled, attempting to make Taylor smile.

Keith opened the door. "Here is some water, baby. Are you feeling better?'' he asked, handing her the glass.

Taylor took a sip before saying, "Thanks, honey. I'm a lot better.''

Tyra hugged her again and whispered into her ear, "Keith is going to be sooo happy. Y'all are going to be great parents. No worries,'' she said, then smiled. "If you are better let's go eat. You need to get something in that tummy.'' She got up from the floor as Keith helped Taylor up.

He helped Taylor to her seat, and they all ate breakfast together. Taylor was able to get through her meal after throwing up once more. After she finally talked Keith into going to work, she decided that it was time for her to go see her doctor. She called to see if they had room for her, and when they told her to come in, she made her way there for the next available opening.

Taylor arrived at the doctor's office. She had to sit and wait for a while before the nurse finally called her to a room. After questioning Taylor to see what was going on with her, she brought her in a cup for a urine sample. Taylor hesitated before grabbing it. She didn't necessarily want to be pregnant, but she was hoping that she was for Keith's sake. She wanted to make him happy, and that was most important to her right now.

She went to the restroom. When she came back, she was so nervous that her hand was shaking as she handed the nurse the cup now filled with urine.

"It's okay, Mrs. Davenport. No need to be nervous. The doctor will be in soon with your results." She smiled.

It took three minutes for Dr. Allen to return with her results. "Good morning, Mrs. Davenport. I have your results and congratulations, you are expecting," she informed her.

"Expecting what?" Taylor asked, still very nervous.

She chuckled. "A baby! You are going to be a mother! We want to go ahead and do a full examination today if that is okay with you. We like to know how mommy is doing as soon as we can. The earlier we find problems, the earlier we can fix them. I will test you for every possible STD and for any abnormalities. Do you have the time right now? It may take another hour or so."

"Yes, I can do it now, but I'm sure everything is fine. I haven't had any problems," Taylor said, now overwhelmed with emotions as she took in the news of her pregnancy.

"I understand, but we want to follow procedures. If you can get completely undressed and put on the gown I will be right back to get things started," she informed her, then left the room.

Taylor undressed, then slowly ran her hands over her stomach. As she thought about the life she was carrying, a tear slid down her face and she wiped it away.

Ten minutes later, Dr. Allen knocked on the door and

walked in, "Are we all set, Mrs. Davenport?" she asked.

Taylor nodded as she thought about what this pregnancy means.

Dr. Allen washed her hands, then put on her gloves. She completed Taylor's breast exam, and then she began her pap smear. After she finished up, she had one of the nurses to swab Taylor's mouth and she began explaining everything to her. "This is OraQuick. It is a rapid oral test that will test you for HIV/AIDS. This test is used for the detection of antibodies to the Human Immunodeficiency Virus. We will just need to take a sample of your saliva and test it. You will get those results in about twenty minutes if you would like to stick around for them. The other tests results, of course, will be back in about a week, and if we find anything wrong with those results, we will give you a call. Do you have any questions for me?" Dr. Allen asked as the nurse finished swabbing Taylor's mouth.

"No, I don't have any questions. I'm not going to wait for the results from the OraQuick test. I'm kinda hungry now, and I'm sure everything is fine with all of the results. Thank you so much, Dr. Allen."

"Not a problem. I would like to see you back in two weeks. After you get dressed, please stop by the front desk and make an appointment. After that you are free to leave," she informed her, and then she prepared to meet with her next patient.

Taylor went to meet Keith for lunch. She was planning to wait on telling him about the pregnancy. She wanted to prepare a candle light dinner and share the news with him then. She knew that he was going to be so ecstatic. He had been waiting for this moment since they had gotten married, and she couldn't wait to announce it to him. She felt like she owed it to him after she had disappointed him by aborting their first baby.

She and Keith had casual conversation over lunch at Raymond's until she got a call to come back in to Dr. Allen's office. They kissed and said their goodbyes, and then she headed back to the doctor's office. They didn't say exactly what they wanted, but it sounded urgent.

When she got there, she headed straight to the front desk. "Yes, I'm Taylor Davenport, and I was here earlier, but they just called me to come back in to speak with the doctor," Taylor informed the young girl at the front desk. The girl pulled her file, then told Taylor to go straight back to the doctor's office. Taylor sat in there and waited for the doctor to come in. She looked around at all of the pictures of Dr. Allen's family, then she saw a big beautiful picture of President Barack Obama and First Lady, Michelle Obama, hanging on the wall behind her desk.

After a few more minutes, Dr. Allen came in and shook Taylor's hand.

Taylor began to feel a little uncomfortable, so she said the first thing that came to mind, "I love that picture you have of the President and First Lady," she looked around at all the pictures before adding, "and all of your pictures really. You have a beautiful family." Her nervousness was heard in her tone.

"Yes, yes, thank you very much. President Obama has proven to be a very intelligent man, filled with great character. He's a great role-model to many generations and so is First Lady... Oh, and my family," she paused, then smiled and

Taylor immediately knew that her family brought her great joy, "yes, family is so important." She was brought back to her present moment after looking at Taylor. Her posture then changed. "Mrs. Davenport," she began, "we called you back in because we have your results from the OraQuick test, and your results came back positive for HIV," she informed her as she looked at her with compassion.

"I don't understand. Positive? What do you mean, positive?" Taylor asked. She tried to wrap her head around what the doctor was telling her.

"Taylor, you are HIV positive." Dr. Allen got on a more personal level with her.

"No, I'm afraid you have the wrong results. I feel fine except for being sick because of this baby. Other than that I have been fine . . . Test me again," Taylor demanded angrily.

"Mrs. Davenport, some people can go years without any symptoms. People can begin having symptoms as early as three weeks after being infected and some can go without symptoms for ten years or more. That is why it is so important to at least get tested once a year. HIV/AIDS does not have a look to it. We have no problem with testing you again, but please understand that if you test positive, it is not a death sentence. Many people have lived long and healthy lives after testing positive. Look at Magic Johnson and there are so many others. The earlier you find out and begin getting treatment, the longer you can live and have a productive life," Dr. Allen informed her.

"I understand that, Doctor, but you are obviously, *not* understanding me. The test results were a mistake. I was a virgin when I married, and I have only been with my husband.

And since we've been together, he has only been with me. There's no need for me to be tested once a year. I am married. I have no doubt that those results are wrong. My husband and I have only been with each other,'' Taylor said with confidence. "Test me again,'' she demanded once again.

"I understand, Mrs. Davenport, and it very well could have been a mistake. So let me get you in a room, and I will get the nurse right in to swab you again,'' she said, trying to make Taylor feel more comfortable about the situation.

"Yes, that will be great. Thank you." Taylor followed a nurse to the room and allowed them to perform another test on her. She decided not to stay for the results, and they let her know that they will call her if they needed to.

Taylor opened the door to her house and headed straight for the bathroom. Everything she ate came up and out into the toilet. She was very disturbed by the first set of results that had come back. She ran the shower water and hopped in. She tried to think if there was any possibility of her being HIV positive, but she didn't believe there was. She knew that she had been faithful to Keith and she had no doubt that he had been faithful to her. *Those results had to have been a mistake*, she thought to herself. She got out of the shower and dried off.

She walked into the room and saw Keith removing his shoes. "I didn't know you made it home," she said to him.

"Yeah, I've been here for a while now. I didn't want to disturb you," he told her.

"Wow, you never seem to care about coming in on me in the shower before. What's wrong? You look drained." She grabbed the lotion from her nightstand after putting on her lingerie.

"I am feeling quite drained, so I left the office a little early. It's been a long day." He walked over to her and kissed her forehead.

"Yeah, tell me about it. I've had quite a day myself."

Keith walked back over to the closet to put his shoes up. "Are you feeling any better?" he asked as he started to undress.

"Well, I did what you asked me to do," she said. "I went to the doctor today, and they tested me for a few things. One of those tests was an HIV test. Do you know they called me back in to tell me that I had tested positive for HIV? I told them that they made a mistake and to retest me." She sat on the edge of the bed, rubbing lotion onto her legs and feet.

Keith stopped in the middle of unbuttoning his shirt, and the room became completely silent. Her words hit him like a ton of bricks.

"Keith, they tried to say that I tested positive for HIV, and I told them it was a mistake." She paused, waiting for his response, but when she got silence in return, she turned to face him. "Right?" She studied his demeanor.

Keith stood still, frozen in place like a statue. His eyes closed with tears running down his face. He knew instantly that those test results were possibly right. He thought about the mistake that he made with Kim and how she had been extremely sick. At that moment he knew in his heart that the information Taylor received from that test was true.

Taylor continued looking at Keith as she shook her head in disbelief. The look on his face was more than enough said and, at that moment, it was as if her heart dropped. "Keith, are you telling me that I'm HIV positive?" she asked, now standing, waiting for his response.

Keith was still frozen in place.

"Keith?" she screamed, needing answers.

He slowly walked over to her and hugged her without saying a word.

"No! Get away from me!" she screamed, fighting his embrace. She now backed away from him as if he were a stranger. Keith walked closer and she grabbed their beautiful, crystal-framed wedding picture from the nightstand and threw it at him. It hit the wall and shattered into thousands of pieces, but it didn't match the shattered pieces of her heart. She fell to the floor, crying hysterically.

"I'm so sorry, Taylor," Keith said. He got down beside her and held her.

"Get away from me!" she screamed while beating his chest and slapping his face. "Get off of me!" she yelled in tears as she continued to fight him off of her.

He let her go.

She grabbed her purse and keys and ran for the door.

Chapter Twenty-Two

Michael had just finished working out when he heard someone banging on his front door. He opened it. "Taylor. What is wrong? What's going on?" he asked, feeling as if it were a déjà vu moment. He had on nothing but his workout shorts and his muscles were ripping through his beautiful dark skin which made Taylor hesitate.

"Taylor. What is wrong?" he repeated. He looked at her from her head to her toes. He knew something had to be terribly wrong considering that she was at his door crying hysterically with nothing but a black lingerie gown on. He invited her in. They sat in the living room as Taylor continued to cry. Michael held her in his arms, attempting to console her. "I'm sorry, Taylor. Let me run and get me a shirt," he said to her.

Taylor held on to his arm which kept him from moving. She rubbed his chest, and then kissed his lips tenderly.

He pulled her away. "No, Taylor," he said firmly. "I don't want you to get confused just because you are hurting right now. You are very much a married woman, and I am your friend. Your husband, he is like a brother to me . . . We will *not* do this," he said to her, meaning every word.

Taylor cried even more. "I'm so sorry, Mike." She had spoken her first words to him since he invited her in.

"It's okay, Taylor. Everything is going to be okay, I promise." He hugged her, and then got up to go to his room to get a shirt.

"I'm HIV positive!" Taylor yelled to him before he was able to leave the living room.

Michael stopped in mid-stride and turned back around to face her. "What?" He walked back over to the couch where she sat. He sat beside her.

"He obviously cheated on me with that whore and brought me home death. I believed him, Mike . . . I believed in him as my husband. I believed him when he said he didn't sleep with her," she said, referring to Silvia and the conversation she and Keith had about her a while back. She shook her head and thought to herself as she remembered that moment. *But his eyes told me that he didn't have sex with her. They told me that he was telling the truth, and I felt that in my heart.* She became even more bewildered.

Michael held her and silently prayed. They sat there in complete silence for an hour. Taylor had cried herself to sleep in his arms. He picked her up and carried her to his bed. When he laid her down, she shivered, and he placed a blanket over her. He got him a shirt and blanket, then went back downstairs to the living room and prepared the sofa for him to sleep on. He kneeled down and began to pray. He prayed for Keith and

Taylor. He prayed for their marriage to survive this. He also prayed that their love for one another would grow even in the midst of their "for worst."

***

Taylor woke up and looked around the unfamiliar place she was in. The smell of breakfast engulfed her nostrils. She walked into the kitchen and saw Michael at the stove. She sat at the table without saying a word. She just watched him as he cooked and sang praises to God. He turned around to grab a plate from off of the counter, and Taylor's presence caught him off guard.

"Wow, good morning," he said. "I didn't know you had come down. I'm fixing you some breakfast. I hope you like it. You know I don't cook much since it's just me here." He smiled.

"What were you singing? It was beautiful and uplifting," she said with tears in her eyes.

"*I'll Trust You* by James Fortune & Fiya. I love to sing that song whenever I'm going through. It may sometimes seem as though we do not feel God's touch, but there is always evidence that He is right there," Michael said to her. He took in her beauty for a moment as the sun shined on her through the kitchen window. He thought that the black lingerie she wore was absolutely beautiful on her. He quickly ran upstairs to get one of his robes for her. He came back and handed it to her.

She smiled and put it on.

He began fixing her plate as they continued their conversation.

"That was the song they sang at the church that day; the day I rededicated my life to Christ. You know the pastor spoke over me that day, and he told me that I was about to go through a storm.'' She shook her head. "God, I didn't know that my storm would hit me like death,'' she said. Her tears now ran down her face.

Michael wiped away her tears. "Taylor, this is not your death sentence unless you claim it to be. Speak life to your dead situation. God can handle this for you, but you have to trust Him.'' He set her plate down in front of her.

Taylor took a couple of bites before running over to the sink, the closest place she could find. She began throwing up into it.

"Are you okay?''

"Oh, I forgot to tell you . . . I'm pregnant,'' she replied, then continued to throw up.

"Wow! I thought it was my cooking.'' He laughed. "Taylor, this is great news! Don't allow anything to damper that.''

"I'm sorry, Mike. I will clean this out.'' She referred to the sink that she just deposited into.

"That's okay, I will clean it up. Just try to put something in your stomach.''

"But, Mike, you can't possibly clean this up. I will get it. I don't want to expose you to anything,'' she argued.

"Know the facts, Taylor," he said, referring to her comment. "I'm going to clean it up," he assured her. "Now eat for the baby's sake."

They sat at the table and finished their breakfast. "This was delicious. You are a really good cook, Mike," she said, taking her last bite.

He laughed out loud. "Now I know that's the baby talking, but thank you."

Taylor shook her head as if trying to shake away her thoughts. "How could he do this to me, Mike?" she asked him out of the blue.

"Your husband made a mistake. He messed up, Taylor. But trust that he didn't do this to you on purpose. I'm sure that he didn't know he had been infected. He would not hurt you intentionally," Mike assured her.

"He should have known that she was carrying something. As trifling as she was at our dinner party. Why would he sleep with her?" Taylor asked. The thought angered her.

"Who are you talking about, Taylor? Who did he sleep with?" he inquired.

"The Latino chick, the one who was in the restaurant that day; I believe her name is Silvia. She even had the nerve to step to me and ask me to share him, knowing that she already had him. I'm sure she knew that she was infected before she even touched him," she explained to him.

Michael firmly said, "Taylor, let's get something straight here. I know a couple of people with HIV and they weren't trifling at all. That's not why they got infected. One of them was infected after being date raped and the other lady was infected at birth and now she's twenty-eight. They are awesome women of God, the same as you." He looked at her closely. "And another thing, Silvia did not sleep with your husband. She may have wanted to, but she didn't. She and I sat down and had a long talk after that day in the restaurant. She finally admitted to me that she did have sex with Trey at the dinner party and she was also very honest with me about what happened between her and Keith. She did not have sex with him, Taylor. I believe that she was being honest with me the day that we talked. She has many issues I know, but she's not the one to blame for this, " he explained.

"I don't understand how he could do this to our family. I can't stay in this marriage, I just can't," she said.

"Remember how you came to my door not too long ago because Keith found out about the secret you kept from him? You were terrified that he was going to leave you. You do remember the secret that you kept from him, right?" Michael looked her in her eyes. "You had an abortion without his knowing and now you are ready to end your marriage because this man messed up, just as you did. No sin is greater than the other no matter how the situation looks to the human eye, sin is sin." He touched her hand. "I can guarantee you that most likely it wasn't a long time affair that he was having. I think it was a result of him being hurt and not responding to it well . . . He made a mistake," he gently explained.

"So, what are you saying? This is my fault, Mike? This

is all on me? I'm the reason why I'm HIV positive?'' Taylor said, as she stood up. She became agitated with Michael at this point.

He gently grabbed her arm. "Taylor, sit down.''

She sat back down in her seat and looked at him.

He continued, "I am not saying that at all. This is not your fault. I'm just saying, think about all the things that you have done against God, but yet He forgave you without hesitation even though you didn't deserve His forgiveness. God understands your pain and He knows that you are hurting, but this is not a reason to leave your husband and turn away from the commitment that you made before God. God loves covenant and that's what your marriage is; a covenant between God, Keith and yourself. You honor God in your marriage and He will prove that He is God in your marriage,'' Mike explained.

"Why do you have to make so much sense?'' She felt a certain peace that amazed her considering her circumstances.

"That's what happens when you allow God to use you,'' he said to her and smiled.

"Yes, I guess you are right.'' She looked at the clock. "Shouldn't you be at work?''

"Well, considering that I run a business that operates without my being there, I don't have to be.'' He chuckled. "I'm just glad I came home early to workout yesterday, or you may have been running up and down these streets trying to find your mind,'' he said. He stood up and pulled her up from her seat, hugging her. He kissed her forehead.

"Keith always does that," Taylor said, comforted by his embrace.

"Does what?"

She looked him in his eyes and said, "Kisses my forehead."

He let her go realizing what she said. "I'm sorry, Tay. I didn't mean anything by it," he apologized.

"No, I know you didn't. You are just being a really great friend, as always." She smiled, and then watched him walk over to the sink. "You must work out a lot?"

"Yes, every chance I get. Train your body to do what you desire it to do. If you desire it to be healthy, train it to be healthy. Thank God that He has given us the ability to do so." He looked back at her. "Taylor, I promise, you are going to beat this," he said to her with a confidence as though he believed it.

Taylor smiled and nodded. She was comforted by his great faith.

He continued, "I understand you need time, and you can stay here for as long as you like, but I do believe that you should at least communicate your whereabouts to Keith. I'm sure he's worried crazy."

"Yes, I will. Thank you so much, Mike. I really appreciate you." She walked up to him and embraced him from behind.

Chapter Twenty-Three

A couple of days had passed since Kim and Trey last spoke.

She was saddened by the fact that she hadn't seen him since he told her that she had been infected. Kim received a call from the hospital and she quickly made her way up there. She walked up to the front desk. "Yes, I'm Kimbrailee Whitmore, and I received a call that my husband, Treyvionne Whitmore, is here," she informed the nurse.

The nurse typed his name into the computer. "Okay. Yes, ma'am, if you take a seat in the waiting area, the doctor will be right with you," she told her.

Kim was drunk with worry as she paced the waiting room floor.

"Mrs. Whitmore?" the doctor called out.

"Yes, I'm Mrs. Whitmore," Kim said as she walked over to him.

A tall dark-skinned gentleman in a white coat walked over to her. He reached out his hand and introduced himself as one of the emergency room physicians. And then: "We called everyone on Mr. Whitmore's list of contacts. He has been in an accident and right now he is in critical condition. He was involved in a head on collision with an eighteen wheeler. His blood alcohol level was extremely high." He paused to make sure that Kim was okay after he saw her grab her chest. After seeing that she was okay, he continued, "He has suffered three broken ribs. His left leg and his left arm, has been broken. He has not responded to us, and he is not breathing on his own. Right now he is in a comma and we are not sure if there is any brain damage. He did lose a lot of blood, but we were able to give him blood immediately. He is in the intensive care unit, room i-555. You are free to go up and see him. Oh, and Mrs. Whitmore, from the looks of that accident, he is very blessed that he didn't die on the scene, so that means that there is still hope. Thank God for grace," he said. He touched her shoulder, smiled, and walked away.

His words were very comforting. Kim walked to the elevator and tried to prepare herself mentally for what was about to come. The elevator doors opened and she got off and headed to Trey's room, i-555. Once she got to the room she slowly walked in, preparing herself for the worse. She looked at his body and quickly closed her eyes for a moment, and then opened them hoping that she was dreaming. Trey was hooked up to all kinds of machines and had a tube in his mouth. She saw the IV hooked up to him and a bag of blood flowing into his system. Tears immediately escaped her eyes. She sat in the chair beside the bed knowing by the looks of it, Trey didn't have very long. Her life with him flashed before her eyes and she began to remember the good times that they once had, even though they were very limited. Then she thought about the times that he had beaten her almost to the point of death. Kim cried at the sight of her husband who lay in the hospital bed lifeless. Then she realized that he'd been lifeless all these years. He had grown cold, so cold that he allowed her to live with AIDS without even telling her that she had possibly been infected. She shook her head at the thought. She was sure that he knew he had passed this on to her years ago.

As she sat in deep thought, she realized that she was beyond hurt by everything that Trey had done to her. She felt the strong desire to go home, take a whole bottle of sleeping pills and chase them with Vodka so that she would never wake up to such pain again. She had become overwhelmed by her transient thoughts of suicide. She left out of the room to get some water. When she headed down the hall she walked right into Keith as he paced the floor.

She took a long look at him. "Keith. What are you doing here?" she asked.

Keith looked as if he hadn't had a minute of sleep in days. "I'm here with my mom. She's not doing well at all . . . What are you doing here?" he asked.

"Trey has been in a terrible accident. It doesn't look like he's going to make it out of this," she said with tears now running down her face.

Keith pulled her to him and hugged her. "Kim, we really need to talk." He led the way around the corner where they could have some privacy. "Is there any way possible that you could be HIV positive?" he asked, looking her straight in her eyes, hoping her answer was no, but in his heart he already knew.

Kim's mouth dropped in shock from his question. She finally said, "I'm so sorry. I swear I didn't know. When Trey saw us together the other day at the house, he told me then that I had been infected." She was hurt by the look on Keith's face. "Keith, it is possible that you are okay. We only been together once, and it is harder for a woman to infect a man," she said, trying to give him a hope that she didn't even have herself.

Keith shook his head. "I'm afraid not. Taylor went to the doctor the other day because she was feeling sick. She tested positive, Kim," Keith said with tears in his eyes. "I can't believe I did this to her." It all began to sink in. "How could I be so stupid?" He turned away from Kim and began walking back and forth, talking to the air. Keith had held on to a little hope, thinking that just maybe Kim was not infected and Taylor's test results were a mistake, but now the truth was out. Reality hit him and it knocked the life out of him. He fell to his knees in tears feeling as though he has taken life from Taylor. He groaned in pain.

His father walked around the corner to find him. "Keith. Are you okay? What happened, son?" he asked, filled with concern. "Your mother finally woke up. She wants to see you. Everything is okay now," his father said to him.

Kim just stood and watched as she shook her head with her hands over her mouth, tears flowing from her eyes. She felt as if this was all her fault.

Keith's father looked back and forth between the two of them and realized that this was not about Keith's mother. His father reached down to help him up. They began to walk to the room together. John looked back at Kim, and asked her, "Are you okay, sweetheart?"

Kim nodded, and he continued to walk Keith down to the room to see his mother.

Keith walked into his mother's room and his tears continued to slip away from his eyes.

"What's wrong, Keith?" his mother asked. "Don't cry for me, I'm fine. God has everything under control." She smiled and reached for his hand. "Thank you for coming, baby, I know this was hard, but this means so much to me. I know that you have truly forgiven me for the pain that I've caused you. I've learned that forgiveness is vital to your health," she looked at his father as she continued to talk to her son, "your father is an amazing man of God. Do you know that I woke up to him praying for me?" She now looked at Keith. "God answered his prayer, baby! You should be happy now. Don't weep for me," she said.

Keith hugged his mother and cried like a baby. He cried for her and for Taylor.

She rubbed his head. "Shhh, it's okay now, son," she said as she attempted to console him. She was happy just to be able to hold him. "I love you, baby," she whispered into his ear.

"I love you, too, Mom," he told her and kissed her cheek.

Chapter Twenty-Four

Keith and his father got out of the car and went into the house. His father asked, "Keith, I don't mean to pry, but where is Taylor?"

"I'm not sure. I've been calling everywhere. I've called all the hotels. I haven't heard from her since Monday and I'm so worried about her . . . Dad, I'm scared," Keith admitted. His tears fell from his eyes.

"Why? What is going on with you two?"

"I cheated on her, but that's not the worst part. I messed up so bad."

His father's eyes were wide with shock. He never would have thought that his son would have fallen into that position. He sat silently and waited for Keith to continue.

"Dad, Taylor was tested the other day, and her test came back positive," Keith informed him.

John sat erect in his seat. "Positive for what?" he firmly

asked.

"HIV . . . I can't believe that I did that to her . . . to us," Keith broke down into tears. "I messed up. I messed up bad, and I can't fix this. I can't make it alright."

Tears ran from his father's eyes as he thought about the depth of his son and daughter-in-law's situation. "It's okay, son. Everything will be okay. Taylor will come back, and God will see the both of you through this." He tried to give him some comfort.

"How is that? I don't think she's going to forgive me for this, and I can't blame her. I took her life," he said. At that moment, his phone rang. He didn't want to, but something told him to answer it. He picked up on the third ring.

Michael's voice was on the other end, "Hey, Keith, I asked Taylor to give you a call to let you know that she is safe, but I really don't believe she was going to call anytime soon, so I decided to give you a call. She is here at my house and she is not feeling that well. I really believe she needs you." He paused as he heard Keith sobbing on the other end. "Look, I will fix dinner tonight, and maybe you should come over and be with your wife. You two need to talk. She needs to be comforted, and she needs you. Oh, and, Keith, she's been wearing some of my old shirts and sweat pants, so bring her some more clothes and whatever else you think she needs. Bring you some clothes as well. You may have to stay here in the guestroom until she's ready to come home. I did tell her that she could stay here as long as she needed to, but I want you guys to talk. She's miserable without you, I know it. I will try to have dinner ready for you guys around seven o'clock," Michael said to him, knowing exactly what he was doing.

Keith thanked him and they said their goodbyes.

Keith felt hope from Michael's call. "Thank God! Taylor is safe,'' he said to his father as he wiped his face. "I didn't even think to check to see if she went to Michael's, but I'm glad she did.   Michael is good people and I trust him.'' Keith was relieved as he explained the phone conversation to his father.

His father hugged him tightly. "I love you, son," he said to him.

"I love you, too, Dad,'' Keith said back to him.

John prayed with Keith and he hugged him once again. He held him for a minute longer before leaving out the door so that Keith could get prepared to be with his wife. Keith packed some of Taylor's belongings together and a few items of his own. He then headed for the shower. He prayed, hoping that God will touch Taylor's heart and that she will forgive him.

***

Before Keith could ring the bell, Michael opened the door. "Hey, man, I've been looking out for you. Taylor's in the bedroom, and I didn't want the bell to disturb her. How's it going? How are you holding up?'' he asked, pointing him to the living room area.

Keith put down the bag of their belongings next to the couch before saying, "Not great. Thanks for contacting me. How's Taylor? Is she okay?'' His concern was solely for his wife.

"She's not feeling that well. I've been letting her have her space. Right now, she's in my room resting. I'm not sure if she has fallen asleep or not, but you are welcome to go check . . . She needs you," Michael informed him. "Oh, and, Keith, this will be a surprise to her. I didn't tell her that I contacted you," he added, warning him to be cautious.

"Thanks so much, man. You don't know how much this means. I really appreciate you."

Michael pointed him to his bedroom where Taylor was.

Keith grabbed the bag that he brought with their belongings and headed to the room where Taylor resided. He walked in and saw her lying down with her back turned to him. She had fallen asleep and had been that way for an hour. Keith stood there and watched her for five minutes as tears ran down his face. He dropped the bag down and walked over to the bed. He kissed her forehead.

She stirred in her sleep and woke up. "Keith. What are you doing here?" she asked. She sat up and pushed herself away from him. She looked as if she was afraid, her eyes weary and sad. The look in her eyes broke Keith's heart.

"Taylor, it's okay. I'm not going to hurt you," he said as he reached for her.

She appeared to be delusional. "Tell me it was all a dream. Tell me I was dreaming. Please, Keith." Her outcry hurt Keith to his heart as he now held her in his arms. He wanted to assure her that it was all a dream, but he knew that it wasn't. It was their solemn reality.

"It's okay," he managed to get out. He held her and tried to comfort her as she continued to cry in his arms.

Then she realized it wasn't a dream at all. It was a real living nightmare that has been haunting her for the past few nights. "Get away from me! Don't you ever touch me again!" she screamed, and pushed him away.

Michael ran in the room to see what was happening.

Taylor had backed herself into the corner. She looked at Keith as if she didn't know him anymore.

Michael slowly walked up to her with his hands up as if to show her that he wasn't going to hurt her. "Taylor, it's okay," he said. "I invited Keith over so you both can talk." He studied her carefully. "You need him, Taylor, and he needs you. You know that."

She fell into Michael's arms as she cried uncontrollably.

"It's okay, Taylor. He's not here to hurt you. He's just here to talk," he said as he consoled her.

Keith walked closer and Michael switched places with him. Keith now wrapped her tightly in his arms as though he never wanted to let her go, and she was comforted by his strong embrace.

Michael, Keith and Taylor sat at the dinner table and ate in silence. Keith watched her as she barely touched her food. She didn't say a word at the table before excusing herself to the room where she has been sleeping.

She took a long shower trying to comfort her self. She got out and walked into the room. She gasped at the presence of Keith sitting on her bed, looking as though he was anticipating her return.

"I'm sorry," he began, "I didn't mean to scare you . . . Taylor, we need to talk." He reached out to touch her hand, but she pulled away. "Taylor, please," he begged. "I know I messed up . . . I need you, Tay, I really do."

His words were met with silence.

"Just talk to me. This silence is deafening and it cuts me to my heart . . . say something . . . anything," he begged of her.

Taylor's tears ran down her face. She felt as if she had been stabbed multiple times and left for dead by someone she trusted.

"This silence between us, I can't stand. This is killing me, Taylor," he whispered loudly.

"Oh, like you killed me," she shot back in anger.

Keith stood and looked at her with tears streaming down his face. Her words cut him deeper than any knife ever could. He left the room without saying another word.

Chapter Twenty-Five

Keith had been staying in Mike's home for a couple of days now, but he still could barely sleep in this unfamiliar place. He felt as though everything he loved was missing. Taylor had been cold with him the entire time that he's been there, so he decided to fall back and give her some space. As he lay in bed, he began to pray that Taylor would just talk to him even if it were just for a minute. At least that would be a start. In the middle of him praying, he heard glass shatter. He looked at the clock which read: 11:05 p.m. He got up and followed the sound that came from the kitchen. He walked in and saw Taylor kneeled down on the floor with her hand on her stomach. He ran to her side to succor her.

"Are you okay? What happened?" he asked, filled with concern.

"I came down to get some orange juice. I drank some and caught a pain in my side, and then I felt dizzy," she explained.

He gently grabbed her left arm and she wrapped her right arm around his neck as he helped her up.

Michael came in with his workout clothes on and his earplugs in his ears, not having a clue as to what was happening. "What's going on? I thought y'all were asleep," he said, pulling his earplugs out of his ears.

Keith helped Taylor to steady herself as he held on to her. "Taylor just had a little incident," he told him. "I'm going to help her to the room, and then I'll come back and clean this up."

"No, stay with her, I got this." Michael looked at Taylor. "You sure you okay, Taylor?" he asked.

"I'm fine now. I just probably need to rest." She looked him up and down in his workout clothes. "Speaking of rest, why are you working out so late, don't you need some rest?"

"Yes, after I finish working out, I will definitely get some rest. I have to burn off some energy first. Then, I will do a little studying. Gotta get my mind right . . . Are you sure that you are okay?" Michael asked again for assurance.

"I'm fine, Mike, I promise," she said. She knew his concern was also for the baby she was carrying. "Goodnight, Mike."

"Goodnight." Michael watched her as Keith helped her up the stairs. He cleaned up the glass that was on the floor, and that's when he saw a drop of blood. He wet a dish towel to clean it up and he threw it in the wash room when he was done. He sat at the kitchen table as he prayed. He prayed that everything will work out for the good of his friends, and he trusted God to work things out on their behalf.

Once Taylor and Keith made it to the room, he hugged her tightly and she was comforted by his embrace. She lay back onto the bed, and Keith didn't say a word as he covered her up. He asked was she really okay and when she said, "yes", he kissed her forehead and stood up to leave the room. He hoped that Taylor would want him to stay with her tonight, but he refused to ask, afraid of rejection.

"Keith,'' she called out to him right before he got to the door. "Was I not good enough for you? Was I not enough?''

Keith was taken aback by her question. "You were more than enough for me, Taylor," he said without turning around to face her.

"Well, what was it? Was I not a good wife?''

Keith turned and walked over to her, then sat beside her. "You are the best wife and friend that God would have ever blessed me with. Don't you for a second believe that my indiscretion had anything to do with you; you are a great wife and you are more than enough for me.'' He looked down and shook his head. "I made a mistake, Taylor, and it only happened once.''

"Who was she?'' she finally asked the question that has been troubling her mind since she found out that he cheated.

Keith dropped his head, knowing that the moment he revealed who she was; Taylor would be hurt even more. He whispered, "Kim.''

She covered her mouth in disbelief. "Kimbrailee Whitmore?'' she asked in a loud whisper.

"Yes. It was when I had found out about the abortion and I became angry. We went out for drinks after office hours and, Taylor, I swear I drank more that night than I ever have. I know that's no excuse and I'm sorry. After that night and having a talk with Michael, I made a promise to God that I will never put another drink to my lips. I promise to never hurt you again. The biggest mistake that I have ever made in my life was the choice of being unfaithful to you," Keith said, tears running down his face. "Please, forgive me. I know that I can't fix this. I know that I can't change your results, but I promise, Taylor, if you give me a chance, I will spend the rest of my life making this up to you." He kissed her forehead and lingered there before saying, "I love you so much."

Taylor sat in silence as tears ran down her face.

Leaning over a little more, he kissed her tears, then her lips tenderly.

She grabbed her stomach and groaned loudly.

"I'm sorry, did I hurt you?" he asked. He put his hand on top of hers as she continued to hold her stomach.

"Keith, I'm pregnant," she whispered to him.

"Are you serious? We are having a baby? Oh, my God, Taylor, this is great news even in the midst of what we are going through," he said. He raised her baby doll top, leaned over and kissed her stomach. "Are you hurting? Do I need to take you to a hospital? I don't want anything to happen to you or our baby." His hand was still on her stomach as he smiled. He was overjoyed by the news. It took his mind away from everything else.

"I'm fine. I catch pains here and there, but I'm fine."

"Wait, is the baby going to be okay considering . . ."

"The baby will be fine," she interrupted. She already knew his concern. "There's no need to worry. Dr. Allen says that women who are HIV positive have healthy babies all the time . . . I went back to the doctor the next day after my results, and she started me on my meds immediately. Of course, my meds would be different from yours considering the fact that I'm expecting. She did say that the baby will be healthy as long as I follow her orders," she informed him. She surprised herself by how calm she was while explaining this to him.

"I went to the doctor the other day," Keith began, "and I've started my meds also. Of course, I don't like the side effects very much, but I'm dealing with them. The doctor explained the virus to me, and we can live long and healthy lives, Taylor. The doctor was thankful that we were able to catch it early on before it progressed. He was saying that early detection can save lives." He touched her hand, and then kissed her stomach again. He looked up at her. "Let's do this together. Let's start our family together. I don't want to be separated from you and our child. I can't take that. We need one another, and our baby needs the both of us in his life," he said, touching her stomach.

"In her life," Taylor said. She smiled, and she knew then that God was working on her heart as she embraced Keith. She asked him to share the space that she borrowed.

Keith lay with her and held her. He silently prayed with his hand on her stomach, and they fell asleep together . . . in peace.

Chapter Twenty-Six

Keith walked into his office and sat down for a minute as he tried to catch his breath. He had just taken one of his meds without eating anything, and he started feeling a little dizzy. He sat there in deep thought, thanking God that Taylor was really trying to stay in their marriage. He understood that it had to be difficult for her, but he was willing to go through the ups and downs with her as long as she was beside him. He got up from his desk to go get some more water.

On the way to the water fountain he passed by Kim's office and stopped when he saw the door cracked. She had been in and out of the office for weeks now. She never came in more than three times a week since she has been sick and so far, she had missed all week. Keith knocked on her door and went in. He looked around and saw a bunch of packed boxes, but no Kim. He turned to leave back out and bumped right into her. "Sorry… Kim, what's going on?'' he asked as he looked around at the boxes.

"I'm leaving,'' she replied. "I can't do this anymore. I'm sick, Trey is lying lifeless in some hospital, and I'm just tired.'' She shook her head at her next thought. "I'm dying, and it doesn't feel good.'' She avoided eye contact with him. She waited a second before she looked up at him. "I'm sorry that I brought this to you and your family. You have to believe me when I say; I didn't know that I was infected.''

"I never once believed that you knew that you were infected, Kim. If you knew, you would not have been so wicked that you would pass it on intentionally. You are far from an evil person, and your intentions have always been pure.'' He looked around her office once again at all of the packed boxes. "What are you doing? I know you, Kim, and you don't want to quit your career. This is your life."

"*Was* my life . . . now I'm tired, and I don't want to face you every day knowing what I did to your family, Keith, it's hard to live with that . . . my heart aches for Taylor, and for you,'' she admitted.

"This is far from your fault, Kim. I played a part in my own decision. Taylor and I are going to work through this. Let me explain something to you,'' Keith began, "Taylor had started going back to church right before I found out about the abortion, and she always tried to talk me into going with her, but my heart was too hard. Then, not too long after she began going, I found out about the abortion. I became angry with her and I was hurt. My actions came from a place of pain.'' He took a deep breath. "One day my mother came by out of the blue. I mean, I hadn't seen this woman in years.'' He chuckled lightly. "It's funny how God sends people into your life at the right moments. My mother talked to me about forgiveness. I was so angry with her and the church that I allowed it to push me away from God. But when she came back into my life, she gave me something real.

She gave me evidence that God is God and that He has never left me. I started going to church with Taylor, and I went through counseling. We have taken what we have learned since then and have applied it to our lives. Finding out this information was definitely not easy for Tay, but she's coming around because she has already been ministered to about forgiveness, and she understands what it means to truly forgive,'' Keith explained.

"I understand, but why are you telling me this?'' Kim asked.

"Because I believe in the power of God. I believe that when you surrender to the will of God, He will make things right in your life. I've grown so much since being under the leadership of Pastor Matthews, and I believe that you should come one Sunday. I promise that the Word will give you hope, and your faith will begin to increase. The first time I went, I was moved to rededicate my life to Christ. After church, the pastor took me into his office, prayed with me and counseled me. He and his wife does that with everyone who comes down and accepts Christ, as well as with those who desire to rededicate their lives to Christ.'' He touched her hand. "You should come, Kim. Your life will never be the same once you truly give it to God. At this place of worship you will grow spiritually like never before because that man gives the Word and he doesn't give it like man sees it, he gives it by the Spirit. What I love about that church is that the shepherd lives his life according to the Word, not his flesh. He's not after your money, or the women there, nor is he after power. He just desires for the congregation to be after the heart of God and to grow spiritually so that everything else in our lives will fall into place. They make you feel so welcomed there no matter what your background is, or what you have going on in your present life.''

He looked deeply into her eyes. "Just think about coming one day because your life doesn't end here." He hugged her and left her office.

Kim sat in her chair feeling a tug at her heart. It was a feeling that she had never experienced before as strongly as she now feels. She sat and contemplated going to Keith's place of worship the following Sunday. Her heart told her to go, but her mind told her not to. They had their own personal battlefield. She desired to feel that hope that Keith had. She desired the evidence of God to be shown in her life, her life that has been so tragic since childhood. She never felt that hope, and her heart desired that. *Help me God*, she silently prayed. *If I'm going to do this, I need your help.* She was going to make it to that sanctuary if it was the last thing she did.

***

Taylor walked into Michael's home and sat on the couch. She sat silently in a daze unable to speak. Michael was at the kitchen table eating some fruit, and he realized that she didn't even notice him there. She was quiet and had a look of disturbance on her face.

He walked into the living room. "Everything okay, Taylor?" he asked, touching her on the shoulder.

Startled, she gasped. "Wow, you scared me."

"Sorry . . . Want some fruit?" He held the bowl out in front of her.

She ignored his question. "I thought you were still at work."

He sat down next to her. "Got hungry, so I had to come eat some fruit," he said. "Have some."

She chuckled lightly. "It's funny how you're trying to encourage me to eat some fruit. The doctor wants me to eat plenty of it." She grabbed a handful of grapes.

"Not only that. God, your Heavenly Father, desires you to live by the fruit of the Spirit." Michael smiled.

She returned his smile. "You always know what to say, and you make so much sense when you say it." She then stared back into space, focusing on the news she had just received from her doctor.

"What's wrong, Tay?" he asked, sensing that she was unsettled about something.

"Well, you know that I went to my appointment today. I didn't tell Keith about it because I knew he would miss work to come . . ." She paused for a while.

"*But* . . . I sense a, but, somewhere."

"But I wish he was there. I had an ultra sound done, and I found out something a bit more than I can deal with right now," she said with her tears now falling from her eyes.

"What . . . What did you find out?" He looked into her eyes deeply before saying, "God will not put more on you than you can bear."

"I'm having twins," she blurted out.

"Wow! That's awesome, Taylor . . . two miracles at

once. That's something to rejoice about.''

She shook her head and said, "Maybe for you, Michael, but not for me. I can't deal with two babies right now. I couldn't even deal with one, remember?'' She became agitated at the thought.

"Look, Taylor, you took one away because of your own selfish reasons, and now God is giving you two more because He knows that you and Keith can handle it . . . together. So, for that, you have a reason to celebrate,'' he said firmly.

Taylor was appalled by his words. It was like the truth slapped her in the face . . . hard.

"God gives us choices. It's up to you to make the right one. He's giving you another chance, Taylor, just work your faith.'' He got up, left the bowl of fruit on the coffee table for her and went to work out in the basement.

Taylor sat in deep thought and ate the fruit that he left for her. She decided to walk down to the basement to talk to Michael. She walked in and saw all of his workout equipment. "Wow, you have a real gym down here. It's nice,'' she said as she looked around. "What are some workouts for a pregnant woman with twins?'' she asked laughing as she picked up a ten pound free weight.

"No, no, no! Don't pick that up. You don't need to be lifting anything," Michael said, grabbing the weight from her.

Taylor looked at him. "I heard you up there, and what you said was so true.'' She then embraced him. She had a desire to kiss him, so she quickly let him go. She turned to touch the weight set that was behind her. "So, tell me, Michael. Why do you work out so much? Ever since I've been here you've been working out none stop it seems," she said, continuing to look around at all of the equipment.

"Honestly. I believe in taking care of the temple that God has given me, so I try to eat healthy and workout. It also builds my endurance, plus it helps me with my stress levels and helps me to release some energy. I've been celibate for years now and, of course, working out helps me with that as well." He laughed shyly.

"That is so honorable. You are a very wise man," she said, impressed by his lifestyle.

"I'm a man who knows that making healthy choices are vital to your health spiritually, mentally, emotionally, physically and even financially. I also know that temptation can get you into trouble, so I've learned to flee from it." When he saw the look on her face he realized that his last statement hurt her. "I'm sorry, Tay. I didn't mean anything by that," he said, pulling her head up to make her eyes meet his.

"No, you meant exactly what you said, and it was the truth. You have been such a wonderful friend, and you have respected me ever since the first day I met you. Your parents raised you well, and you have become such a great man. I know they would be so proud of you. You are going to make a great husband one day." She smiled brightly.

"Thanks. I miss my parents so much, but I am thankful for everything that they have instilled in me. Because of that, I know that they live on through me. And, yes, I plan to be a great husband." He smiled.

Taylor looked at his smile, and it reminded her of when they were in elementary school. He was so handsome to her. She began to feel dizzy, and her knees buckled allowing her to fall, but Michael caught her. He helped her to the love seat that he had in there.

"You okay?" he asked.

"I'm fine. Dizziness is just one of the side effects to one of my meds . . . I probably need to get a bite to eat," she informed him.

"Okay, I will fix you something to eat. Are you sure that's all it is?"

"Yes, that's all it is. You know that wasn't enough fruit for me. I'm eating for three now," she said laughing.

He helped her up the stairs and to the bedroom, then he went to prepare her something to eat.

***

Taylor had finished the meal that Michael had fixed for her, and then she went to lie down. She still felt dizzy and nauseated. She thought maybe hopping in the shower would help her to feel better, but she felt too weak to get up and stand for that long.

Keith had gotten off work and walked in the room to check on her. "Hey, Taylor, you okay?" he asked. He watched her as she lay on the bed holding her stomach.

"I'm fine," she said. "I was about to take a shower, but I'm feeling kind of weak right now, and I don't think I could stand for a long period of time. So I decided to lie here and rest for a minute.'' She now rubbed her stomach.

Without a word, Keith went to the bathroom and began running some bath water for her. He came back into the room and picked her up off the bed, then walked her to the bathroom. He put her down and started removing her clothes. He stopped and stared at her for a moment. He couldn't resist kissing her neck softly, then her nose, her lips, then her collar bone.

Taylor's body responded to his kisses and his every touch.

When he felt her body quiver, he said, "I'm sorry, Tay. I shouldn't have.'' He continued to remove the rest of her clothes.

Taylor missed making love to her husband, but she closed her eyes and chose to repress her feelings.

He checked the water and helped her into the tub. He got on his knees and began washing her back. He stopped when he got to her stomach. He touched her stomach and tears of joy formed in his eyes.

Taylor leaned over and kissed his lips tenderly. "We are having twins,'' she announced to him.

Keith now sat flat on the floor with his hands over his mouth, tears running down his face. He was overjoyed by the news.

Taylor gently grabbed his hand and placed it back onto her stomach. She repeated, "Twins, Keith." She now brushed her lips against his tears, and then she kissed his lips softly.

"I love you, Tay," he whispered into her ear.

A single tear ran down her face as joy filled her heart. She knew without a doubt that Keith loved her. He made her feel that with every single touch.

He continued to wash her and massage her shoulders. He refrained from even attempting to make love to her, even though he desired to.

After he finished bathing her, he helped her out of the tub and dried her off. She now lay on the bed naked as he gave her a light massage with lavender scented massage oil. Her skin was so soft under his touch. As his fingers kneaded her shoulders and back, she moaned at his touch. She'd missed that touch so much. When he finished, he brushed his lips against her back and neck, then he ran his fingers down her right side all the way to her waistline.

Her breathing became heavy as she desired her husband.

He then ran his tongue up her spine and she gasped at how good it felt. He ran his fingers down her side once again, then they began to explore her body until he heard her say, "Keith, wait." She grabbed his hand. "Not yet, I'm just not ready."

Keith dropped his head and slowly nodded. He swallowed hard before saying, "I understand, Taylor, and I refuse to rush you in any way." He helped her slip into her Victoria's Secret negligee. He then helped her to lie down onto the bed and he covered her up. He asked, "Do you need anything else?" He wanted her to say that she needed him.

She replied, "No," her voice soft.

He kissed her forehead and left the room.

Taylor felt so relaxed. She basked in the tranquility of the moment and she fell asleep peacefully.

Keith went into the kitchen and fixed himself a glass of water. He was riled up from what had just happened between him and Taylor a few minutes ago. He had been anticipating the moment that he would make love to his wife again and he felt as though he had that moment right there within reach. He was disappointed, but he understood how she felt.

Michael came in and took him away from his thoughts. "Hey, man. What's up? You want to catch the game?" he asked. "You know it's the playoffs tonight, Saints vs. Cowboys. It's a pretty good game too." He grabbed himself a bottle of grape juice from the refrigerator.

"Naw, I'm good. Don't even feel up to watching the game tonight," Keith said, taking a sip of water.

Michael studied him for a minute. "Long day?"

Keith replied, "Taylor just told me that we are having twins. That's great and all, but I'm seriously hoping that we can get back to being like we once were. I want our children to see us happy and loving one another." He sighed as he thought about what had just occurred between the two of them. "I wanted her so bad tonight, but I didn't want to rush her. I know she's not ready for that emotionally. Taylor has her up and down moments. One minute we are good, the next, she seems so angry with me. I know she's still not ready to go back home . . . I guess too many memories.'' He turned and looked at Michael. "By the way, man, thanks so much for allowing us to stay here. It has really helped. I believe it would have been even harder for us to get to this point if we were at home alone trying to work through this.''

Michael nodded and said, "You are very welcome and it was no problem at all. I gave you both a key and invited you both to stay here for a reason. I knew it would take some tension away. Taylor was not going to stay there at home with you, I already knew that. And I knew that if I invited you to stay here, she wasn't going to leave just because you were here. She's comfortable right now by not being in the environment which she initially felt hurt. I wanted you both to be under the same roof. You can't reconcile if your house is divided and we all know that a house divided, will not stand. Sometimes you need a mediator. Consider that to be me.'' He smiled. "I've enjoyed talking to the both of you and Lord knows I enjoy the company, but what's real is that I want your marriage to work and that's going to take you and Taylor working together to make that happen. Marriage is a beautiful ministry designed by God. It's going to take a lot of time for Taylor, and it will be a long process, Keith, but your marriage will work out. You just have to keep the faith, and work that faith. You remember, before you got it right with God, you had a lot of disorder in your life. With disorder comes judgment. We have two options in life. Get right, or get left. Just continue to keep God in His rightful place in your life, and everything else will fall into place,'' he said. He took a sip of his grape juice.

"That is so true . . . You have been counseling Tay and I since we've been here. You should really consider going into counseling one day,'' Keith said. He chuckled, but he was very serious about his comment.

Michael thought about Keith's statement before saying, "As a matter of fact, Pastor Matthews asked me to be the facilitator of a group of people who are dealing with addictions. Of course, I'm not a licensed counselor, but the pastor was like, 'the Lord desires to use you in the area of counseling, son. You don't need a license. He has called you by name, he has already ordained you'," he said, imitating Pastor Matthews as he chuckled. "To be honest, I felt that call a long time ago, but I didn't pursue it. But God continued to pursue me. Sometimes we feel as though we are not qualified to do certain things in life, but when God qualifies you, that's all that matters. When Pastor Matthews came to me about that, I knew it was nobody but God. You see, He uses the prophet for confirmation. I told the pastor that I would be honored. I'm not technically counseling. I'm just facilitating a group of people who need help with the redirection of their focus. I'm getting enough practice in up there with my employees. Working with people . . . man, I tell you, too many people, equals too many problems. Anyway, how is work going with you? How are you handling the stress? You know with your condition, your body doesn't need to be under too much stress," he said with compassion.

"It's going pretty good. I haven't told anyone yet about... well, you know." Keith sighed heavily. "I don't know how they would react, and I don't really know what to say and how to say it. People will begin to look at me differently, and you know how that goes."

"Well, Keith, it doesn't matter how they would react. Just because you are HIV positive doesn't mean you are not the same good hearted person or hard working man. Your condition doesn't have anything to do with who you are. It does not define you or who God has called you to be, and it doesn't stop what He has in store for you.''

"Yeah, maybe you are right, but you know people will be people,'' Keith said. All of sudden he felt extremely tired. He leaned on the counter for support.

"Are you okay?''

"I'm fine, just tired. I probably just need some rest, that's all.''

"Yes, you probably do. Rest is so important for your mind, body and spirit. Don't give Satan any room to attack. Even Jesus rested,'' Michael told him.

Michael helped Keith to the room, and then he checked on Taylor who was fast asleep. He went back to the den and enjoyed the rest of the game.

Chapter Twenty-Seven

The day that Keith had spoken with Kim about going to church really weighed heavily on her heart. She went that following Sunday and her spirit was truly blessed beyond measure. Before the day Keith spoke with her, she was planning to leave her job and not only that, she had planned to end her life. She felt as though God used Keith that day to minister her. The fact that he could stand there and communicate with her showed her that he had no hostility towards her. She knew then that the God he was talking to her about is powerful. When she attended church that following Sunday, it was like a worship service she had never experienced before. She received the Word from Pastor Matthews as he preached about Jesus and the Samaritan woman at the well. Her heart was truly blessed.

As Pastor Matthews preached the Word, Kim's spirit began to stir. She could not sit still with this man of God speaking to her. She went down to the altar during altar call and fell to her knees as the Pastor's wife spoke into her spirit. A group of ladies along with the pastor's wife took her to the back and prayed with her. It was as if Mrs. Matthews knew what Kim was going through. From that point on, Kim's life would never be the same. She had been to church for the past two Sundays and she, too, sat in a couple of counseling sessions with Pastor Matthews and his wife. She had gone to the doctor and started her meds and she was feeling great. She returned to work full-time and she even started looking like herself again.

Trey had been in a comma for a while, but Kim continued to pray for him as she sat by his side every night. She would normally go up there for the seven o'clock visiting hour, but this time, her spirit led her there for the three o'clock visiting hour. She sat in the chair right next to Trey as she held his hand and began to pray. She heard the door creak open and she looked up. She saw a beautiful young woman holding the hand of a young boy.

"I'm sorry. I didn't mean to disturb you,'' the young woman said, and then she turned to leave back out.

Kim's words stopped her, "No, you are not disturbing me. Please, come in," she said, studying the young woman.

The young woman slowly walked in and stood on the other side of Trey's bed with tears in her eyes as she held the little boy's hand.

Kim sat in complete silence as she watched the young woman and her son. She didn't have to open her mouth for Kim to know that she was the reason why her husband spent so much time away from home. The young woman didn't say a word as her tears now ran down her face, they told her story. Kim continued to watch her as she leaned over and picked up her son.

"How old is he?'' Kim asked.

"He's two and a half,'' she replied.

"He's handsome . . . What's his name?"

She hesitated before finally saying, "Treyvionne Lamont... Whitmore . . . Jr." More tears fell from her eyes. "I'm so sorry, Mrs. Whitmore, but it is not what you think," she said, putting down her son. She walked over to where Kim sat.

"What do I think?" Kim asked, curious of what the young woman thought.

"That I'm not a good person," she said to her.

"I don't think that at all," Kim responded back to her. She stood up to look her in her eyes. The girl expected Kim to raise her voice . . . slap her . . . spit in her face . . . something... anything, but Kim did nothing other than reach out her hand and introduced herself, then she waited for the young woman to do the same.

Their hands met, "I'm Keisha Fullerton. They called me when he first arrived. I guess I was someone on his list of contacts. I've been coming to bring Jr. to see him during the day."

Kim looked down at her husband's spitting imagine. "May I?" she asked.

Keisha nodded.

Kim bent down to pick up Trey, Jr. She broke down in tears as he kissed her cheek. She instantly felt connected. She hugged him in her arms without saying a word.

"Mrs. Whitmore, has Trey told you?" Keisha asked.

"Told me what, that I have AIDS? Yes, he informed me right before his accident . . . Did you infect him, or did he infect you?" Kim asked her, curious to know the answer.

"I'm not a whore if that's what you're thinking. I had a boyfriend when Trey and I met. My boyfriend wasn't very good to me at all. I was beaten so badly at times, I was unrecognizable. While working in a club Trey became my number one client and he treated me very well. Never once did he tell me that he was married until after I had already fallen in love with him." She looked over at Trey's body, and then she looked back at Kim. "I wanted to stop seeing him, I swear I did, but I was already in too deep. It was sooo hard to let go of someone who I thought loved me. He rescued me from my relationship and took very good care of me. I was young with nowhere to go. What was I to do? I didn't know my boyfriend had infected me. I didn't even know that he had sex with other men and I certainly had no idea that he had full-blown AIDS until he died. It wasn't until the funeral that I found out that pneumonia had taken his life. Then, one of his homeboys came up to me after the funeral and told me to get tested. At that very moment, my life changed drastically," she said. She began crying hysterically at the thought of her own death.

Kim hugged her as she continued to hold Trey, Jr. in her arm. He rubbed his mother's hair, attempting to comfort her.

"I had already infected Trey by the time I had found out," Keisha continued. "I swear, I had no idea my boyfriend had sex with men. Nobody knew except for the men he was with... I'm so sorry. I didn't mean for any of this to happen." She cried out to Kim.

"Is he okay?" Kim asked as she held up Trey, Jr.

"He's fine, thank God. I found out right after I became pregnant with him. They immediately started me on my meds," Keisha told her. She watched her son in the arms of the woman whose life she'd played a part in destroying. "As a matter of fact, he doesn't take to anyone very well and look at him, he's clinging to you. That amazes me," she told her as she rubbed her son's back.

Kim shed more tears. "I can't have children," she informed her. She hugged Trey, Jr. even tighter.

"Well, I bet he would love to spend time with you," Keisha said to her and smiled. She looked at this woman as she held her son. She thought about all the times she had begged Trey to tell Kim about their situation. "I begged Trey to tell you about everything, especially about being infected. It wasn't fair to keep that information from you. I even thought about picking up the phone, or even knocking on your door to tell you myself."

"How long have you been with him?"

Keisha looked down at the floor, not really wanting to answer that question. "About four years," she informed her.

"How long have you known he was married?"

"I don't know, maybe about three." She looked at Trey's body, and then returned her focus back to Kim. "He told me right after I found out that I was pregnant. I wanted to stop seeing him, but there was something so strong that held me to him."

"Wow, it sounds like you loved him more than I did. I

fell out of love with him a long time ago. Perhaps sometime after he put me in the hospital for the third time because I was beaten so badly that the doctor didn't expect me to make it. Or maybe it was when he put the gun to my head and told me that he would kill me. Or, no, wait. Maybe it was the night that he raped me several times. Or could it have been the day that he told me I had AIDS." She paused as she went back to that day, which was such a vivid memory, and then she said, "He said it so coldly, as if it meant nothing to him." She came back to her present moment. "I'll stop there because the list could go on forever." Once again, Kim's tears had escaped her eyes and ran down her face.

"I'm so sorry, Mrs. Whitmore," Keisha said.

Kim handed her back her son and walked over to her husband's bed. "There's no need to be sorry. I'm the one who's sorry. I've been sorry for a long time. I allowed him to do this to me all these years, but you know what, my heart has been healed and I've been delivered. It is because of Jesus that I've been set free. I've let it all go, and I've given it to God, which is why I am able to stand here in this room asking God to spare his life," Kim said as she looked at her husband's lifeless body. She looked back at Keisha before saying, "Now that's love." She now returned her focus back to Trey.

Keisha walked closer to her and softly said, "I have no family, no friends and I know this sounds crazy, but I was thinking maybe . . ."

Kim's eyes stayed on her husband. "Yes, I would love to be your friend. I would love to be in you and your son's life," Kim said, interrupting her. She turned to face her. "I want to be clear about something. I don't blame you for any of this." Kim took Keisha into her arms and embraced her.

Keisha sobbed as she embraced her back. There they stood several minutes before letting one another go.

They exchanged information and said their goodbyes. Kim's heart desired to keep in contact with Keisha and her son. Keisha left with Trey, Jr. and Kim sat back down in the chair beside her husband. She held his hand and began to pray as she prepared to leave.

Trey's hand began moving in hers. Kim slowly looked up and saw him looking at her with tears in his eyes. He was in so much pain, in more ways than one . . . but that wasn't the reason for his tears.

Kim's mouth dropped as she stood up. She reached for the Nurse button, but Trey stopped her.

He pulled the tube from his mouth.

"No!" she yelled. "What are you doing? I'm going to call the nurse."

She reached for the button again, but paused when she heard, "I'm . . . sorry . . . Kim," he said to her as he began coughing. He continued, "I was so very wrong . . . and . . . I'm sorry . . . for everything."

Kim fell to her seat, shocked because he has never apologized to her.

He had her full attention and she listened to him as he continued to talk, "You reminded me so much of my mom, so passive and submissive. I loved that about you. I never wanted to be like my dad who was an abusive drunk.'' He began coughing some more before saying, "He use to beat me and my mom so badly. I had so much hate for that man, and then I became him. I turned out to be just . . . like . . . him . . . a heartless, abusive, no good, lying, cheating, drunk.'' He coughed more. "My childhood wasn't pleasant and I made my adulthood just as unpleasant by bringing my childhood into it. Please, don't you for a second believe that I didn't love you; I just didn't know how to show you. That's how my father taught me to love.'' He paused, trying to catch his breath. "Kim . . . I'm so sorry . . . Please, find it in your heart to forgive me." He continued to cough and every inch of his body ached, including his heart. He groaned as he suffered. The pain was so unbearable. It felt as if something was squeezing the life out of him.

Kim got up and reached for the Nurse button once again.

He grabbed her hand, stopping her. "Kim, please . . . forgive me for everything.'' he asked sincerely.

"I forgive you, Trey. I forgive you because God forgave me and commanded me to forgive you . . . I accepted Christ into my life as my Lord and Savior. After all you have done to me, Trey. After all you put me through. God has given me the heart to forgive you. Now you must forgive yourself . . . and your father.'' She waited before saying, "And even me." She thought about her unfaithfulness to him. "God forgives, and we must forgive.'' She paused and looked into his eyes deeper. "Christ died for you and God raised Him from the dead for you. He loved you just that much. He died on that cross and God raised Him from the dead, just for you. All you have to do is turn away from your sins and repent. Ask God for forgiveness and accept His love for you. For He so loved the world that He gave His only begotten son for you, Trey. The wages of sin is death, but the gift of God is eternal life through Christ, His son. All you have to do is open your mouth and confess Him to be Lord and believe in your heart that God raised Him from the dead and you shall be saved. You can ask Him into your heart right now, if you truly believe,'' Kim said as she stood over him, holding his hand.

Tears ran from his eyes. "I can't, Kim. It's too late. I've done too much. I've done so much wrong in my life. There is no way that He will forgive me. I've caused so much hurt and I've played a part in damaging the lives of so many people. I've exposed so many women to this virus. I can't see Him forgiving me or loving someone like me. I can't possibly ask Him for forgiveness.''

"Yes, you can and it's not too late. For all have sinned and has fallen short of God's glory. It doesn't matter what you've done in the past. The only moment that matters, is right now. He's given you another chance. God loves you, Trey, and He is faithful enough to forgive you for all you've done. All you have to do is call out to Him and He will answer you,'' Kim assured him.

Trey began to cry uncontrollably as his heart was pierced by her words. "God, please forgive me, for I have sinned. I've done so much wrong in my life and I know that I don't deserve your love, but right here, right now, I call on you. I need you. I forgive myself and my father with all my heart. I believe that you sent your son for me. I believe He died for me and I believe you raised Him from the dead for me. I accept Him into my heart today.'' He sobbed even more. "Thank you for your son and thank you for my wife. Thank you God for keeping me even when I didn't deserve to be kept,'' Trey called out to God from his heart and he continued to cry uncontrollably. He no longer felt the pain that was once in his body. He looked at Kim. "I forgive you, Kim, and I love you so much,'' he said to her. She continued to hold his left hand. He reached up and wiped away her tears with the other.

"I love you, too, Trey,'' she said as she continued to cry. She kissed his lips passionately for the first time in years. As she felt the presence of God in the room, she laid her head on her husband's chest and began to pray with him. She and Trey felt peace and it surrounded them in the room. When she finished praying she listen to his heartbeat, and then she felt him as he took his last breath. Tears flowed from her eyes and joy filled her heart, knowing that her husband had given his life to the Lord. She was thankful that she was led there for the three o'clock hour and that she was able to lead her husband to salvation before his death. Now he would spend eternity with God and not away from Him, and for that she was grateful.

Chapter Twenty-Eight

Kim sat on the front pew as Pastor Matthews performed the eulogy. Many came up and spoke about her husband and how he was this great man who played pro football and played the game well. Little did they know; he wasn't anywhere near being a great husband. Many had no idea that he was a philanderer, or that he was abusive. The image he portrayed in the public's eye was immaculate. Tears fell from Kim's eyes, but not because she was saddened by her husband's death. Her tears came from a place of peace and joy. She was joyful that her husband had accepted Christ right before his death. She had peace in knowing that he would be joining the Father in Heaven. Her joy also came from the forgiveness that had taken place in the hospital room the day he died.

Trey had a big life insurance policy that Kim didn't know about. Kim, his son and even Keisha were all going to be well-taken care of. She sat and wondered how her marriage would have been if Trey would have accepted Christ long ago. She just knew that they would have had a much better marriage if it was Christ-centered. She began to think about living in the world without a husband and she cried even more as she thought, *Who will want to marry me now? I'm a woman with full-blown*

AIDS? Then she made a conscience decision. *I will not allow my condition to hold me back. I am going to live my life to the fullest, and I am going to be happy and whole with, or without a man.*

Her thoughts were interrupted when she felt Keith touch her hand. He leaned over, hugged her and gave her his condolences. She didn't even realize that people were going around for the final viewing of the body. She looked around and realized this was it. This was the end. This was her chance to see him for the last time and to say her final goodbyes. After everyone had a chance to view the body, an usher came over to Kim as she wept loudly.

"Do you want to go up?" the usher asked.

Kim shook her head.

"Are you sure?" he asked as he held out his hand to her.

Kim then gently grabbed the usher's hand and stood to go say her final goodbyes. She cried loudly as she leaned over and kissed her husband's lips.

She stood there for the longest as two ushers tried to gently pull her away from the body. Taylor sat on the back row as she watched through tears of her own, only her tears came from the thought of it one day being her husband lying in a casket. The thought of death weighed heavily on her. She was pulled away from her thoughts when she felt her husband let go of her hand. He stood and walked back up front where Kim stood crying uncontrollably over Trey's body. Taylor watched as she saw her husband's hand touch the back of the woman who he had once been unfaithful with.

Kim felt Keith's touch and she turned to him. She cried on his chest as he embraced her. "It's okay, Kim. Everything is going to be okay. I promise," he said, trying to console her. He walked her back to her seat and sat with her as they got ready to close the funeral procession.

Michael was sitting next to Taylor and saw that she was hurt by Keith leaving her side to be with the woman who had caused her so much pain. He grabbed her hand. "She's hurting, Taylor. You have to understand that," Michael said to her.

Taylor looked him in his eyes and nodded as if she understood, but in her heart she was extremely hurt.

At the burial, Taylor watched as Keith comforted Kim once again. Keith held Kim in his arms as she continued to cry. Taylor continued to watch through tears of her own, and then she saw him kiss her forehead. *Oh, my God, he loves her*, she thought to herself. She turned her head and closed her eyes, unable to watch any longer. Tears fell from her eyes even more. She began wishing that it was Kim in that casket instead of Trey.

Michael walked up and hugged Taylor as if he knew the truth behind her tears. She pushed him away. "My husband should be comforting me, Michael, not you," she stated angrily.

He watched her as she walked away and headed to the car.

Michael then walked over to where Kim and Keith stood. "Hey, Keith, your wife needs you," Michael said as he pointed to the car.

Keith didn't even hesitate as he ran to the car to check

on his wife.

Michael hugged Kim. "I'm truly sorry for your loss, Kim. If you need anything, give me a call."

"Thank you so much, Michael. And that night at the dinner party, I appreciate you for that. Your words were really comforting,'' she said.

Michael smiled and nodded. "You're welcome."

She hugged him again. He got ready to walk away, but then she grabbed his hand. "There's something about your spirit that really brings comfort," she said to him and smiled. She meant every word.

Michael smiled and walked away.

***

The ride home was long and the silence was deafening. Taylor hadn't spoken a word to Keith since she assured him that she was okay at the grave site. He didn't want to force her to talk to him because he knew that she was going through her mood swings. Taylor could be extremely sweet one minute, and extremely angry the next. He knew that her mood could go from zero to sixty within seconds. He thought she was having one of her moments, but in actuality it was because her mind was telling her that he was in love with another woman, and that was the reason for her silence at that moment.

They walked into their quiet home, which they had moved back into about a week ago. They would still sleep in separate beds at times when Taylor was in one of her moods.

They hadn't made love since she received the results that she was HIV positive. She still wasn't emotionally ready for that, and Keith didn't even try because he knew that she wasn't ready. Taylor headed straight for the guestroom. Ever since she came back home, sleeping in their room, in their bed, where they made passionate love, was not an option. Not only did that room bring back great memories, it also brought back the memory of the pain and devastation she experienced the day she learned of her husband's indiscretion that resulted in her positive HIV test results.

Keith stood in the doorway of the guest bedroom as he watched Taylor lie across the bed on her back, rubbing her stomach with her eyes closed. "Are you okay, Taylor? Do I need to get you anything?" he asked.

She shook her head and rolled over onto her side with her back to him. Keith was about to walk away until he heard, "Are you in love with her, Keith?" Taylor asked, tears running down her face, staining the bed.

He turned around. "In love with who, baby?" he asked, now confused.

"I think you know who . . . Kim," she said. She wiped the tears from her eyes as the thought pained her.

He was flabbergasted by her question. "No . . . not at all. I am in love with you and only you. Why would you ask that, or even think it?"

"Well, let me rephrase that. Do you love her?"

"Why are you asking me this, Tay?"

"Just answer the question, Keith . . . Do you love her? Yes, or no?"

"Yes. I love her as a friend, nothing more, nothing less."

Taylor quickly got up and pushed past him as she ran to the bathroom with her hand over her mouth.

Keith was right behind her as he always was. He rubbed her back as she leaned over the toilet throwing up.

"Stop!" she yelled. "Just stop acting as though you care. *Do . . . not . . . touch . . . me!*" She emphasized each word as she pushed his hands away from her, and with every word breaking his heart. "Why didn't you just think? You couldn't have just worn a condom, Keith?" she screamed as she thought about him making love to another woman. "You should have protected me! You should have protected our family!" she yelled through her tears, her mind reverting backwards to the time she got her results.

Keith balled up his fist. Hitting the bathroom door, he left out. Her words hurt him to his core. "You want me to leave, Taylor, fine I will go!" he yelled to her with tears streaming down his face. "Is that what you really want me to do? I will give you what you want. Just tell me, Taylor. What do you really want me to do and I will do it. I just want you to be happy." He paused, fearful of what her answer to his next question would be. "Do you want out of this marriage? Do you really want me to leave?" he asked, making his way back to the bathroom. He was hoping that Taylor's decision wouldn't be one that would leave him completely heartbroken.

"What marriage? It stopped being a marriage once you stepped out of it!" she yelled out in anger. She felt sharpness in her stomach and cried out in pain.

Keith ran to her side.

She continued to cry as pain struck her body even more. She saw blood on the floor as she attempted to stand.

After seeing the blood, Keith picked her up without hesitation and took her to the car. He headed for the hospital where Taylor passed out in his arms as he carried her into the emergency room screaming for help. They ran some tests and decided to keep her overnight, just to be safe. They did an ultra sound and checked the heart-rates of the babies, and everything was fine. The doctor was very concerned about Taylor's blood pressure and she placed her on bed rest after performing a stress test on her. She put her on a strict diet and changed some of her medications. The nurse and doctor then left the room.

"You scared me, Tay," Keith said. "I didn't know what was happening. I was afraid that I was about to lose you and the babies." He shook his head. "God knows I can't stand the thought of that. I would lose my mind if anything ever happened to our family." He gently grabbed her hand. "Forgive me. I don't mean to stress you out or anything. I love you, I just wish you knew how much." He kissed her forehead. She could feel how much he loves her every time he kisses her forehead, and that's why when she saw him do that to another woman, it scared her. He touched her stomach and brushed her lips with his. "Please, Tay . . . Don't say you want out of this marriage," he said to her with an apology and love in his touch as he stroked her cheek. Taylor knew right then and there that her husband was in love with her and only her. She could feel it in her very soul. There was no need to worry about another woman ever taking her place.

She put her hand on top of his as it now rested on her stomach. "In spite of what we are going through, I have never stopped loving you and I never will. The love I have for you is unconditional." She looked deeper into his eyes. "Keith, remember when you asked me to promise you that I would make our marriage work, for better and for worst, no matter what happens? Well, I made you that promise and giving up on this marriage is not an option. I am willing to make our marriage work no matter what. It's just that I've been feeling so stressed and I know that I have been saying some really stupid things to you, but the truth is; I'm so scared. Satan has been attacking my faith and I've been living in fear of everything lately. When I sat back there and saw Trey in that casket, I thought about, what if that was you . . . I'm scared of you not being here with me, or me not living long enough to see our children grow up. I'm scared of not living my dream." She paused. "Fear has taken over me," she confessed and cried out to him.

He squeezed her hand tightly. Without a word spoken he assured her that there was no need to fear.

Michael overheard her as he walked into the room. "Well, fear and faith can't reside in the same place," he stated. "One will rule over the other. Don't allow your situation and your circumstances to weaken your faith, Taylor. God is the author and finisher of our faith, so just trust Him." He assured her that there was no need to fear. He brought in a Subway sandwich, a bottle of water and a bowl of fruit from home. "You doing okay?"

She nodded.

Michael handed Keith the Subway sandwich and water, and then he placed the bowl of fruit on the counter for Taylor. "I thought maybe y'all could use something to eat,'' he said as if he read Keith's thoughts.

Keith had called Michael as soon as he and Taylor got to the hospital and he was surprised that Michael brought food because he didn't mention the fact that he was starving. "Thanks, I had just taken some medicine on an empty stomach,'' Keith said to him.

Michael nodded to Keith, letting him know that he was welcome, and then he looked at Taylor and said, "Satan is going to continue to attack your faith. He knows that God is about to work another miracle in your life and Satan wants to weaken your faith. You will have according to your faith and faith is an action word. It was that woman's faith that made her touch the hem of Jesus' garment, and it was her faith that made her well. Jesus spoke those words Himself, so that lets you know that it takes having faith in Him for your healing,'' Michael continued. Taylor received his words of encouragement with a smile as they touched her heart. Michael prayed with them and left them in peace.

Once Michael left, Taylor invited Keith to lay with her in the hospital bed.

Keith looked at the hospital bed and laughed. "Tay, I don't believe I can fit, baby,'' he said.

"Yes, you can. Get in,'' she said, raising the cover.

He got in bed with his wife and they both fit in perfectly. As he lay with her, she grabbed his hand and placed it on her stomach so that he could feel their babies moving. Feeling his babies doing all that moving around brought tears to his eyes. He was thankful that they were okay, and it made him say, "Wow. Are they trying to get out?" He chuckled.

"Yes, they can't wait to see their pa-pa!" she exclaimed.

Kissing her lips, "And don't forget about momma," he said.

Keith silently prayed that God would spare his wife's life. He felt as though he deserved to be sick and that he deserved death, but not his wife. He was the one who deserved judgment, not Taylor. She was an innocent bystander who he felt didn't deserve this . . .

Chapter Twenty-Nine

Taylor watched Keith from the doorway of their master bedroom. Just getting out of the shower, he had nothing but a towel on. Her eyes traced every inch of her husband's body. His muscles were ripping through his beautiful honey-colored skin and it was as if she had never seen him in just a towel before. She desired to have him. It seemed like forever since they had made love. She walked over and embraced him from behind, which caught him by surprise.

"What's wrong, baby? Are you okay?" he asked as he held her arms that wrapped around him.

"I'm ready," she said to him, and then gently kissed his back.

Keith turned around to face her. He looked in her eyes, her words catching him off guard. "Are you sure?"

She nodded. "Yes."

Keith began kissing her softly. Once they made it over to the bed she took his towel from around his waist, revealing one of her favorite parts of his body.

He gently touched her stomach. "Is this safe? Will they be okay?'' he asked, filled with concern about the babies she carried.

Taylor's stomach was growing more and more every day. Weeks had passed since she had her episode and had to be taken to the hospital. She was doing much better and Keith made sure that she was stress free. Right now she needed her husband. She desired him. She had been punishing herself far too long as she watched her husband walk around her looking as good as he was. She had allowed the space to grow far too wide, and now it was time to fill that space. Oh, she was more than ready.

Taylor smiled at his words and how handsome he looked with concern on his face. "Yes, it is safe, and they will be fine. No worries . . . I want this, Keith. I need you right here,'' she kissed his neck and added, "right now." She kissed his lips.

Keith reached into the nightstand and pulled out a condom as he thought about the safety of his children. This time Taylor did not protest. He slipped it on and began kissing every inch of his wife's body, pleasing her in every way. Taylor was drunk with anticipation. She moaned as soon as they made one. Keith was very gentle, not wanting to hurt the babies. He enjoyed being with his wife. He enjoyed pleasing her. He took his time with her and made sure that she was well pleased with each one of his gentle strokes.

Taylor released every bit of tension that she has felt over the past months. She dug her nails into his back and whispered into his ear, "I'm all yours, baby.'' She kissed his neck and as he got deeper, her nails dug deeper.

She moaned a little louder and as Keith began to climax, he felt the babies begin to move, which made him ask, "Tay, are they okay?"

"They are great, Keith. You didn't do anything wrong." She kissed him. "They can't see us." She laughed softly.

"Do you think they felt us?" he asked with all seriousness.

"And if they did? Keith, trust me. They are fine," she said as she rubbed the sweat from his face.

He lay down beside his wife and touched her stomach. The babies were moving so much that he was afraid to move, thinking that if he made one move, they would want to come meet their parents a little earlier than planned. Taylor rested her hand on top of his as she lay before him naked.

She stared at the ceiling. "I've been thinking, Keith, and I believe that we can beat this. I believe that we can be healed. I've been reading scripture and that Word has really gotten into my spirit and it has been on my heart. I believe that God will work a miracle for us, for our family."

Keith didn't say a word as tears filled his eyes. He understood Taylor's hope, but his faith wasn't as strong as hers. He knew that this was something that he brought on himself and to his family. Because of that, he felt as though he didn't deserve to be healed. It was a sensitive subject to him, so he chose to remain silent.

She squeezed his hand as if she felt his doubt. She was hoping to reassure him. She looked him in his eyes as tears now freely fell from them. It was now her turn to kiss away his tears. The look in her eyes begged him to have faith, but the look in his, told her that he didn't.

She kissed his forehead. "I believe, Keith, and my faith will not fail. I won't allow it to. God promised that I can be healed, and I believe Him with my whole heart. This virus will not bury me, and it doesn't have to bury you,'' Taylor said to him and she believed every word she spoke.

Keith was still, completely silent, paralyzed by fear.

She looked him in his eyes. "I stayed with you in this marriage because I love you, and when you love someone, you don't just walk away. I know you have made some mistakes, but, Keith, I made a vow before God to love you for better and for worse, in sickness and in health, until death. I took those vows seriously. I am still here because of my love for God and my love for you.'' She kissed his cheek. "Love will conquer all things . . . It never fails,'' kissing his lips, "we will beat this, baby.''

Keith swallowed hard and closed his eyes.

Taylor sensed his fear and it compelled her to say, "There is more that God has for you to do. Do not give up, Keith. He requires more of you and you will not leave this earth until His work is complete in you, but you have a choice in the matter. All you have to do is trust Him. You have to choose to do that.'' She didn't mind Keith getting silent on her, but she wanted him to receive what she was saying.

When Taylor went into worship the other night, God spoke to her. She had fallen to her knees as the shower water ran over her body. She cried, prayed and worshipped God, and then she went into praise. As she worshipped and praised God, her babies leaped in her womb. She knew that the babies she carried were blessed beyond measure. She also knew that what she was going through now was going to be her testimony. But when she went to God earlier in prayer, He told her, "YOU HAVE TO FORGIVE HIM WITH ALL YOUR HEART AND YOU HAVE TO FORGIVE HER. THERE'S A BLESSING IN YOUR FORGIVENESS." Taylor realized then that she still held some resentment in her heart for Keith and Kimbrailee. That was the day she truly released it and broke free. This was the reason why she could lay with her husband today and have a heart-to-heart.

Chapter Thirty

It had been months since Trey's funeral, and Kim was doing considerably well. She was taking her medications properly and feeling great. She was also looking better than ever. She looked and felt like a brand new woman. She was happier now than she has ever been. She had become a praying woman, and it was apparent in her attitude about her life. She continued counseling with Pastor Matthews and his wife, and she had also begun speaking at different engagements that dealt with HIV/AIDS awareness. She spoke life to those who had been infected by this virus and she spoke awareness to those who have been affected by this epidemic.

Kim was sitting in her office going through files when she heard a knock on her door. She looked up and Taylor had already come in. Kim didn't know what to expect when she looked into the eyes of the woman whose life she'd caused so much pain in. Taylor had not spoken a word to her since she found out about her and Keith's infidelity. She didn't even give her condolences at Trey's funeral.

"Hi, Kim, I just wanted to come by and tell you what a

great job you did at the speaking engagement last night. I was really touched. God is really using you to bring awareness by sharing your story.'' She walked up to her and touched her hand. "It takes courage to do what you are doing. You have shared your hope with so many people around you and for that, you are a true blessing.''

Instantly Kim knew that Taylor had forgiven her. Without a word, Kim stood up and hugged Taylor so tight, it was as if she was hugging her for dear life. She cried because she had prayed for this moment, and now it had come to past.

Taylor gave a little laugh as she hugged her back. "I forgive you, Kim, with all of my heart,'' she said.

"I know. You didn't have to say a word. I felt it in your touch and I heard it in your voice,'' Kim said. She continued to embrace her.

The knock on the door startled Kim for a moment, and they both watched as Keith came into her office. He looked between the two and was relieved by what he saw. He exhaled knowing that things were only going to get better from here.

"Taylor, I didn't know you were here, babe. Everything okay?'' he asked. He walked over to her and touched her stomach, and then he kissed her tenderly on her lips.

"Everything is great, honey,'' she said, and then she looked at Kim. "I was just congratulating Kim on a job well done last night.'' She smiled at her, her smile genuine and warm.

"Oh, yeah, Kim, you did awesome,'' Keith told her.

"Thank you so much. You both don't understand how much that means to me. I didn't even know that you guys came... Oh, yeah, Keith, I need a favor. Keisha hasn't been feeling well lately and she wants me to take custody of Trey, Jr. in case anything goes wrong. Do you mind drawing up some custody papers for me? I will pay you."

"Not a problem. I will draw them up immediately and no need to pay me. I got you. You two have become pretty close, huh?"

"Yes, we have," Kim replied. "She's a great person and she's a great mother to Trey, Jr. I can't blame her for any of this. She was young and she made some bad choices in her life, but she has grown a lot." She smiled.

She thought about how much she and Keisha has grown since attending church together every Sunday. After seeing how well Kim responded to her when they first met, it compelled Keisha to get to know the God Kim served that made her be able to forgive her without hesitation. Keisha had been a great support system for Kim ever since. She went to every engagement that Kim had and it was as if they had become the best of friends. And Trey, Jr. seemed to have fallen in love with Kim and she was so joyful that he had taken to her so well. Keisha knew then that she would leave her son in great hands. Kim thanked Keith and Taylor once again before they left her office.

Taylor and Keith went and enjoyed themselves over lunch. They talked about the babies and they were so excited about getting the babies' room prepared for their arrival. When the doctor told them that the babies should be here in a week, Keith was ecstatic. He was so ready to see the faces of their children and he couldn't wait to hold them. Taylor wanted to be surprised by the sex of the babies, so she told the doctor not to inform them of the babies' sexes. Keith didn't agree because he wanted to buy every baby outfit and toy that he saw. He would always tell Taylor, "Baby, I need to know what colors to buy and what kind of toys."

Even though he didn't know the sexes of the babies, it didn't stop him from buying out the baby clothing and toy department of every store. He bought baby girl and baby boy stuff. He decided that, depending upon what they have, he would just give away what they didn't need. Even though his meds had him tired and sick quite often, nothing could steal his joy. He was ready for his babies and he counted the days for their arrival.

Keith made it back to his office and to his surprise, Mr. McCallister was there waiting to see him. He didn't really understand why he had come in since his case was completed. Keith invited Mr. McCallister back to his office.

"What can I do for you, sir?" Keith asked with a perplexed look on his face.

"Son, have you seen the news?" McCallister asked.

"No, I haven't. What's going on?"

"Well," Mr. McCallister began, "ever since I was found not guilty, I had been getting threats from the young man who was having an affair with my wife." He paused as if he was still trying to accept the death of his entire family. "After all this time, the police couldn't find him, but this morning he was found dead. A young woman, who he had been seeing, shot and killed him.'' He sighed deeply as he shook his head.

"Wow. I guess justice was served,'' Keith said to him.

"No, son, it wasn't. I just hope the young man was saved. I knew it was coming, but not like that. I didn't wish death upon him. My hope was for him to get his life right with the Lord," Mr. McCallister said to him.

Keith paused for a minute and realized how great this man was who sat in front of him. He thought to himself, *That insane man killed this man's entire family, but his only desire was for the man to get his life right with Christ.* Keith knew that his faith was not as strong because if it was him, he would have killed the man himself. This man sat in front of him as though he was grieved by the man's death.

McCallister studied Keith for a moment. "How have you been?'' His question cut into Keith's thoughts and brought him back to the reality that he was sick.

"I'm fine . . . making it, you can say . . . I don't know, hope to get better, I guess,'' Keith rambled.

"Which one is it?'' Mr. McCallister asked, confused.

"I'm HIV positive, sir," Keith said for the first time to anyone in that office.

"Okay, but you are still living, right?'' Mr. McCallister paused briefly. "That's a reason to have joy within itself.''

"Yes, you are correct and I am very joyful. I have a set of twins on the way!'' he said, now with excitement in his tone.

"That's excellent. God has a plan and purpose for you and your family. I wouldn't worry about anything else. You have a life to live . . . for God and for your family," Mr. McCallister told him as he stood.

Keith was still seated and was in deep thought. He stood after a minute and saw Mr. McCallister out. He reached his hand out to shake McCallister's hand, but to Keith's surprise, McCallister hugged him. "Everything will work out fine. Just keep faith," he said as if he could read Keith's thoughts. He smiled at him and walked away. It's as if God sent him at the right time.

He seems to always send the right people when you need a word of encouragement, Keith thought to himself.

***

Taylor was making herself a sandwich when Keith came up behind her and wrapped his arms around her stomach.

"Baby, I told you not to lift a finger," he said. He got the knife from her and began spreading the Miracle Whip over the sandwich for her.

He kissed the side of her neck and she moaned at how good it felt.

"How about we forget about this sandwich and I just eat you?" she said after turning to face him. She kissed his lips tenderly.

When he kissed her back her stomach caught a sharp pain. Keith touched her stomach and felt the babies start moving quite a bit. "Wait, maybe you need to eat . . . Have you eaten anything since lunch?" he asked.

"Yes, Keith, I've been eating all day. These babies don't need anything else. They are trying to kill my figure," she said laughing, and then she groaned at the next sharp pain she had. "Wait, maybe you are right . . . I need to eat. These babies are kicking me like crazy. They must be mad at me," she said as she held her stomach in pain.

He helped her walk over to the table to sit down, but then she grabbed his hand, squeezing it hard. She was having another sharp pain. "Keith!" she called his name as she felt something running down her leg. She looked down, and Keith followed her eyes down to the puddle of water on the floor. "I think my water broke." She smiled so that he wouldn't panic, but she wanted to cry from all of the pain she was in.

Keith picked her up and took her to the car. He ran back in the house to grab her packed bags, and then he came back to the car. He silently prayed as he sped down the street. He had Taylor in total fear of his driving.

They arrived safely at Memorial Hospital where Keith stood beside her as she delivered their set of twins. Keith was in tears the whole time. Dr. Allen asked him if he wanted to take a seat because she thought he was going to faint during the delivery. There, he stood watching them clean their babies. They handed him the baby boy and brought the baby girl over and handed her to Taylor.

Keith broke down as he held his beautiful baby boy in his arms, his pride and joy, his first born. He couldn't control the tears that flowed. The room of nurses smiled at how happy he was. He had waited for this moment and here it was. He prayed over his son, and then he walked over to Taylor and looked at his two favorite girls. He broke down even more. He leaned over and kissed Taylor's forehead, and then he kissed his baby girl's forehead.

"I love you, baby . . . so much," he said to Taylor.

"I love you too . . . pa-pa bear," she said, smiling. Her tears of joy were overflowing.

They switched babies, and Keith held his baby girl, loving every minute of watching her kick in his arms. She was the apple of his eye. He had his boy and his girl. That was more than enough for him.

"What are we going to name them, baby?" he asked Taylor while looking at his baby girl.

"How about I name baby boy, Justin, and you name baby girl . . ." She paused, waiting for him to give her name.

"Justice," he said without hesitation. He looked at all three loves of his life and smiled. "Thank you, God!" he whispered as he looked up toward Heaven.

The babies were as healthy as can be. Keith considered that a real blessing. He stood in the window on the nursery floor as he made funny faces at the two new additions to his family. He silently prayed for his babies and for Taylor. He prayed that his wife be spared from the illness she carried. Then, he prayed for his babies to live a full and healthy life. He was thankful that they were . . . HIV negative.

***

Everyone came to the hospital to visit with Keith and Taylor. They couldn't wait to see the babies. Taylor had met Keith's mom a few months back and instantly fell in love with her. They spent quite a bit of time together while shopping and preparing for the babies. Now, here she is holding her grandbabies in each arm. Taylor and Keith were happy to see that his mom had gained all of her strength back. The doctor said that her cancer was in remission, but let her tell it, she was completely and totally healed. She said that her body was healed the night she woke up from that coma to Keith's father praying for her. She was doing extremely well and she, Keith, Candis, and their father had restored their broken relationship.

Candis and Tyra each got one of the babies from Janice. They were so excited. Tyra was happy to have her niece and her nephew here at the same time. She considered it a double blessing. Taylor's parents and Keith's dad just watched as the babies got passed from arm to arm. Mike entered the room with a bunch of balloons and some flowers.

"Congratulations!" he exclaimed. He shook Keith's hand and walked over and hugged Taylor. He sat the flowers down onto the counter, and then he went and stood by Candis as he watched Justin squirm around in her arms. He saw how healthy he looked, like a little football player already. Then he looked across the way at Tyra who was holding Justice.

"They are so quiet and peaceful," Tyra said. She kissed baby Justice's hand.

Candis spoke, "We are sitting here and y'all haven't even told us their names." Her eyes filled with tears of joy as baby Justin held her finger.

"Justin and Justice!" Taylor and Keith announced in unison.

"I'm glad you are all here together," Taylor began. She looked back and forth between Tyra, Candis and Michael. Then she looked back at Keith who stood at the head of her bed. He smiled at her and she returned her focus back to them. "We've been talking and we would like you all to be the Godparents of Justin and Justice," she announced to Michael, Tyra and Candis.

They each accepted with great joy.

Keith looked Taylor in her eyes and kissed her lips, a silent thank you for giving birth to their beautiful children.

Chapter Thirty- One

Taylor smiled as she watched Keith walk around the room holding Justice in his arms as he fed her. She sat on the bed rocking Justin in her arms. They had been really great babies for the past seven weeks and they were growing so fast. Justin had finally fallen asleep and she leaned over to put him in his basinet. She continued to watch as Keith walked back and forth while singing softly to Justice. Justice was a true daddy's girl already.

Taylor could see the joy in Keith's eyes every time he held their children. She continued to watch him and she thanked God. They were truly blessed beyond measure. Keith has been such a great father and has helped her every step of the way. He wakes up in the middle of the night, feeding the babies and rocking them back to sleep and she was thankful to have him beside her. He made sure that she was always free from stress.

Justice had finally fallen asleep and Keith kissed her forehead and placed her in her basinet. He turned off the lamp and kissed Taylor's forehead. "Rest well, honey," he said to her. "We only have about two hours to sleep before they wake up again." He chuckled.

She kissed him passionately, and then said, "I don't want to sleep tonight. It's been over six weeks, Keith. We are good to go, baby." She kissed him again. "My body has been yearning for you."

Keith began kissing his wife. He took his time as he released some of her tension with each touch. He reached into the nightstand and grabbed a condom. He took his time with her. It was as if it were their first time. She wrapped her legs tightly around his back and with her hips she told him that she was enjoying the moment. His fingers intertwined in her hair. She moaned loudly as Keith's rhythm got a little faster. She wrapped her legs tighter around him as she showed him how much she loves him. She moaned even louder this time, waking up Justin. He cried just as loud as her outcry. Keith was about to stop until he heard her say, "Keep going, Keith." She kissed his neck. "Let him exercise his lungs, baby." She continued to moan quietly now, trying to control herself.

Keith continued as they kissed each other passionately. When it got to a certain point she couldn't control it any longer, and then Keith, too, began to moan as he was bringing the moment to an end. Justice began crying as she heard her father's voice. Keith and Taylor both laid there for a minute as they tried to catch their breath. Taylor kissed his neck and he kissed her forehead. He fixed his pajama pants and got up to get his baby boy. Taylor got up to get her baby girl and they settled them down.

Once Justice had fallen back to sleep, Taylor placed her back in her basinet and ran to the bathroom to vomit. She was transitioning from one of her meds and the new one seemed to have her sick all over again.

Keith placed Justin, who was now fast asleep, back in his basinet, then ran in bathroom behind Taylor to comfort her. He had gotten use to getting up in the middle of the night to rub her back as she threw up. Neither of them was getting the proper amount of rest that they needed, but they thanked God for the twins' Godparents. They each had a key to come in and help Taylor and Keith with the babies when they needed them.

Keith has been the greatest husband and father. He never missed an appointment during the pregnancy, except for the ones that Taylor didn't tell him about whenever she was having one of her moments. He was there for every appointment and for whatever Taylor needed him for. He was every bit of the man she needed and for that, she thanked God. She knew that God had to be pleased with the man he has become.

Keith carried her back to the bed even though he felt weak himself. He promised to be the best husband and father that he could be. He didn't want to ever disappoint his wife again as a husband, and he definitely didn't want to disappoint his children as a father.

***

Keith and Taylor's parents, Tyra, Candis, and Michael took turns helping Taylor with the babies as Keith went and worked half days at his office. Keith was sitting in his office when he heard a knock on his door. Kim stuck her head in. When Keith smiled, she walked in. Without a word spoken, she sat down in one of the chairs in front of his desk. Tears formed in her eyes as she looked Keith dead in his eyes. He sat and waited.

"She passed away this morning," Kim finally said. Tears now fell from her eyes and she wiped them away.

Keith paused. "Who? Keisha?"

"Yes, and now I have a son to raise." She looked down at the floor, then back up at Keith. "I'm so scared. I've never been a parent."

"Neither have I and I'm doing just fine and so will you. There's no need to be afraid of that. You are going to be fine, just believe in yourself." He tried to assure her.

"You are so right, everything will be fine. Everything will work out," she said, trying to convince herself. "How are your babies doing? Growing, I bet." She smiled. She had come to the hospital to see them right after they were born, but she hadn't seen them since they had come home.

"Oh, God, Kim, they are so beautiful . . . my greatest accomplishments. It amazes me sometimes when I look at them, each one of them is a true gift from God." He now spoke with so much joy in his tone.

"That's great. You and Taylor are so blessed."

"Yes, I can definitely agree with that."

Kim got up to leave the office and when Keith called her name, she looked back with tears in her eyes.

"You, too, are very blessed," he said as if he could read her thoughts.

She turned around and walked briskly back to his desk as he stood. She wrapped her arms around his neck, a silent thank you.

Chapter Thirty-Two

$\mathcal{K}$im sat on the front row with Trey, Jr. seated beside her. She saw Keisha's body lying in her casket and she was beautiful even in death. Trey, Jr. cried out as he saw his mother's lifeless body and Kim put her arms around him as she attempted to comfort him while shedding tears of her own. She held the letter in her hand that Keisha had left her with a poem attached. The letter read:

I know that I have told you many times that I was sorry for the situation that I put your family in, and for what all I put you through, but here I am again. I am truly sorry. Words can't begin to express that. When I saw how you forgave me without hesitation, I knew that there was something different about you. I thought that you were strong enough to carry the burden you carried, and then you helped me to realize that you weren't the one carrying that burden, it was Jesus. You introduced me to the greatest gift of all and that gift was salvation through Jesus Christ. You helped me to understand that God is faithful enough to have forgiven me of my sins, both known and unknown.

As soon as I met you, I fell in love. You had become not only someone I looked up to, you became my friend. A lot of the qualities that Trey saw in me were some of the same ones that he saw in you. Your kindness towards me brought tears to my eyes many times. Thank you for every encouraging word and for every act of kindness. Your heart is so beautiful. Please, don't change who you are for anyone. People may not always accept you, but keep your head held up no matter what life brings.

When I told people that I had been infected, they looked at me as though I was poison and wasn't fit to live. They were scared of my touch and from their reactions you would think that if I breathed on them, they would have instantly died. No one understood my hurt, my pain. Looking at me as though I was nobody and I deserved what came to me. But God, He is a God of grace and mercy. He looked beyond my faults and met my need. If only people knew, they would understand. I am not this virus. I am a child of the King . . .

In the letter, Keisha had requested Kim to read a poem that she had written. She wanted it read at her funeral and at any speaking engagements that she had. This was Keisha's way of sharing her story and helping others who had been infected . . .

I Am NOT This Virus

You look at me as though I am poison and I'm not fit to live.

You don't understand my hurt, my pain, yet you judge me still.

I am not my situation or my circumstance.

I just wish that you would give me a chance.

I see the stares and hear the words passed.

Those words cut like a knife and tries to steal the joy that I have.

I am not this virus or what brought it about.

I am someone of worth, without a doubt.

Be careful, death does not discriminate, just be prepared.

If you ever become sick you will find out who really cares.

You look at me as though I'm nobody and I deserved what came.

You judged me and didn't even know my name.

The world is cold and will leave you for dead.

But I chose life instead.

I am not this virus or who you say that I am.

I am a child of the King, saved by the blood of the Lamb.

I have found real love and someone to take away my pain.

He has lifted every burden and Jesus is His name.

I am not this virus or who you say that I am

I am a child of the King, saved by the blood of the Lamb.

Every one of my sins has been forgiven and even after death, I will still be living.

Living with my Heavenly Father

Your words and stares that tried to kill me, now I can't be bothered.

You judge me but don't understand who I am.

I am not this virus or who you say that I am.

I am a child of the King, saved by the blood of the Lamb.

Chapter Thirty-Three

Keith woke up and began getting ready for work. He went to hop in the shower and while he was in there, he started to feel extremely lightheaded. He quickly rinsed the soap from his body and got out. He fell onto the floor and Taylor woke up when she heard the loud thud. She ran into the bathroom to see what happened. When she saw Keith on the floor, she rushed to his side.

"Are you okay, baby? What happened?" she asked.

"I'm good, baby," he replied. "I will be fine. Just go back to bed."

"Babe, you are not fine. Just let me help you up." She grabbed his arm attempting to help him up.

"No, Tay I'll be fine. You need to lie down. You are not well yourself. . . I got this," he said, pushing her hand away.

"Keith, I am just trying to help you, baby . . . Maybe you should just call in today."

"Tay, I said I was fine!" he yelled at her, pushing her

hands away once again.

She jumped at his forcefulness.

Taylor sat on the floor beside him as tears formed in her eyes. She was surprised and hurt by his actions. She knew that he had been getting frustrated from having to take his meds daily and from some of the side effects. She and Keith both were not feeling well at all last night, so Tyra came over and took the babies back to her place to spend the night. Keith seemed to be getting weaker and weaker not only physically, but in his faith as well. Taylor, too, had become more and more sick from the new meds the doctor put her on, but she was not about to lose faith.

Keith finally mustered up enough strength to pull himself up and he allowed Taylor to help him to the bed where he lied down for a while. Taylor lay beside him and silently prayed for his strength. After a few minutes, Keith got back up and began to get ready for work even though he didn't feel like going in. It was as if he had become angry at the fact that he was feeling weak. He didn't feel like the man of his house anymore which hurt him to his heart. He had days where he was feeling energetic and he cooked for Taylor and played with his babies, but then there were days when he felt too tired and weak to move.

After he got dressed he sat on the bed next to Taylor. He leaned over and kissed her forehead. "I'm sorry, Tay, for my outburst. I don't know what I was thinking. I love you so much, and I want to be around to show you just how much?"

"And you will be, baby," she said. She kissed his lips tenderly, letting him know that she believed that with all her heart.

Keith had left for work and Taylor had fixed her something to eat, and then took her meds. She began to feel sick and she quickly ran to the bathroom. She began vomiting and crying, all at once. She was in pain at this point. She silently prayed for the feeling to subside, and then she felt a touch on her back.

"You are okay, Taylor, just breathe," Michael said. He kneeled down beside her and whispered into her ear. He rubbed her back with one hand and pulled back her hair with the other. "God has already healed your body by the stripes that were placed on Christ's back. All you have to do is receive it by faith. He tells us plainly in His Word, Taylor, 'Surely he has borne our grief and carried our sorrows; Yet we esteemed him stricken, smitten by God, and afflicted. But he was wounded for our transgressions, He was bruised for our iniquities; The chastisement of our peace was upon him, And by his stripes we are healed,'' he whispered into her ear.

Taylor began to feel a great comfort. Her heart was open as she continued to cry out.

"God's will is to heal and He desires you to prosper and be in health. It is up to you to receive that healing and it is up to you to allow your faith to make you whole. The blood flowing through your body right now is the blood of Jesus. Receive your healing, Taylor," he continued to whisper into her ear and into her spirit. He had her wrapped tightly in his arms with her back to him and he laid hands on her and began to pray.

Taylor felt a shift in her body and she knew a miracle had just taken place as she received healing into her spirit and her body. She continued to cry out in worship. She spoke a sweet utterance as she thanked God for this miracle. She embraced Michael as she cried tears of joy. They continued to worship God in the midst of His presence. She knew that Michael had been led there by the Spirit and she was grateful that God heard her cry.

***

"The doctor will be in to see you momentarily, Mrs. Davenport," the nurse said after she had taken her vitals.

After Michael left, Taylor headed for the doctor's office and she has been sitting in the waiting room for an hour. She felt excellent and she was ready to give her testimony. She knew that God didn't bring her out of this for nothing. She had a marvelous testimony and she was ready to share it with the world.

"Hi, Mrs. Davenport, your vitals were great. So tell me. What can I do for you today?" Dr. Allen asked.

"I would like to take another HIV test," Taylor said.

Dr. Allen looked at her with a puzzled look on her face. "Okay," she said with uncertainty in her tone. "You want us to retest you?"

"Yes!" Taylor said with excitement.

"Okay . . . but may I ask why, Mrs. Davenport?"

"I just would like for you to test me again."

"Okay, I have no problem with that. I will get the nurse right in," she said, and then left the room.

The nurse came in and performed the OraQuick test on Taylor. She then informed her that she could be seated in the waiting area until the results were ready, which should take twenty minutes. This time, Taylor was going to patiently wait. They called her to come back into the room after thirty-three minutes. Taylor sat in the room and after five minutes the doctor came in. Dr. Allen had a dumbfound look on her face as she looked at Taylor's chart.

"Mrs. Davenport, it looks as though your results came back . . . negative," she said, now looking in Taylor's face. "But I'm going to get the nurse to retest you if that's okay. We just want to be sure that we have the right results. Okay?" She paused, and then continued, "This time after your test, you can just sit in this room and wait."

"Well," Taylor began, "I can assure you that those results are right, but feel free to retest me . . . for your benefit."

"Yes, I understand and I will get the nurse right in," Dr. Allen said. Doubting Taylor's words, she left the room.

The nurse came and tested her again. She patiently waited once again for the results.

The second set of results had come back and Dr. Allen came back into the room. She stared at Taylor for a moment before asking, "Mrs. Davenport, you have been taking all of your meds correctly, right?"

"Yes. I have."

"Well, we will test your blood next and those results should be back within forty-eight hours," Dr. Allen said.

"You didn't say what the last set of results were, Doctor."

"They turned out to be negative as well, but I want to do a blood test just to be sure, and we will go from there. We have never had that happen in this office, so we just want to make sure we are testing you properly . . . Is that okay?"

Taylor nodded. "If that would make you more comfortable, then feel free, but those results are correct," she said with confidence.

The nurse came back once again, but this time she took blood. Shortly afterwards, Dr. Allen came back to explain a few more things to Taylor. By the conversation, Taylor could tell that Dr. Allen was one of little faith, if any at all.

"If you are trying to figure out why those results are negative it is because of the stripes that were placed on my Savior's back. I have been healed by none other than the blood of Jesus," Taylor said with absolute.

Dr. Allen lightly chuckled. "Okay, Mrs. Davenport. We will call you when the results from your blood test come back."

"Look, Doctor, you may not know where I am coming from, but I guarantee you, one day you will. It is so funny that when I first got my results that turned out positive, I asked you to test me again and you really didn't understand why. But now when I come in and they turned out negative, you want to test me over and over again without me even having to ask you to. I am healed, Doctor, and it's not from any kind of medicines that you have prescribed me." Taylor got up and grabbed her purse. "You said you've never seen this happen in your office before. Well, I

suggest you write this miracle down in your records.'' She
smiled and left the office.

Dr. Allen looked down at the chill bumps on her arms
and she knew that there was something different about Taylor's
situation. She didn't know how to explain it, but she was curious
to know more.

Chapter Thirty-Four

Taylor, Keith and the rest of their family sat together at Holy Temple Ministries for Sunday evening services. Justin and Justice, now seven months, were being passed from arm to arm. They were simply beautiful, and at seven months they loved sitting in the presence of the Lord.

"Now Faith is the substance of things hoped for, the evidence of things not seen," Pastor Matthews said from the pulpit. "I once heard a wise man say that hope has to have faith in order to have evidence. God is a God who loves faith and if you go up from Hebrews 11:1 to Hebrews 10:38, it talks about the just living by faith and it also talks about not drawing back in your faith. You mustn't draw back in your faith no matter what your situation or circumstances may be. No matter how it looks, you must have faith that God is bigger than your circumstances. God is a God who can handle it when you trust Him with it. You have to look with your spiritual eyes instead of your physical eyes. Satan is after your faith. He wants to destroy your faith."

"Amen," was shouted out everywhere as people cried out to God.

Pastor Matthews took a sip of water, and then continued, "Satan wants to destroy you and kill your testimony. He wants to keep you from your destiny, but God. . . Somebody should have shouted right there because I know somebody in here has had a 'but God' in their lives, somewhere. You must keep your faith and don't allow your faith to fail. God is a God who won't fail you, but you must have . . .''

Everyone all over the building shouted, "Faith,'' in unison.

"Abraham was a man of great faith. Sarah was a woman of faith. Job was a man of Faith. Ruth was a woman of faith. Daniel was a man of faith. Mary was a woman of faith. David was a man of faith. It was faith that made the man take up his bed and walk. It was faith that made the woman touch the hem of Jesus' garment and it was her faith that made her whole. How many of you want to be whole today? All it takes is faith in Jesus. Attach your hope in the Word to your faith in God and watch Him work it out for you. Faith comes by hearing and hearing by the Word of God. Without faith it is impossible to please God. You have to take that step. Faith without works is dead which tells you that you have to work your faith. Step out in faith. Come on down to the altar. God desires for you to be whole. He desires to work miracles in your life, but it takes faith. Make that step of faith today,'' the Pastor said. He stepped down out of the pulpit to meet people where they were.

People cried out all over the place as they raised their hands in worship. Some people praised God with singing, dancing and some praised Him with silence, but they all worshipped Him in Spirit and in truth. Many made their way to the altar. The choir sang *I Believe* by James Fortune & Fiya and many were brought to tears.

Silvia was seated on the back row. She began to feel a tug at her heart. She wanted to move, but something was holding her back. Tears burned her eyes as she tried to force them back.

Pastor Matthews continued, "Some of your hearts are filled with un-forgiveness. I can feel you in here. Come on down to the altar. Some of you need healing, but God is not going to force healing into your bodies. You must have faith that He can and will heal you. Come on down to the altar. Give all your worries, all your troubles, all your problems to Jesus. Let go and He will take care of it for you, but you have to trust Him. Don't come down here and try to take your heavy hearts and your troubles back with you. Leave them here, at the altar. He can and will work it out for you. God works behind the scene, but what He does is greatly seen. The evidence of God surrounds us and He has proven Himself to be God. Get into His very presence right now.''

Many laid out before God in worship. Healing and deliverance was taking place all over the building.

Silvia got up and ran out of the church doors. Once she got out, she gasped for air. Her heart was racing. She began walking until she heard someone call to her, "Silvia.'' She stopped in her tracks. Before she could turn around she knew who it was. She put on her shades to hide the tears in her eyes. "What is it Michael? This is not for me,'' she said without turning to face him.

"You've allowed so many men to hurt you that you won't even trust the one who can heal you . . . You can't run forever, Silvia.''

She now turned to face him. "Well, good thing I ran track in high school . . . so, I think that I can endure the race.'' She turned back around and headed to her car.

Michael watched as she got into her car and drove off into the sunset.

***

As Taylor and Keith were heading out of the doors of Holy Temple Ministries, she had accidently bumped into the person beside her.

"Excuse me,'' Taylor said after bumping into them, and then she looked up and realized who the person was. "Dr. Allen? How are you? Is this your first time visiting this church?''

Dr. Allen looked at her and said, "Yes, it is, and I am glad I came. Let me tell you, Mrs. Davenport . . .''

"No. Call me Taylor.''

Dr. Allen continued, "Well, Taylor, I now understand where you were coming from when we spoke in my office. You see . . .'' She paused, and then exhaled. "I had a patient to come into the emergency room one day from a heroin overdose. She went into a seizure and I had to sedate her. With her jerking out of control, after sticking her, the needle jumped out and went all the way into my finger. I mean, I felt that needle deep down to my bone. I already knew this woman from previous visits and I knew she was HIV positive." Tears formed in her eyes. "I was so scared. I immediately got tested, it was negative. I tested a month later, it was negative. Then, I tested five months later and it was negative. Right after that last test I heard a voice say, 'MY GRACE IS SUFFICIENT'.'' She took a deep breath as tears fell from her eyes. "I mean, Taylor that test should have been positive and I know it. I went and spoke with one of my colleagues about what happened and about the voice that I heard. It was so loud and clear. I had never picked up and read a Bible a day in my life, but my colleague went to scripture and that's when I saw those exact words, 'My grace is sufficient', and I knew in my heart that God had spared me. God knows just how to get your attention. My colleague led me to Christ that day in his office and I was led to this church today. I went down and joined, so I think that makes us family, my sister,'' she said, and then she embraced Taylor.

"God is truly an awesome God,'' Taylor said. As tears fell down her face, she embraced her.

Chapter Thirty-Five

Three Years Later

*K*eith sat in the living room and watched through the slide doors as Justin and Justice play with their toys outside in the back yard. Michael and Taylor began throwing water balloons at them. Keith laughed as he watched them run around screaming as if strangers were after them. His babies were so happy and filled with joy and had no knowledge of this illness that took over his body. As he would play with them for a little while from time to time, he would get so tired that he would have to sit down to rest and it would never fail that Justice, a true daddy's girl, would always ask, "Daddy, what's wrong?" He would never answer.

He wanted to keep them with no knowledge of his illness. He wanted them to only have joyful memories of their father. He knew that Taylor had been healed and the day he found out, he praised God with tears flowing from his eyes. He didn't expect God to heal him, but as long as his wife had been healed, delivered and set free, that brought him great joy. He continued to laugh as he watched his children play.

He stood up and went over to the mantel and looked at all of the pictures of his family. He looked at the wedding picture of his mother, Janice, and his father, John, and he smiled. He was thankful that they had reconciled and remarried. He had never seen them as happy in their first marriage together as they were now. That also brought him great joy. He then heard his babies screaming which broke into his thoughts. He went to the slide door and opened it.

"Daddy!" Justice exclaimed. She ran over to him and he picked her up into his arms. He hugged her tightly without saying a word.

Taylor walked over to him and kissed him. "Hey, baby! I didn't know you woke up from your nap." She paused, studying her husband. "Are you okay, honey?" she asked, still out of breath from chasing the twins.

Keith didn't say a word as he continued to hug Justice. He kissed Taylor's forehead and lingered there.

"What's wrong, baby?" Taylor asked, knowing there was something different about him. She looked at him for a moment and noticed that he had a certain glow about him that she had never seen before.

Michael walked over to them. "Everything okay, Keith?" he asked.

Silence . . .

"Daddy!" Justin exclaimed, now tapping on his knee. "Play with us!"

Keith now grabbed him up into his other arm and hugged him. He stayed in that position for a minute. He put them both down and began playing with them. They played for about an hour longer. Tired and weak, Keith went and sat down in the lawn chair.

Justice ran over to Keith, Justin right behind her.

"Daddy, what's wrong?" Justice asked.

Keith put both of them on each of his knees. "I love you both sooo very much and nothing will ever change that." He looked at Justice. "You are so beautiful, baby girl," he said, and then kissed her forehead. He now looked at Justin. "And you, son, are going to grow up to be such a great man," he said, and then hugged him tightly.

"We love you, daddy!" Justice and Justin exclaimed in unison. Justice kissed his cheek, and he smiled.

He put them down and they went back to playing. He watched them as tears filled his eyes. He stayed outside for a little while longer until he felt extremely tired. He barely felt like moving. He stood up and fell back in his seat.

Michael ran over to him. "Are you okay?" he asked out of concern.

Keith grabbed Michael's arm. "Would you help me to my room?"

Taylor walked over to him and whispered into his ear, "Keith, have you been taking your meds?"

When Taylor was giving him his meds, she made sure that she gave them to him daily and she gave them to him on time. But about two months ago, he told her that he wanted to take them on his own. She knew that he was having one of his "let me be the man moments", so she trusted that he would take them properly. But as she watched him get weaker and weaker, she wasn't so sure that he was taking them the way that he was supposed to.

"I'm okay, Taylor. Mike is going to help me upstairs,'' Keith said, avoiding the question.

Michael helped him upstairs to his room.

Taylor brought the children in the house to watch a movie in the den. She pressed Play on the DVD player and *The Lion King* began to play. She waited for Michael to come back downstairs to be with them, so that she could be with her husband. She could sense that he needed her.

Once Keith and Michael got to the room, Keith hugged him. "Thank you so much for stepping in my place when we needed you. You have been a true blessing to my family," he told him.

Michael had come over every day to play with his Godchildren and he made sure that they were all taken care of. He helped Keith out around the house and he kept the environment comfortable for him. Michael could sense that Keith was tired and he made sure that he was there for him whenever he needed him.

"I'm thankful to be a blessing. You, too, have been a blessing to me. You are like a brother to me and I will always be here for you and your family,'' Michael responded.

"I will hold you to that . . . I love you, man," Keith said. Never had he told him that before.

"I love you too,'' Michael said, and then embraced him. His spirit told him what his mind didn't want to accept.

Michael headed downstairs and Taylor went up to be with her husband. She lay next to Keith in bed. She grabbed the remote and pressed Play and the movie that they attempted to watch the night before, began to play. Her woman's intuition told her to go look in the medicine cabinet, so she did.

She stormed back in the room. "Keith, what is this? What are you thinking, baby?'' She tried to hold back her tears. "This is why you are so weak . . . You haven't been taking your meds.'' She held up three of his prescription bottles, each of them completely full.

He pulled her into his arms and the prescription bottles fell from her hands onto the bed. He kissed her. "I'm fine, Tay, just lay with me.'' She lay down beside him and he kissed her lips. "Thank you for being a wonderful wife.'' He kissed her again.

Tears stung her eyes as she looked into his eyes. She said, "Thank you for being a wonderful husband.''

She hugged him for dear life as they lay together. They allowed the movie to watch them as they both held each other tight. Keith watched his wife in silence. She was just as beautiful to him as she was the day he met her.

"I love you so much, Taylor. You and our children are my greatest joy." He sighed deeply and looked off into space. "I'm tired, baby. I want you to be happy with no worries and I want our children to grow up and be happy and whole. I don't want y'all to have to worry about a thing. I love y'all so much."

"We love you, too, baby, but I don't like it when you talk like that. There is no need to worry because you can beat this, I know you can. I have faith, but my faith can't work for you. You have to believe and have faith for yourself," she said.

"I love you, Taylor."

"I love you, too, Keith. I just don't want you talking like that. We'll be fine. We are going to sit here, watch this movie and enjoy each other."

"That sounds great." He kissed her forehead, then her nose, and then he gently kissed her lips.

Keith silently prayed as they held each other. He was tired of this battle and he was ready to be with his Heavenly Father. He knew his family would be left in great hands and he had comfort in knowing that.

Taylor watched the movie and laughed here and there even though she wanted to cry from the feeling that came over her. An hour had passed and she realized that she had fallen asleep and Keith hadn't said a word.

She rubbed his arm. "Keith?" she called to him.

No response . . .

"Keith, baby?" her voice trembled. She closed her eyes and took a deep breath. She then opened them, hoping to see his chest rising and falling, but instead she saw that he was no longer breathing. She put her hands over her mouth, attempting to hold back her desire to scream from the hurt she felt. She silently prayed as she tried to calm herself. She didn't want to cause her children to panic or be saddened by what she knew. She sat for a minute as tears began to fall from her eyes onto his face, covering it. She rubbed his face as she looked at him. She again noticed that he had a certain glow about him. He looked peaceful, which gave her a little bit of comfort.

She took a deep breath and counted to ten. "Michael!" she yelled downstairs to him.

No answer . . .

"Michael!" she yelled out again.

Michael told the children that he would be right back, and then he ran up the stairs, his heart heavy from what he felt in his spirit. He ran into the room. "What's wrong, Taylor?" he asked.

"Call . . ." She paused and took another deep breath. "Call 911."

Michael walked over and touched Keith's neck to check his pulse. "I'm sorry, Taylor." He paused trying not to choke on his words. "He's gone," he whispered with tears in his eyes.

Taylor nodded. "I know," she said, tears streaming down her face.

Michael called the emergency unit.

Taylor sat in the middle of the bed beside her husband's body. She held his body tightly in her arms and gently kissed his lips as she continued to cry.

Michael sat next to her and held her. "To be absent from the body, is to be present with the Lord," he whispered into her ear as he shed tears of his own.

That Word gave them both some comfort.

Extended Version:

To Everything There Is a Season

(I Shall Wear a Crown)

Chapter Thirty-Six

*T*aylor was lying in the middle of her bed, holding her children that were on each side of her. She held them tightly as they slept. She looked over at her clock: 3:40 a.m. This was another night that her mind wouldn't rest and her heart seemed to skip beats. She wished that her husband was beside her, holding her, but he wasn't; and now this was her solemn reality. A tear slid down her cheek and she angrily wiped it away. She looked at her son, Justin, then at her daughter, Justice. *How could you leave us, Keith? Why would you do that to us?* She thought as more tears escaped her eyes. *You were supposed to always be here!* It was as if death was the enemy and she wanted revenge as the thought of it taking her husband angered her.

She gently slid herself away from her children who slept peacefully. She got up and sat on her chaise lounge as the moonlight shined upon her. Her mind reverted to thoughts of how her heart begged her husband to breathe again as she held him in her arms three days ago. *God, please, let this be a nightmare that I will be waking up from in a few minutes. Make this all go away. Please, God, whatever you want me to do, I will do it. Just give me my husband back. Please, give the love of my life back to me. I can't breathe without him.* She wanted peace, but she couldn't find it as the reality of her husband's death weighed heavily on her.

She got up and opened the drawer to her nightstand. She pulled their family photo album from the drawer and sat back down on the chaise lounge. She slowly opened the album and began looking at the pictures. She paid close attention to the still moments and wished that she could turn back the hands of time so that she could kiss her husband once more. She covered her mouth attempting to conceal her sobs. She turned the page and an envelope fell out onto her lap. She held it as she read: *Taylor* beautifully penned on the front of it. She gasped, knowing it was something that her husband wrote and she wondered when it was written. She slowly opened it and read:

Taylor,

I know that if you are reading this, my spirit has departed my body, but know that I am always with you because I know that you will always carry me in your heart. I am at peace and all is well with my soul. Life has to take its natural course and death is a part of that. God was ready for me, Taylor, and He called me home. I have lived my life and I have enjoyed it. I died happy and fulfilled. God allowed me to fulfill His purpose in my life and I am thankful that He allowed me to live as long as He did. I have fought a good fight and I have run my course. I enjoyed the journey, but we all have to leave the same way. I enjoyed my life with you, Taylor, and I loved you with all my heart. I've gotten to see a lot of things in my life and I've shared so much with you, but the truth is; I was not yours to keep. I belong to God. I am leaving behind my legacy and I know that God will take care of what is left behind. Whenever our children ask about me, just tell them that I loved them very much and I always will. You all were my joy. God was ready for me, Taylor, and believe it or not, so was I. He prepared me for this moment. I love you more than words could ever say. You touched my life in a way that no woman has and for that, I love you and thank you. Know that God will never leave you nor forsake you. With that in mind, I want you to live a happy life every moment you breathe. That is my last request to you. I love you, baby, and I always will.

Love always,

Keith

Taylor heard her door creak open, so she hurried and folded the letter back up and placed it safely in the envelope and back into the photo album. She gently closed it.

"Taylor, are you okay?" Tyra asked as she walked in closer. She and Michael had been sleeping over ever since the evening Keith passed away.

Taylor's tears continued to flow. She shook her head. "Why did he have to die?" she whispered through her tears.

Tyra walked over and hugged her sister. "Oh, Taylor, I'm so sorry." She cried.

Taylor cried on her shoulder. "This is some kind of dream and I'm going to wake up. My husband is not dead. I can feel it."

Tyra held Taylor's head up and looked into her eyes. The empty look in her eyes made Tyra look at her strangely. "Taylor," she slowly said. "You have to face this. It's not a dream.'' She then whispered, "Keith is dead and you have to come to a place of acceptance.''

"No,'' Taylor said angrily. She pushed her sister's hands away from her face. "I will not accept that . . . I won't... What am I supposed to tell our children?''

"Tell them that their father loved them very much.''

Taylor looked at her sister after she spoke the very words in the letter from Keith, her tears flowed even more and Tyra wrapped her in her arms tightly.

Chapter Thirty-Seven

Keith's body lay still in the beautiful pearl-blue casket and flowers surrounded it. Two beautiful doves were in a cage next to it. The family walked in slowly as Pastor Matthews recited Psalm 23: "The Lord is my shepherd, I shall not want . . ." he continued as the family viewed the body. Taylor walked up to the casket and leaned over it. She rubbed the side of her face against her late-husband's face, and then gently kissed it. She cupped his cold face in her hands and gently kissed his lips. Her tears poured onto his face, covering it. She rubbed his face as she listened to Pastor Matthews, "As I walk through the valley of the shadow of death, I will fear no evil. For thou art with me, thy rod and thy staff, comfort me . . ." his words faded as her knees buckled.

Michael caught her and led her over to the pew. He sat down beside her, holding her as she laid her head on his shoulder, crying.

Tyra held Justin and Justice's hand. She sat on the pew next to Taylor and Justice climbed into her mother's lap. Justin sat on Tyra's lap and laid his head onto her chest. As he watched his mother, he became curious about her tears.

Justice wiped the tears from her mother's eyes. "Mommy, why are we all watching daddy sleep?" she asked. "Why are you crying?"

Taylor looked at her daughter and cried even more.

Candis walked over to her and gently picked Justice up from her lap. "Come on, baby. Sit with me," she said to her.

"Aunt Candi, why is mommy just watching daddy sleep?" Justice asked, curiously. She looked back towards the casket. "Daddy, wake up!" she yelled out.

Some of the members assembled began to shed tears as they saw how Justice responded to the death of her father.

Candis' tears fell as she said, "Baby, daddy is not going to wake up right now." She walked out of the church, still holding Justice tightly in her arms. She didn't want her to cause a disruption. She repeated, "Daddy's not going to wake up right now, okay?" She sobbed heavily.

"Why not? Doesn't he know that people are watching him, and why is mommy crying?" Justice looked at Candis, realizing that she was crying too. "Why are you crying, Auntie Candi?"

"Justice, we will talk about it later, but right now, you have to be quiet when we walk back in the doors of the church."

"Candis, are you okay?" John asked as he gently took Justice from her arms.

"Yes, I was just trying to keep Justice quiet," she said.

"Pa-pa, what's wrong with mommy and Auntie Candi?"

"It's a sad moment right now, sweetie, but everything will be fine." He walked back through the doors with Justice in one arm and with his other arm wrapped around Candis as she sobbed loudly.

Pastor Matthews stood in the pulpit. "This is a time to celebrate life. God is an awesome God. Look at how many lives brother, Keith, touched." He looked around the packed sanctuary. "This man was a powerful man of God who stood for what was right. We didn't know Keith's heart, but by his walk, I believe he was a child of God. Those who have accepted Christ into their hearts shall inherit the Kingdom of God. That's a reason to rejoice and celebrate, for Keith is with the Father in Heaven."

"Amen's," were shouted out everywhere.

Pastor Matthews continued, "We cannot stop God's work. We all have to leave here the same way and death is natural. We just need to be ready for whenever death takes place in our lives. We must understand that we all are just passing through. We are not here to stay. Keith was not ours to keep. He belonged to God and He called him home. He lived his season here on earth. This is a time for celebration. Go with me if you will to Ecclesiastes 3:2-8." He waited a minute.

Everyone turned in their Bibles to the scripture.

He continued, "The Word says, 'To everything there is a season, and a time to every purpose under the heaven: A time to be born, and a time to die; a time to plant, and a time to pluck up that which is planted; A time to kill, and a time to heal; a time to

break down, and a time to build up; A time to weep, and a time
to laugh; A time to mourn, and a time to dance; A time to cast
away stones, and a time to gather stones together; a time to
embrace, and a time to refrain from embracing; A time to get,
and a time to lose; a time to keep, and a time to cast away; A
time to rend, and a time to sew; A time to love, and a time to
hate; a time of war, and a time of peace.'''" He took a sip of
water.

Taylor continued to shed many tears.

Pastor Matthews continued, "To everything there is a
season. Death is natural and God knows what He's doing. He
makes no mistakes. Keith lived his life for God and his family
while he was here on earth. He made a difference in his
community and he made a difference in the lives of others. He
may have made some mistakes in his past, but he got it right with
God and that's all that matters. He served his purpose while here
on earth. The evidence of God was all through Keith's life. He
lived a life that was pleasing to God, and he was a man after His
very heart, but it was time. The Word tells us plainly, to
everything, there is a season; A time to live, and a time to die.
Many of us don't want to hear about death, many of us don't
want to accept it, but that is a part of life. To this fine family,''
he looked at Taylor, and continued, "God will never leave you
nor forsake. Being without Keith may be difficult, but know that
God is with you. He will comfort you and bring you peace in the
midst of it all. Keith no longer has to worry. He no longer has
to suffer. He has fought a good fight. He is in a better place; a
place of rest and a place of peace. He's resting in peace because
he knew the Father. That's a reason to rejoice. To God be the
glory. Weep if must, but know that God is still right there.''

Taylor cried even more as she thought about the words in Keith's letter that the pastor also just spoke. Michael held her tightly, attempting to comfort her. Tyra gently rubbed her back with Justin still in her lap.

Janice cried in the arms of John and Candis now held Justice in her arms as she sobbed.

Kim sat on the back row holding Trey, Jr. She wiped away her tears as she listened to the comforting words of the pastor.

"Love never dies," Pastor Matthews continued, "and because of that, Keith lives on."

A female from the choir stood up and began singing beautifully, "I shall wear a crown . . . I shall wear a crown . . . When it's all over . . . When it's all over . . ." The choir now joined in, "I shall wear a crown . . . I shall wear a crown . . . When it's all over . . . When it's all over . . . I shall see his face... When it's all over. . . I'm going to put on my robe and tell the story how I made it over . . ." They continued singing the lyrics to *I Shall Wear a Crown*. "Soon as I get home . . ."

"How many of you know that Keith is wearing his crown. Have peace in knowing that he's with the Father. No more sorrows. No more pain. No more worries. No more heartaches and disappointments. He's with the Father. God has already prepared a resting place. He's resting with the Father. Let us celebrate in this place."

The choir continued, "When it's all over . . . I shall wear a crown . . ."

Many broke down into tears.

Taylor leaned over in her seat and Michael pulled her back up and she cried in the nape of his neck. Tears ran from his eyes. He was already missing his friend.

Pastor Matthews continued, "If you don't know Jesus as your Lord and Savior; now is the time to get to know Him. Death does not discriminate and it has no age limit. But when you have that relationship with Jesus, you will live forevermore. You shall wear a crown in a place where there are no sorrows. There will be no more hurt and you will worry no more. There will be no more pain and suffering. All you have to do is make the choice to get to know Him. This is a personal call. Come on down to the altar. If you need prayer, come on down to the altar. The death of a loved one is never easy, but we serve a mighty God. Those who are left to grieve know that He will comfort you. He will be your comfort when you wake up in the middle of the night. He will wrap you in His loving arms. Continue to trust Him. Come on down to the altar. Whatever you need, He will meet that need. Today is a great day to give your lives to Jesus. Come on down to the altar.''

Many came down and gave their lives to Jesus.

***

Keith's family and friends sat around in the living room as they told joyful stories about him. They all laughed and some laughed so hard at some of the stories, they cried. Michael looked around and saw that Taylor was missing from the group. He went upstairs and knocked on her bedroom door.

No answer . . .

He twisted the knob, eased the door open and slowly walked in. He saw her sitting on the bed. "Taylor," he called to her, "are you all right?" He then saw the prescription bottles in her hand. "What are you doing?"

"I . . . I should have made sure that he was taking his meds," Taylor whispered as she looked down at the bottles in her hand. "As his wife, I should have taken care of him. I should have made sure that he was taking his meds. I failed, and this is my fault." She cried.

Michael quickly approached her and pulled her up from the bed and into his arms. "No, this is not your fault. You didn't fail and you are not to blame for this. Keith chose not to take his meds. That was his choice, but it was God's choice to call him home. He was ready," he whispered into her ear. "His death had nothing to do with you, so do not blame yourself."

"Why?" she squalled. "Why did he leave us?"

Michael held her tightly in his arms.

Justice and Justin walked in and Taylor pulled away from Michael's embrace and quickly wiped her tears.

"Mommy, when is daddy coming home?" Justice asked.

"Uncle Michael, are you going to spend the night with us again?" Justin asked.

Michael nodded, his words caught in his throat.

"Are you staying until daddy comes back?" Justice asked.

Taylor walked over and sat on the bed. She patted it. "How about you two come sit up here with me?" she said to the twins.

They ran over to her and happily jumped up onto the bed.

Taylor hugged them and smiled as she looked at them. As she rubbed Justice's silky black hair, a tear fell from her eye.

"Why do you keep crying, mommy?" Justice asked after seeing her mother's tears fall.

Taylor wiped away her tears. She had been avoiding this moment. "I have something that I need to tell you," she began, "your daddy is not coming back." She choked on her tears. "He's in Heaven with God and he told me to tell you," she released a sob, "that he loves you very much and he always will."

"If he's with God, then why are you crying?" Justin asked.

She shrugged and smiled. "Because I miss him."

"I'm going to miss daddy too," Justice said. "But Uncle Mike said that when people go to be with God, that's a good thing. He said that they are always happy because they are always in His presence." She looked at Michael. "Uncle Mike, doesn't that mean that daddy is happy?"

Michael nodded. "Yes, baby, that means he is very happy."

"But won't he miss us?'' Justice asked.

Michael answered, "But he knows that God will take care of you and that brings him joy. He also knows that he will see you again.''

"Come sit with us, Uncle Mike, and tell us some stories about what God and my daddy are doing in Heaven!'' she exclaimed while scooting over and patting the bed.

"Well,'' Michael began as he sat next to them on the bed, "right now, God is hugging your daddy tightly in His arms and He is saying to him, 'Servant, well done'.''

A Note from the Author

First of all, thank you so much for taking the time out to read this book. I hope you enjoyed reading it just as much as I enjoyed writing it. It is my prayer that it has touched your life in some shape, form or fashion. God had given me this vision several years ago, and I stepped out on faith and began to work my faith. I was divinely inspired to write this storyline and it is my very first novel, by the grace of God. In this book there is a message of faith, hope, love, forgiveness, salvation, healing and deliverance. This is a book that addresses what having great faith in God can do. It is so easy for our faith to weaken when we begin to focus on our situations and circumstances instead of focusing on God. God can bring you out of anything when you truly trust Him.

God tells us plainly in His Word that faith comes by hearing and hearing by the Word of God. We must study His Word and get it into our spirits. We must increase our faith and understand that our faith determines our outcome. One way that we can build our faith is by studying the Word of God. It is so important to stay in His presence through worship, praise, prayer and reading and studying His Word daily. You can worship and praise your way through any storm that life brings.

God also tells us plainly in His Word that faith without works is dead. We must learn to work our faith. We work it by living the Word, not just speaking it. Peter had to step out onto the water in order to walk on it and it was fear that caused him to sink. Satan tries to distract us with what we see around us and blind us to what God sees in us. God created you to be great, excellent, and awesome. He desires for you to prosper in all that you do. Be who He has called you to be, not who the world wants you to be.

God has given us the ability to speak a word and move the mountains in our lives, but we must have faith that when we speak it, the mountains will move. I just want to encourage you to trust God with all of your life's situations and circumstances. He can handle them better than we can. God has also given us free will. Life is all about choices and in this book you will see how some of the choices that the characters made had a major impact on their lives and the lives of the people around them. It is so important to make wise choices in every area of our lives. Seek God in everything and wait to hear from Him before making your decision. All it takes is one mistake and that one mistake can be life altering. Live your life on purpose and with purpose. Live as though your life depends on it and make wise choices.

I want to encourage you to get a physical by your primary physicians at least once a year and please, get tested at least once a year. Know your status. Knowing can save your life. Make healthy choices and live a healthy life because you know you can. Be the difference and make a difference. For more information on HIV/AIDS go to: www.knowhiv.com

It is my prayer that God's will be done in your life and that you be blessed beyond measure. May your faith increase daily and fail not. Again, thank you so much and be blessed. Remember, God has great things in store for you. Pray, praise, and prosper. Choose to walk in faith. To God be the glory.

Miracles and Blessings,

Terri T. Thrash

Imagine. Innovate. Inspire.

Be Creative. Be Unique. Be You.

"I write to Encourage. Empower. Inspire."

"A vision is just a vision until you make the choice to do something with it." ~ Terri T. Thrash

Ulterior Motives

A taste of Ulterior Motives... Enjoy!

Silvia was headed for the checkout line with a bottle of grape juice in her hand. She turned the corner and as she looked up, she looked right into the eyes of the man who has haunted her memories for the past twelve years. She instantly released the grape juice from her hand and it crashed to the floor, shattering to pieces. Grape juice and glass covered the entire floor around her. Her mind went back in time as her eyes burned with tears and the hate grew stronger in her heart . . .

"Hey! You are not supposed to touch, remember?" she whispered in a seductive tone, her lips brushing against his ear.

Silvia was used to men trying to grope her as she danced for them. She was one of the most beautiful exotic dancers that Boss Gentlemen's Club had to offer. Her breast were full, thighs were thick, small waist, voluptuous bottom and a beautiful face to go with all of that. She was the one who all the men came in and requested for their sexy entertainment.

Jazzy was her stage name, the Latin Mamacita. She was one of what they called the, "top notch," exotic dancers. She was also one of those who refused to go beyond dancing. She allowed them only to watch her in her little uniforms and her sexy lingerie as she danced for them. They desired to have her, but knew that they never could. She was a little different from most of the other girls there. While many of them took off all of their clothes and had sex with their clients, she never did.

She was never interested in any of her clients, but there was something about this man that intrigued her. He was mysterious and beautiful with his light-skin, beautiful wavy hair and gorgeous green eyes that seemed to stare into her very soul as he looked back into her eyes. But she kept her clients, clients… nothing more nothing less. She has never gotten her feelings involved and she wasn't about to start now. This was about business, not pleasure, at least not for her.

She was just doing what she thought she had to do in order to pay her way through college. This brought in fast money, and she was hooked once she was hipped to the game. At the tender age of seventeen she began her journey as an exotic dancer. Now, at the age eighteen, she was one of the very best at what she did after being there for only a year. She could do all the pole tricks, floor dances, chair dances, table dances and lap dances as if she was a pro. The other girls said that she had an advantage because she had that Latin blood flowing through her veins. She was blessed with the "sexy gene" is what they always told her.

She continued to give this man a lap dance as she looked into his green eyes which were fire red at the moment, but still gorgeous. She began to redirect her focus not wanting to get drawn in by this man who had her amazed by how attractive he was. She began to look around the VIP room at the other five men who drank their liquor and watched as she gave this man what he wanted. Each one of the men reeked of liquor, especially the one she was on top of now. She felt his manhood rise to attention as she continued his lap dance.

"Hey!" she exclaimed as this attractive man touched her again.

"What? I'm buying," he said, grabbing her arm as he looked into her eyes.

Little did she know, he found her just as attractive with her beautiful flawless skin, dark-brown eyes and gorgeous long hair. She was one of the most beautiful women that he'd ever seen. She tantalized him as she circled her hips around while on top him. Lust had taken full control of him as she danced for him. There was something hypnotic about her and his desire was to have her and he wasn't willing to tame it. Oh, yes. He wanted her and whatever he wanted . . . he got.

"Let go! You are hurting me!" she screamed as his grip tightened and immediately bruised her arm. He slapped her and she fell onto the floor, crying hysterically.

He got up and grabbed her by her throat. He then squatted down next to her to look her in her eyes to let her know just how serious he was. "Look! Me and my boys are here to have a good time and I chose you to show us a good time. So, you *are* going to show us a good time." He paused. "Aren't you?" He spoke calmly as his grip tightened around her throat. He nodded as if coaxing her on what to say.

Frightened by the look in his eyes, she nodded slowly. Her heart seemed to skip beats, scared of what he may do to her next. She knew that she was in a bad situation. She could feel it. Her heart began to get heavy as the man continued to look her dead in her eyes. His deafening silence warned her that she'd better not do anything that he didn't tell her to do, like run to that door, which is what she desperately wanted to do.

He saw the fear in her eyes, then he whispered, "Good girl." He loosened his grip a little and gently kissed her lips as he now reached down below and fondled her with his other hand. No man's hands had ever touched her in that place before! His lips brushed her ear as he whispered exactly what he wanted her to do. He then released her throat from his grip.

"I'm sorry, but I can't . . . I . . . don't . . . do that." Her voice now trembled with fear.

He grabbed her by her hair. "Well, tonight you are. It's your lucky night. There's a first time for everything. Right?" He chuckled, and then let her go. He unzipped his pants, then sat back in his seat.

Even though this was one of the most attractive men that she had ever laid eyes on, she was not willing to do what he asked of her in front of the other five men who were in the room. She wouldn't be willing to do it even if they were alone. Of course, men looked at her as if she were nothing but a stripper. But she still possessed some innocence in that she had never performed any sex acts of any kind. She was a virgin, never touched. She carried a gift.

After taking a minute to look around the room, tears filled her eyes. She watched as the other men talked among themselves and continued to drink.

The green-eyed man-turned-maniac grabbed Silvia again by her throat. "What are you waiting for?" he growled.

Tears now fell from her eyes as she got on her knees, looked around the room one final time as her heart told her to get prepared. She finally began to do what the man commanded her to do. After six minutes into it, without stopping she looked up at him and stared into his eyes as her own eyes begged him to tell her to stop and leave so that she could turn and never look back at this shameful moment. He stared back into hers, his eyes empty and cold. He leaned his head back and continued to moan while grabbing the sides of the chair as Silvia continued to please him.

He grabbed Silvia by her hair as his pleasure neared its peak. She stopped and his eyes turned into slits as he looked at her. His eyes told her that she just made the biggest mistake of her life because he had not given her permission to stop. Now she would pay for that mistake. He slapped her and she fell back onto the floor. He got up, grabbed her and began dragging her behind the couch.

She tried to grab hold of something so that she could pull herself away from him . . . anything in order to keep him from doing what she feared was coming next. Her hands grabbed nothing but the air as he continued to drag her. She kicked and cried out, "Me ayuda . . . Por favor . . . Help me!" as the other men now watched in total shock. Fear had taken full control of her.

"Don't worry about it. I'll finish it," he told her as he spread her legs and pulled her underwear to the side. He got on top of her and forced himself into her body without her consent. She kicked, she pulled and she scratched and tried to scream as he covered her mouth. She was in excruciating pain as he moved in and out of her body. She felt as though she was going to die with each one of his strokes.

She was trying to fight but he was far too strong and she started to feel much too weak. She ripped his shirt and saw the tattoo of a scorpion on his chest. Two other guys came and held her down as they waited for him to finally finish. He slid himself out of her and looked down at all the blood that now covered him. He knew that it came from her. As he took his hand from over her mouth she wailed loudly from the pain she was in. Her mind, body and spirit cried out from all the pain, and every bit of her ached.

He stared at her, then quickly got up and zipped his pants. His eyes were fixed on hers and were now apologetic as if he realized that he had just taken something precious away from her and that was not his intention. She lay on the floor crying uncontrollably as she looked up into his green eyes with eyes that pled the question "Why?" She looked at the man who now towered over her, the man who left her empty and broken . . . the man who took a part of her. He touched her in a place no man has ever touched her before and bruised her in a way that no man had ever bruised her.

Lost for words, he left the room ashamed of what he had just done. The other five men each took their turn with Silvia without hesitation. That night, she was severally beaten by one of the men and was left for dead after she blacked out on the floor. She could not clearly remember the faces of any of the men except for one and she had good reason to remember his.

That night she was rushed to the hospital where she spent the next three weeks. She was devastated. The hospital offered her counseling but she refused. A part of Silvia died the night she was raped and beaten. She was left with nothing but a broken spirit and a cold hard heart. The men never paid for what they did to her that night; but she promised herself that if she ever came across the one who she felt killed a part of her on that dreadful night, he would pay, even if he had to pay with his own life.

She snapped back to her present moment as the world around her seemed to go in slow motion. She watched the woman pushing the buggy and the man who stood beside her with a bouncing baby girl in his arms. There he stood tall, handsome, slender yet muscular, light-skinned, wavy hair and with green eyes that now stared back into hers. She stood still and glared at the man who had left her bruised and broken.

"Ma'am, are you okay?" the clerk asked her. She was concerned by how distraught Silvia appeared.

Silvia stood frozen in place, still as a statue. She wanted to run. She wanted to walk away. She wanted her feet to move, but they were stuck in one place. Her brain couldn't register how to move them.

"Be careful ma'am! There's glass everywhere and I don't want you to cut yourself! Just be still so that you don't get hurt," another worker said, as he swept the glass from around her feet. At this point Silvia's feet wouldn't stay still. She backed away with her eyes locked on the man's green eyes. She did an about face and ran from the building and to her car. Once she got there, she broke down into tears. She sat there for a while, beating the steering wheel as if it were to blame for her pain.

She sped off, rubber burning. It was as if running away was going to leave behind the thoughts of this man from her past. She tried to bury her thoughts . . . her hurt . . . her hate . . . all at once, but it grew uncontrollably and somebody was going to have to pay for her pain. Now, she was ready for sweet revenge . . .

Reader's Group Guide:

Reality and Purpose sessions (R.A.P. sessions) for readers

1. Taylor desired quality time with her husband. What was your first impression of her? Can you relate to her character? Why or why not? In this story, Taylor's love language is quality time. What is your love language?

2. Taylor's sister, Tyra, was introduced in chapter two. What did you think about their conversation in that chapter? Should Tyra stay out of Taylor and Keith's marital affairs? Why or why not? Do you think that friends and family have a place for input in one's marriage? Explain.

3. In chapter three, do you think that Taylor was attempting to use seduction in order to entice Keith to go to church with her? Explain.

4. Pastor Matthews prophesied to Taylor and told her that she was about to go through a storm. What did you think her storm would bring? Explain. What was your first impression of Michael and why?

5. What was your first impression of Kimbrailee Whitmore? Can you relate to her character? Why or why not? When you met Treyvionne Whitmore in chapter six, how did you feel about his character?

6. What did you think that Taylor's dream was trying to tell her in chapter seven? Should she have talked with Keith about her dream? Why or why not?

7. In chapter eight, Keith involved his sister, Candis, as well as Kim and his dad in his marriage. Do you think

that he should have involved them? Why or why not? Do you think that they helped or hurt the situation? Explain.

8. What was your first impression of Silvia Martinez? When she invited Trey out to the porch with her, what did you think was going to happen? How did you feel about Michael's conversation with Kim and Keith at the dinner table? Why do you think Keith responded to Michael the way that he did?

9. It all went down in chapter eleven. How did you feel about everything that transpired in this chapter?

10. When Silvia saw Keith at the Mi Amore Hotel and began talking, drinking and dancing with him, what went through your mind? Did you think that something was going to happen between them? Why? What do you think happened in that hotel room? How do you think Keith should have handled the situation?

11. In chapter fourteen, Keith went to Silvia's office to inquire about what happened between them at the hotel. Did you believe Silvia when she explained to him what happened? Why or why not? What did you think about him and Michael's conversation over lunch that same day? Did you think that this was the beginning of a new friendship between him and Michael?

12. What was your first impression of Keisha Fullerton when her character was introduced? How did the scene where Trey was physically abusing Kim make you feel? When the police showed up at their door, did you think that Kim was going to tell the truth about what was really happening behind the closed doors of her home?

If she would have, what do you think would have happened? Since it was apparent that Officer Townsend knew something was going on, do you think he should have questioned Kim alone, before leaving her there alone with Trey?

13. How did you feel about Keith's mother, Janice, after she was introduced in chapter seventeen? How do you think Keith felt about her showing up at his door after many years of being MIA?

14. Keith poured his heart out to Taylor in chapter eighteen. He told her about his feelings about the church and "church people". Could you relate to how Keith was feeling? How do you feel about "church people"?

15. Keith finally got his life in order in chapter nineteen, and then Silvia comes back into the picture, trying to start confusion. Silvia played somewhat of a mind game with Taylor and Keith in this particular scene. Do you think that she was just attempting to cause a problem in their home, or do you believe that something really did happen between her and Keith?

16. In chapter twenty, Keith was in trial for the McCallister's case. Did you think that McCallister was guilty when he was first introduced in chapter eighteen, or did you believe that he was an innocent man? How did you feel about the outcome of the case?

17. What did you think was going on when Taylor had become sick in chapter twenty-one? When the doctor gave her results, did you think that her results were a mistake, or did you think that the results were correct? How did her results affect you?

18. Taylor goes to Michael for comfort in chapter twenty-two. Do you think that it was appropriate for her to go to him? Why or why not? Do you think that it was appropriate for him to invite her to stay with him for as long as she needed to before he contacted Keith?

19. In chapter twenty-three, Kim had gotten a call that Treyvionne was in the hospital. Do you believe that Trey reaped what he sowed? Explain?

20. When Michael invited Keith to come stay with Taylor in his home in chapter twenty-four, did you think that it was a good idea? Explain? How did you think Taylor was going to respond and what did you think was going to happen? What do you think you would have done?

21. How did it make you feel when Trey poured out his heart in chapter twenty-seven? Do you think you would have been as compassionate with Trey after all that he put you through? Why or why not? How would you have responded to Keisha? Do you think that Kim responded to her well?

22. When Kim was crying at the casket and Keith left his wife's side in order to comfort her, in chapter twenty-eight, what went through your mind? Did you think that Keith loved her more than just as a friend? What do you think about Taylor's reaction to his actions in that particular scene? How do you think you would have felt if you were in Taylor's shoes and why?

23. How did you feel about Keisha's letter to Kim and her poem in chapter thirty-two? What were your feelings toward Keisha? How did you feel about Kim taking Trey, Jr. into her home and raising him as her own?

24. What was going through your mind when Michael came into the bathroom with Taylor, in chapter thirty-three? What did you think was going to happen at the doctor's office when Taylor went to get tested again? What did you think about Dr. Allen's reaction to Taylor's results?

25. What do you think was going through Silvia's mind when Pastor Matthews was giving the message as she sat on the back pew in chapter thirty-four? What do you think made her get up and leave? What did you think about Dr. Allen and Taylor's conversation? Do you think that God has a way of getting people's attention? How did He get yours?

26. What was going through your mind in chapter thirty-five as Keith looked around at his family's pictures and as he played with his children? What did you think about the conversation he had with Michael? What did you think about his last moments with Taylor? How did the ending of chapter thirty-five make you feel and why?

27. How did you feel about chapter thirty-six and thirty-seven? How did Taylor's response to her husband's death make you feel? Do you think that the death of a spouse is one of the hardest things to get through? Why or why not?

28. What message(s) did you receive from Evidence and how did the message(s) affect you?

Bad News

A Short Story by Terri T. Thrash

Bad News

If only I had the power to turn back the hands of time, I swear I would not have slept with her. Brent Newton thought to himself. His friend Cornelious had told him that the girl he had cheated with was rumored to be HIV positive. She was so beautiful, sexy, exciting and inviting. She didn't look sick, but now here he was sitting in a chair in the waiting room, staring at the cold white walls. The young lady across from him caught his attention. She smiled, but he was unable to return her smile because of the worry that took over his mind. She looked similar to the girl who was partially responsible for his being here in this clinic. But the girl who sat in front of him is much skinnier and her skin was covered with sores. *Could I be infected? Is it possible?* His mind went back in time . . .

With her legs wrapped around him, he reached over the side of the bed and pulled a condom from his pant pocket. He tore the wrapper open.

Grabbing his hand, "We don't need it. It feels so much better without one, baby." She kissed his lips, staining them with her red lipstick. "Trust me."

He looked into her beautiful brown eyes for a minute, then kissed her. She gently took the condom from his hand and threw it onto the floor. She ran her hand up his spine and kissed his neck softly, leaving behind traces of her lipstick and before he knew it, they were engaged in sexual activity.

As the tempo of his strokes sped up, she whispered into his ear, "I told you that it's better without them." She moaned.

As he was bringing the moment to an end, her red lace underwear at the top of the bed caught his attention and that's when he saw his reflection in the headboard mirror . . .

"Sir," the nurse began, bringing him back to reality, "would you please come with me? Your results are ready." She had a slight smile as if it was forced. "Have a seat, sir. Someone will be in with you in a moment." She avoided eye contact, which lead him to believe that the results weren't good.

A lady came in dressed in a black suit. "Hi, Mr. Newton, I'm Liza Phillips, one of the counselors here at County General." She reached out to shake his hand.

Oh, no, a counselor this can't be good, he thought to himself.

"We have your results. Mr. Newton, I'm sorry to tell you this, sir, but you tested positive for HIV." She paused to make sure that he was okay.

This educated handsome business man who was full of laughter, life, ambition, and now a deadly virus.

"Mr. Newton, are there any other sex partners that could be infected? If there is, you can provide us with their names and we will contact them to come into our office to be tested." She gave him time to think, then she continued, "You do know that there is no cure for HIV/AIDS, but with early detection and the proper medications, you can live a healthy life . . ." She kept on and on about what HIV/AIDS is, the different medications, how to prevent others from getting it, and how to live a long and healthy lifestyle. Her words just went in one ear and out of the other. He just stared at the dying roses on Mrs. Phillips' desk. "Mr. Newton, are you listening to me?" she asked.

He nodded, "Yes." His throat tightened. "I just need to get some water."

He left out of her office and rushed to the bathroom down the hall. All of his lunch came up and out into the toilet. Sweat running down his face, he instantly felt sick.

Oh, God, I can't go back in that office, I just can't. I got to get out of here. He stared in the mirror as he tried to catch his breath. The man in the mirror, he didn't recognize anymore. He rinsed his face with cold water, ran out of the bathroom, down the hall and into the parking lot. He got into his car and sped off, rubber burning. "What am I going to tell Jamie? Baby, I'm HIV positive? No, wait! Jamie, I'm sorry, but I cheated on you about six months ago?" he kept talking aloud trying to figure out how to tell Jamie, his fiancé, that he put her at risk of this deadly virus that he now carries. He practiced it over and over. "Wait, those results can't be right. I am not HIV positive." He was in denial, but then he thought of the possibility of them being right. "God, why me? You need to fix this," he spoke angrily. "Please, make it all right. No more messing up, I swear. I will never cheat again if you just make it all right." He tried to bargain with God as if he could.

He pulled into his driveway and sat in the car for a minute as he tried to stop his heart from pounding.

The love of his life met him at the door. "Hi, honey, I'm cooking up your favorite for dinner!" Jamie exclaimed as she took his briefcase and loosened his tie, kissing him softly. "Babe, I had the most amazing day! I got the promotion. I am now V.P.!" She screamed throwing her arms around her fiancé's neck. She saw the disturbed look on his face, then said, "Baby, what's wrong? Sit down, you don't look so good. Are you okay? I'm sorry, I was going on and on about me. So, how was your day?" she asked question after question, filled with concern.

Mr. Newton, I'm sorry to tell you this, sir, but you tested positive for HIV, kept playing over and over in his mind. "No, sweetheart," he answered. "Everything's fine, I'm just a little tired, that's all . . . but look at you, beautiful! A promotion? I knew it was coming." He paused, then kissed her. "So what's for dinner?"

Each and every one of you, are very important to me and I would love to connect with you.

Find Terri:

www.facebook.com/Terri T. Thrash

www.twitter.com/@MsTerriTThrash

www.instagram.com/@divinely_inspired_writer

email:divinelyinspired28@yahoo.com

For exclusives, up and coming literary works, events and more, please visit Terri at www.TerriTThrash.com

Thank you for your love and support!

I love me some you!!!